A Hidden Heritage

Prologue

Princess, A Hidden Heritage is a fantasy tale in the distant past of a land with many secrets. It is based on the arrival of a young girl with unknown gifts to change back the times of this long, suffering land, Lystonia. Her name is Princess, and she was left at the entrance to a religious order, where she was found as a new-born, with just a necklace with the name Princess imprinted on it. She is beautiful just turned 18 years with deep brown eyes and an athletic figure. Her character is very calm, and she has a way of calming any confrontations and arguments within the order. She has an aura that hides a hidden secret, even to herself.

The Priory where she now lives with numerous young trainees of the order, both male and female, is amid a deep forest, a distance from the nearest town. The head of the priory is Orpheus, an old man who is not pestered by the authorities for a reason no one knows. The female Superior is a hard lady named Damsen in her late forties.

The land where they live was once a prosperous country, but is now ruled by a neighbouring country Urania, ruled by Lord Manion, who destroyed the Royal family and political heads of Lystonia and now taxes the country into poverty. His second in command is a powerful mystic names Kaaron. Urania sends tax collectors, supported with military to raise these taxes, using force when necessary, or even when not. Amongst the military group is a handsome young man named Alexander the Brave. He is different from the other soldiers and tries to stop the bullying and has reached his position in the command as he has been brave in battle in the past.

The towns people often hide some of their supplies at the priory as the Priory is tax free and rarely visited. This helps them through the tough winter months. This has been increasing since Urania has been at war with other neighbours.

This tale is the awakening of a new leader of Lystonia and her adventure to unite all the lands against Lord Manion and to eventually rule over all the lands. With new powers, she unites the continent regardless of countless adversaries, she overcomes everything to be a much-cherished leader. She is supported by her closest friend Rebecca and initially a wild mountain man called Geraldo.

Princess

A Hidden Heritage

Chapter one

It is a rainy, windy day in a wooded area of the land called Lystonia, where alone stands an ancient castle now acting as the Priory. Members of the Priory are struggling to bring in equipment from the surrounding land into the Priory walls. This includes cattle and chickens which need gathering up and moved into pens. Princess, a young junior girl left at the Priory Gates at birth, is amongst this group of workers. She is adept at catching chickens, which is no mean feat. As she catch's them, she passes them to Rebecca, a close friend, who places them in a pen on wheels. Princess has finally caught the last chicken, cheered on by her fellow helpers, when she hears a noise coming from the surrounding bracken. She wonders if she has missed a chicken, but then a ragged group of strangers appear, carrying bundles of belongings and looking in dire need of help. Princess calls to Rebecca and the others to help them. As they approach, they see the line of strangers is stretching into the woods, dozens of them. Princess and Rebecca help the leading family, two parents and two young children, the others follow.

She leads them through the Priory gates and tells Rebecca to climb to the parapet to see if there are any others coming. Rebecca immediately does as she is asked, as the Mother Superior, called Damsen appears from the building and instructs the Priory juniors to take everyone to the main hall. They are all lead away as Princess calls up to Rebecca, "Anymore?" Rebecca "No" but then she sees movement and shouts out "Soldiers, close the gates, quick." Princess rushes to the massive gates and starts to close them, she can see the riders approaching at a pace. The first door closes, and it is a rush to close the other when as from behind her a gust of wind which blows the gate shut and the thick wooden bar falls into place to lock it. Through a metal grid, Princess sees the soldiers pull up and the leader approaches the gate. His name is Alexander, an officer for the army of Urania, the country now in control of this land.

He slowly approaches the grid in the gate and calls out. By the authority of my Lord Manion of Urania, I demand you release the peasants we are chasing to us. The head of the Priory Orpheus, an old man dressed in a dark robe and rope belt, comes to the grid, and answers him, "you know you have no authority on these grounds, now be off with you, and take your rabble of men with you." Alexander replies, "Those peasants all owe taxes, and if not released, we will burn the town down, if not this priory." Orpheus responds, "Good luck with that." He then closes the grid and leads Princess into the hall. Alexander is speechless and calls to his men, back to the town. They all turn and ride off. As they leave, Princess enters the main hall and Rebecca approaches her. There's over 50 of them, 15 children. Princess taking control, "OK, let's arrange some warm food and check for injuries." As the juniors proceed with their orders, an old man approaches Princess, "Thank You, thank you, we were desperate, we did not want to bring trouble to the Priory, but we had nowhere else to go, there are many dead in the town." Princess "Oh no, and many injured I am guessing?" I am afraid so, the man replied, we had no choice but to leave them." "Ok" Princess responds," nothing can be done for now, but help me organise these people." "I can do that, thank you my dear" he replies. Princess leaves him and goes over to Orpheus. "Sir, it seems that there are many injured in town, what can we do?" she asks. "Nothing for now, I am afraid, we must care for those here." he points to the children. "Go and look after them, see if they all have relatives or not. "Oh yes, of course," she answers as she walks over to the children huddled in a corner. She sits down with them and takes out a piece of paper and pencil. "Hello children, my name is Princess and," she is interrupted by a little girl" are you a real Princess," Princess laughs and says" No it is just my name like yours, so let's start with you, what can I call you?" "Carol," she answers as Princess points to the next child and proceeds to take all their names. She comes to a young boy, aged around 15, "Charming" he says, "Prince Charming". The children all laugh. "He's Tom the butcher's boy" one child says. Princess laughs and replies" I thought my dreams had come true she laughs." She then gathers the children around a large table and Rebecca places hot bowls of soup in front of them. Rebecca tells them "Eat up, then we will get you cleaned up and to bed for you all." The children grab a handful of bread and tuck into their meals.

Meanwhile Orpheus is talking to Damsen. "Place the men in the barn and work out sleeping arrangements for the women" and the kids can share with the Juniors." Damsen "Some kids might want to stay with their parents," "Not tonight" Orpheus states, we need to organise first. "Very well ", Damsen replies and walks over to the men standing be the fire. She leads them towards the barns as the women look after the children and tidy the hall.

Night falls and all is calm as Princess lies in her bunk talking to Rebecca. "We have to do something about those left in town." Rebecca replies "What, we can't go up against soldiers." Princess replies" well somethings got to be done, I can't stand by and leave them to those animals". Rebecca explains "They won't think twice about cutting your throat, or worse!" Princess adds "I don't know that captain seemed different from the others, maybe we can talk to him". "Rather you than me" Rebecca states "He didn't get to be a Captain by being nice." "Yeah, maybe you're right, I'll sleep on it. She blows the candle out "Night." Meanwhile Orpheus is in his office with Damsen. They are drinking a small drink, like sherry. Damsen asks "What are we going to do with everyone, they can't stay here indefinitely." "No!" Orpheus replies but the soldiers won't stay forever, they have other towns to plunder. They know they have no chance of gaining entry here." "I hope not" Damsen mutters. "I'll go and do a security check to make sure everyone is down for the night." "Ok, good idea, good night" Orpheus replies. Damsen leaves as

Orpheus open a large old book titled Kings and Queens of Lystonia.

Chapter two

The Town, called Meerdown where the refugees have come from. It is still late, and the soldiers have raided the bars and are all drunk. Any women left behind are being passed around and ravished and the floor is littered with bodies of dead or unconscious men. A young man who looks like a mountain man is tied up to the roof beams hanging by his wrists. His body has many cuts and bruises and there are several arrows and knives stuck in him, none however lethal. Every so often as a soldier passes him, he kicks out and receives another wound for his collection. Everyone is laughing at him and throwing drink and food at him. A drunk soldier walks up to him "Where's the gold you animal" he shouts, as he hangs on to his waist, adding extra weight to his arms. "Where's the gold!" At this moment Alexander enters the bar and pulls the soldier of the mountain man. "Dead men don't talk, cut him down and lock him up" he orders. "Shall I get another then?" the soldier asks. "No go and check the boundary fence if you want something to do" Alexander orders. "But…. but" the soldier stutters. "Now" Alexander barks. The soldier leaves as some other men cut the mountain man down and carry him away. Alexander leaves the bar carrying a bottle of rum and walks towards a larger house in town. He kicks the door in and is met by an attractive lady who is obviously one of the wealthier people of the town. "You've taken everything, there's nothing left" she quietly says. "Not everything" Alexander replies and pulls her close to him and kisses her forcibly on the lips. Now come with me. He leads her upstairs to her bedroom and takes out his knife and presses it across her throat. He then tells her to undress. "She slowly starts to undo her buttons as she quietly whispers "You're late "as they both fall onto the bed.

Morning arrives and everyone in the Priory is active trying to sort families out. Some Juniors are with the children in the courtyard singing songs. The men are helping repair the barn and other items and the women are preparing food and cleaning. Everyone wants to make their presence valued. Princess is in the courtyard watching everyone as Damsen comes over to her. Damsen asks" you do not look happy, what is wrong, these people are all safe and well." "And the others" Princess responds, "what about them"? We can't look after everyone, that's not why we are here, we have done are part and soon they can return home and rebuild". What about the others, what about them"? Princess asks. "The town has its own doctors, nurses, forces, they are not helpless, but we certainly cannot go there." Princess "Why not, they would not dare attack us, surely"! Most of the soldiers will be drunk by now and will not care if you come from here, trust me, be patient and wait till they leave." Princess explains "I can't just stand here doing nothing, it's unbearable." "It's all in your mind, you have no idea what is going on, so be patient and wait as I said" Damsen orders. Princess shrugs and walks off to see Rebecca. She is helping a man with a wound to his arm, she is placing a bandage on it. Rebecca looks up and sees Princess "I'll be finished here in a minute if you want me." "No rush" Princess says. She looks around the priory, seeing the walking wounded as they go about their business helping. "All done" Rebecca announces as the man stands up and flexes his arm. "Perfect, thank you missy." "No problem" Rebecca replies, and she stands and walks over to Princess. "What are you thinking about, you've got that look in your eyes." I was just thinking, how long will these people be here, when will we know if it is safe to go back to town"? "That is not your problem Princess, they are not your responsibility." "Then why do I feel so," Princess admits. "I have to talk to Orpheus" she states as she walks off.

Orpheus meanwhile is talking to some of the men about the previous day. "How many men do they have"? he asks. "At least 50, all on horseback, they were so quick and unstoppable" one answers. "Well hopefully they will leave soon if they cannot find anything else to take" Orpheus sighs. At this moment Princess enters the room. "Sir can I have a moment please" she asks. "Excuse me please," Orpheus gestures to the men as they all stand and leave. Princess closes the door and sits in front of Orpheus's desk. "So Princess, what is worrying you"? "It's the people in the town, who knows what is going on there and we are just closing a blind eye to it." "Princess, there is little we can do but help the ones who made it here, the others I am afraid are on their own." Princess grabs the edge of the desk, "I can't just sit by whilst these people need our help." Orpheus slams his hand on the desk "You cannot go and that is final, now go and help the ones we can help." He waves her out and she stands, and leaves crest fallen. She closes the door behind her as Orpheus opens the draw to his desk. He takes out two thick wrist bracelets with a crest on. He looks at them and puts them back.

Meanwhile Princess is with Rebecca and sulking over what Orpheus has said. "You know we can't just ignore the towns people, don't you"? she asks Rebecca. "But Orpheus has refused, that is it, over" she replies. "I'm going to sneak in tonight and see what is happening there" Princess announces, "are you coming with me"? "Do I look crazy. Not in a million years" Rebecca replies. "Ok, well cover for me then, don't tell anyone, promise"! "But… Ok, just don't take long." She complained. Princess rushes to her room to gather things she may need. And waits for darkness.

Several hours later as most are asleep, Princess creeps out the Priory dressed in a black cloak with a hood. She creeps away and disappears into the dark forest. As she moves towards the town, she is startled by all the noises of the forest, amplified by the dark stillness of the night. After around 45 minutes she reaches the town boundary and looks around for any movement. She creeps closer to the centre and can hear the soldiers, still drunk, loud, and violent. She approaches the bar and peeks through the window. The mountain man is back hanging from the joist. He is looking in very poor condition with even more wounds. Two buckets full of water are tied to his ankles to increase the strain on his body. A guard throws a glass of beer at him. "Where's the gold, where's the gold" he barks. "No gold" the man mutters, as the man throws another glass at him. "Where's the silver then, there must be something here, we weren't sent here for nothing." "No gold, no silver" again the man mutters. The soldier frustrated, punches him hard in his stomach as the man spits blood. "You're no good, get me someone else" the soldier shouts as Alexander again enters. "Didn't I tell you to not injure him anymore"? he asks. "That was yesterday, Sir, I thought he might have changed his mind now" the soldier informs him. "And has he changed his mind"? he is asked. "Not yet Sir, but I'm working on it" the soldier replies. This is all watched by Princess who passes by the bar towards the doctors' surgery. She slowly enters the surgery and is shocked to see the doctor dead in his chair behind his desk, his hands pinned to the desk by scalpels and his throat slit. She winces and goes to the doctors' store cupboard. She opens her bag and fills it with medicines and bandages and turns to leave as she hears someone enter the building. She hides under the desk as two soldiers enter the surgery and make straight for the store cupboard. It is obvious they are looking for drugs and when they find what they are looking for, rush of to use. Princess is surprised by the lack of discipline in the soldiers, but then thinks this is normal in occupied countries. She exits the surgery and makes her way to the school. There is a guard on the hall door, so she assumes there are captives in there. She creeps along the building and peeks in through the window. She sees at least 30 women all safe but obviously they have been attacked with their clothes ripped and bruises. There is no sign of any men. She moves on and comes to the sports field. Here she is shocked to see dozens of men cross eagled tied down on the field. Some are untouched but others are in a horrific state. She is surprised that they have no guards, but then, they are secure, so why bother. She crawls along the ground towards the first man. He is conscious and begs her to release him. She takes a sharp knife out of her belt and cuts through his ropes. Once free, he runs off to her pleas to help. In seconds he is gone. She moves to the next man who is in a bad way. He is semi-conscious with bruising all over his body and face. His eyes are

9

swollen closed. She cuts him free, but he is too weak to leave. She gives him a drink of water and moves onto the next man. He is fitter and again she frees him and asks him to help the other man and head for the Priory. He agrees and she moves on to the next, again an injured man is freed and supported by a healthier man. She moves on when a spotlight appears, and princess is lit up. She is quickly surrounded by soldiers and taken away. She is taken to the police station where she is thrown in a cell while the soldiers decide what to do with her. "We better tell Alexander, "One says. "You tell him and where the prisoners went" another replies. "Oh yes" the first responds. Princess chips in "He's going to notice anyway, so you might as well get him, he won't be happy if he finds you are mistreating a member of the Priory." "How do we know you are from there" he argues. She opens up her cloak to reveal her uniform. "Go and get him quick" he shouts to one of the men. "You better tell him we treated you well." She sits down and waits.

Shortly after, the door swings open and Alexander marches in. He heads straight to Princesses cell. "Who are you and why are you here" he shouts. "Well as you can see, I'm from the Priory and I came to see what was going on, Oh and freed a few men." "What! Where were you lot during this," he shouts at his men. "We were on our rounds Sir; we are undermanned here" was the reply. "More likely in the bar with their fellow soldiers, beating up on one guy, very brave" Princess calls out. "That's enough from you missy" Alexander tells her. "Take her to my quarters and I will question her there, and don't lose her". "Yes sir" the men reply as they unlock the cell and march Princess out. Alexander watches as they leave, he hits the wall, he then follows them out.

Upon reaching Alexanders quarters, Princess is pushed forward and onto a chair as Alexander enters and sits opposite her. "Everyone out," he orders as the men leave. "So, what now, am I your captive"? Princess pleads. "Let me think, why, why are you here, this is nothing to do with the Priory" Alexander asks "I'm very sorry to ruin your evening, I guess I can always go home "she taunts. Why did Orpheus allow you here, it's not what was agreed". He asks. "Agreed"! "What agreement"? We don't interfere with Orpheus, and he does not interfere with us. It is a long-standing agreement, which you have now broken." "Oops sorry" she shrugs. "You can always let me go." He stands up and takes her jaw in his hand. "I don't think so." I wanted something to convince the people to tell me where the money is, and now you may have just given me that push." He releases her, as she adds, "I don't know anyone here, they owe me nothing really, I'm sure I will be useless to you." He replies, "Well you need to be punished for your actions at the very least, so let me think, what to do with you"? he calls for the guard. They enter. "Lock her up in a cell till the morning, I'll decide then. They drag Princess back to the station and throw her in a cell. In the next cell is the mountain man, lying on the floor covered in blood. She goes over to the cell wall and calls to him. "Are you awake," he mutters and rolls over, his eyes are forced shut from swelling and his hands shaking. "My God, what have they done to you, and why you"? He mutters, "someone told them I hid the gold in the mountains, and they want it, there is no gold, I keep telling them." He then loses conscious.

The following morning a fire pyre is built, and guards are forming a solid circle around the town square. The few towns people who are active are standing behind then wondering what is happening. Alexander enters the square and stands in front of a large chair placed central to the square. He motions, and Princess is dragged into the square by guards and forced onto her knees in front of Alexander. He announces to the crowd. "This female is guilty of freeing prisoners and uprising, the only punishment regardless of her position is death, prepare her," he orders. She is dragged to the fire Pyre and tied to it. A guard carrying a burning stick approaches her. Just as he is about to set light, a bell is heard, and Orpheus followed by eight of the juniors enter the town square and he approaches Alexander. Orpheus stands before him and proclaims" You do not have the authority to fulfil this punishment, Princess is under the protection promised by your own Lord Manion, he will hear of this action if you proceed"! Ha! There is no evidence that she is one of yours, and she certainly acted like no Priory Junior, I am sure he will agree with my actions, now proceed." He points to the soldier with the flame. Orpheus" waves" Wait, if you insist in this action, please let me give her, her only belongings, from when she was left on our doorstep." Alexander waves to the soldier to wait and turns to Orpheus. "Very well give her the trinkets and then leave." Orpheus agrees and goes over to Princess and takes out two bracelets from his bag. He goes behind her and places them on her wrists and then kneels in front of her. He raises his arms and makes a short prayer. "May the power of Lystonia be released through it's only remaining saviour." He then stands and takes the flame from the guard and lights the pyre. It quickly sets alight, and we hear the shrieks of the women watching as the flames quickly engulf Princess, yet no sound comes from her. Suddenly from the centre of the pyre comes a bright light beaming upwards to the sky and then circling the square and then shooting down engulfing all the soldiers except Alexander. They instantly disappear, turning to ashes. The flame dies down and standing boldly over the pyre is Princess, glowing and looking glorious, although naked. The towns people rush forward and all lower to their knees. Orpheus takes his cloak of and wraps Princess in it then takes Princess's hand and leads her towards Alexander. Princess shouts to him" You have been left to run home and return to your Lord Manion and tell him to leave our lands or we will destroy him and his land, now leave. Alexander stutters "B... but how... you are just." "She is our Princess, by name and position, cared for by us till this day when our ancient gods return to forgive us for our past. Leave now or feel her power," Orpheus announces. Alexander turns and rushes to his horse and rides off followed by the jeers and taunts of the town people. Rebecca rushes to Princess and gives her a hug, "How on earth"? she asks. Princess "I have no idea, Orpheus placed the bracelets on me, and I just felt the spirits of my past family and relatives, The rest you know." Orpheus tells one of the juniors send a message to the Priory to bring the other villager back. Rebecca rushes of and grabs a horse left by the soldiers. Princess then remembers the Mountain Man. "Wait here, I have to check on someone." She rushes of to the cells and sees him still on the floor, she grabs the keys and grabs a glass of water and goes to him. She raises him onto her lap and helps him drink. His eyes open and he mutters, "Am I dead"? "No, we will get you better, can you stand." She asks. "I don't think so" he says. "Ok, stay still and I will get help." She goes to the door and calls a couple of the young boys from the Priory. They rush over and she gestures them to carry him to the doctors. As she re-enters the town centre, the towns people surrounds her. They are all touching and praying for her. Orpheus comes over to her, "We have to talk." "I guess so," she answers. "Meet me in the town hall in thirty minutes, which will give you enough time to sort out your mountain man". "Ok" she replies.

Princess enters the doctor's surgery and approaches the Mountain man. "Hi, how are you feeling" she asks. "Feels like I've been run over by a herd of buffalo," he answers. "Well let's see if we can make you feel better." Princess cuts of what remains of his shirt and inspects the numerous wounds. Rebecca brings a bowl of ointment and starts to wash the wounds. He winces but grins and takes it. Princess goes to the medical cabinet and takes out some pills. This will help reduce the pain, but the next bit will hurt. She takes out a needle and starts to sew up the wounds. All in all, eight gapping wounds. Rebecca holds a cold compact against his eyes to reduce the swelling. "Ok, try and lie down and get some rest" Princess tells him. He tries to smile and lies down. "I'll return later, OK"! Princess turns and leaves the surgery.

Princess walks across the town centre, glancing at where the Pyre once was. She enters the Town Hall and meets Orpheus sitting at the head of a grand table. As she enters, he stands up. "Princess, please take your seat," he moves away from the seat and offers it to her. "What, why"? "This is your rightful place

Princess as the Heir to Lystonia ". Orpheus states. "You weren't left on the steps, you were left by your mother to protect you from Lord Manion, she kept her whole pregnancy secret so only a select few knew about your life and your whereabouts." "But why did you not tell me." She pleads. "It was for your safety; we knew your powers would not appear until you reach adulthood. So, it was safer to keep the secret to the few, not even you." He sits next to her. "But now the secret is out, and Lord Manion will take immediate action." "Oh my god, what have I done." Princess explains. "We must organise things immediately; we will have to move to the Capital for starters" he explains. "What, how! It is so far away" she questions. Exactly, that's why we must leave as soon as possible, hopefully tomorrow. "Fortunately, they have provided us with plenty of horses." Orpheus adds, "Now I suggest you go back to the Priory and pack any of your belongings you will need." What belongings, all I have is here," she taps her bracelets and necklace. "Good then we will leave in the morning, I will send some ravens to let them know "he informs her. "Who know"? she gasps. "Those who have been waiting for you Princess, there are many waiting." "I must get my things together at least, so I will see you later." Orpheus leaves and Princess sits in her chair trying it out for size as Rebecca enters. "Princess, she calls, what exactly is going on"? "Well apparently I actually am a Princess, and I am leaving for the capital tomorrow, you will join me, won't you"? "Try stopping me" Rebecca replies as they wrap their arms around each other. "Oh, the mountain man is asking for you"? "Ok, guess I better get over there. Are you coming." "I'll meet you there, I have a few things I need to do first." Princess gets up and leaves for the surgery.

Orpheus is back in the Priory and is writing letters to send off by ravens. A junior enters his office." Sir you called." "Yes, can you send these of immediately to all the main centres, thank you." He hands a bunch of rolled notes to him. "Excuse me Sir but is it true that we are leaving for the capital"? the junior asks. "Yes, some of us." Orpheus replies. "Excuse me Sir, but could I be one of the members to join you." "Why not, I will see you in the morning" Orpheus responds. "Yes Sir" the junior cries as he rushes off. Orpheus continues with his plans for leaving and picking items he needs to take, including the large book.

Back at the Doctors surgery, the Mountain Man is looking much better and sitting up on the bed. Princess enters and moves over to him. "You are looking better, I was thinking, we don't even know your name, we can't call you Mountain man ha-ha" she laughs. "It's Geraldo" he tells. "Well Geraldo, I'm glad you are feeling better, unfortunately I will be leaving tomorrow, but I will make sure you are looked after" Princess tells him. "Well thanks for all your help, I hope you will be safe." Geraldo says." Hopefully, we will meet again in the future, but I need to go and get ready now" Princess says. She leaves as Geraldo watches her depart, he pulls the bandage from his head throws the sling away and he also leaves.

Chapter three

Next morning Princess looking magnificent with her long blond hair blowing in the wind and a bronze breast plate and matching head band worn over leather tunic and tight trousers, followed by Orpheus, twenty Juniors and ten men from the town dressed in armour are all in line waiting to exit the town through the entrance arch. The remaining towns people are cheering as the small group slowly move out. Princess is looking around at everyone somewhat blushing at the cheers flowing her way. They slowly leave the sight of the town and disappear into the woods, heading for the Capital. On a hill above watching over them is Geraldo. He slowly moves his horse on, in parallel to the group. After a few miles Orpheus leans over to Princess," so how did you wake up this morning, must feel like a dream I guess"? Princess taps her forehead and replies "It certainly was different, especially when some ladies entered my room and started to dress me, I had to send them away. Ha-ha Orpheus laughs "well get used to it, it

15

will be even worse once you reach the Capital." "I never thought of that, they won't all be bowing to me will they." "Well, I believe the ladies will curtsey" he laughs." "Oh, my goodness, I won't be able to keep a straight face." She replies. "You'll get used to it, you have to be strong, as you have a country to build, and not long to do it in, it won't be long before Lord Manion responds to your appearance, he's had it his own way for a long time now." "He better not try and enter our country; I won't let him"! she claims. "Good that's the character we need at the front, there are plenty of men ready to support you, but they have been leaderless for a long time now." "So, who will lead them" she asks. "I have sent messages out to all my old contacts from the days when our army was formidable" he replies "But for now, enough talks let move on" as he digs his heels into his horse's side and gallops of followed by everyone else.

Meanwhile in the distant land of Urania, the news from Alexandra has reached Lord Manion. He bursts into Kaaron's work room where he is mixing potions. "What is this news" Manion barks as he throws Alexanders news on Kaaron's desk. "You said they were all dead, who is this Princess"! He shouts. "My Lord, it appears we were misled, but it is just a single girl, the whole Royal family could not face up to us and our power, you have nothing to worry about, I assure you, my Lord." "You better be right" he shouts as he turns and marches out. From down the corridor he could still be heard "We will see what Alexander has to report."

Kaaron moves over to his library and opens a large book of the Lystonian Royal Family, like Orpheus's book. He looks up the last King and Queen and close family and notes their powers. The King controlled fire, the Queen water, the Kings brother wind, and his sister nature. Each had been killed individually by spies or open battle, but none together. Individually none could match the power of Kaaron and his dark magic. He smiles and thinks to himself, a sole girl has no chance, especially with no army. He closes the book and moves back to working on his potions, He takes a small bottle of liquid and throws it out the window, it is followed by a large explosion and the building rocks. Books and bottles fall around his. "That'll do" he says to himself as he leaves the room and heads for the court room where Lord Manion is receiving news from Alexander. Alexander is on one knee as he gives Manion his report. "We had visited a few villages when we heard of a large hoard of gold in a nearby town. We headed there and searched, there was little obstruction to us, we found little, but someone told us that a mountain man had hidden cases of gold and silver in the mountains. We found him and started interrogation. He was very stubborn and after two days and many beatings had given up nothing. Meanwhile some towns people had escaped and ran to the Priory headed by Orpheus. He gave them sanctuary and locked the gate. I never tried to enter as per your previous orders my lord, so we returned to the town. We continued looking and interrogations and that night a single girl, now known as Princess, sneaked into the town and rescued some men. Fortunately, she was caught, and after questioning, I passed sentence on her to be burnt in the town centre. As I waved to proceed a band lead by Orpheus entered the centre and questioned my orders. I made it clear that she was clearly guilty, and the punishment was death by fire. He did not argue but asked to give her last personal belongings, a couple of bracelets, I did not think anything of it and allowed him. Strangely, he himself took the flame from my man and lit the Pier. Then suddenly there was a great light, and a beam entered the heavens and then whirled around engulfing all my men. They just disappeared. Orpheus told me a go and give you a message." "And what is this message" Manion demanded. "Do not enter Lystonia or be destroyed, he seemed very confident" Alexander stated. "Confident"! Manion shouted "Confident, wait till we flatten that country and kill everyone, I was too easy on them before, but now they dare to forbid me, me"! he shouted as Kaaron comes forward "My Lord, it seems she has inherited her father's power, but as we know, that is all, she is alone and so were they when we defeated them, she is not a problem, as long as we prepare carefully". "Alexander, arrange a battle plan to present to me by tomorrow, I want this matter ended without delay." Manion orders. Alexander stands" As you command my Lord," and he leaves. Manion sits on his thrown and scowls at everyone as they back away and Kaaron moves up to talk to him. "My Lord, please let me guide Alexander and work out a plan to nullify her power, their army is non-existent." "Very good" Manion explains and waves him off.

Back on the road in Lystonia, Princess and her group are making camp. She is sitting within her tent on a large chair brought on a wagon with supplies. Before her is a table with a map on it. She is with Orpheus and Rebecca, who is now her constant companion. Orpheus is showing her the map which is of both Lystonia and Urania. He is pointing out areas where the enemy can attack through. "I'm not a military person Orpheus, I don't know what to do with this information. We have no idea if we even have an army" Princess says despondently. "Trust me my Princess, you will have an army" he replies reassuring her. At this moment, a guard enters and announces the presence of a large man dressed in full armour. He enters and lowers to the Knee, his helmet held under his arm. "My Princess, may I offer my services," Orpheus moves over to him and takes his hand. "My Princess, this is Lord Durent, he was one of your fathers' greatest generals, He has received my message as promised and others will follow". Princess tells him "Please rise Lord Durent and thank you for coming to our side." "Not only myself my Princess, as soon as the news arrived that you actually exist, my men rallied and are currently gathering all their hidden equipment and will meet us outside the Capital gates. I would be proud to lead you into your new Capital"." It would be my honour Lord Durent, now join us and remove some of your armour, I am sure you are hungry after your journey here" Princess gestures to Rebecca to get him a drink and some food. Rebecca pours him a drink and tops up Princess and Orpheus's drinks, then leaves to get some food. Orpheus leads Durent over to the map and they study it while Princess looks outside the tent at the small group supporting her. Everyone is busy, but they also look happy for the first time in many years. She leaves the tent and starts to walk amongst everyone. As she approaches them, they immediately stop what they are doing and bow or curtsey. She naturally reacts to stop them, but they carry on. She smiles and moves onto the next group. As she leaves each group, they are even happier and work harder. Suddenly a musician starts playing and everyone starts singing and dancing around the central fire. Orpheus and Durent stand at the tent entrance. Durent turns to Orpheus "So tell me, can she handle all this". Orpheus "If anyone can, she can. You should have seen her when she first used her power, she didn't even know she possessed it, she was magnificent, and you can see the effect she has on everyone". "I hope so" Durent mutters. "Everything will be ok; I am confident in her". Orpheus replies as Princess re-enters the tent." Well gentlemen, everyone seems happy, so if you don't mind, I am going to get some sleep". "Of course, Princess, please have a good night". They both leave.

Chapter four

The Capital called Pargon is very active with everyone rushing around preparing for the arrival of Princess. Word had spread like wildfire and the roads are covered in flags and bunting. The area in front of the palace is filled with people patiently waiting and on the bandstand a band played encouraging everyone to dance and sing. Outside the city, thousands of men had assembled, maybe as many as three thousand. All of a sudden, a trumpet blasted out and the men all climbed on their horses and get into columns. Then the church bells start to ring, and children rush down the street crying out" She's coming, she's coming". The crowd start to part so the entourage can move forward. Through the arch gates, Princess appears leading her entourage and then the three thousand mounted guards. Slowly she enters the city as everyone cheers and throw flowers at her. She waves royally and is surrounded by four guards to make sure nothing happens. The atmosphere is electric with cheers and singing from the music from the band. As she approaches the palace the gates open, and she rides in, the troops pair off and surround the city centre. Princess, Orpheus, Durent and Rebecca all unmount and are led into the palace. The gates close and the crowd rush forward, heads poking through the gaps in the railings. Then a cheer erupts as the balcony doors open and Princess steps out and the cheers explode into a crescendo. She waves and is then joined by Orpheus, Durent and Rebecca. They all wave and then Princess raises her hand. Everyone quickly hushes and she places her hands on the balcony railing. She announces "Today I come to you as a simple person, blessed with a name of a Princess. Never did I ever believe that this was in fact my heritage. I swear by all mighty god, that I will try and fulfil my duties to you, if you truly wish me to rule over you." A loud cheer breaks out from the crowd, and everyone is waving back at her. Again, she raises her hand, learning quickly how to control a crowd. Everyone again goes quiet. "As I join you, we find we are indeed in troublesome times. It looks like Lord Manion is again going to invade, and again we must stay strong and quickly prepare to defend our country, families, and friends. Will you join me in this battle for survival." Again, on que a cheer erupts in agreement and the mounted soldiers smash their shields with their swords. She raises her hand again and proclaims, "Then I will be honoured to lead you in this defence and remove this vial invader from our land, I thank you for your belief and support." Another cheer goes up and she turns and leaves the balcony followed by Orpheus, Durent and Rebecca who locks the doors behind her. The crowd celebrate into the night and the soldiers all move into the old barracks and prepare their lodgings. The four are all in the balcony room as a maid enters the room and asks, "Your majesty, would you like to view your room, it has been fully prepared for you". "Oh yes, Beccy do you want to join me" Princess responds and the two leave. The two men remaining move over to a small glass table and pour themselves two drinks. Orpheus "Well I think that all went rather well, don't you"? "Yes, but this was just a welcome, how will everyone react when the fighting starts" Durent responds." One step at a time, one step at a time. How many men do you think you can raise in a month say"? Orpheus questions. "Hard to say, but I would hope comfortably fifteen thousand, although not many will be fully fit, so we have a lot of work to do." Durent replies. "Well, you concentrate on raising the men and getting them battle fit." Orpheus commands. Durent interrupt him with, "Fifteen thousand will not be enough, we might have to look elsewhere, and we will need money for that, mercenaries are not cheap or easy to acquire, you are going to need to find some money from somewhere, or this can all end up as a bad dream". "Well, I guess I have my work set out for myself as well then" Orpheus responds. They clink glasses.

Up in Princess's bedroom, the two girls are jumping on the massive four poster bed and exploring. They open a wardrobe, and it is full of long dresses, which it is assumed belonged to Princesses mother. She takes one out and holds it against herself. "What do you think" Princess asks. Very elegant your highness as she takes a bow, they both fall back on the bed. Princess looks up and sees a door over in the corner. "What's that," they both get up and go over to open it. As the door opens it reveals another bedroom with a slightly less opulent bed. "You can sleep here next to me Becky," Princes excitedly pulls her in. "If that's what you want, I don't mind being downstair with the others." Rebecka suggests. "No way, I can't spend all my time shouting out for you or hunting for you." "I think the idea is you ring a bell actually" Rebecca explains. "Not for you, you are like a sister to me, better, you are a best friend too, and who else can I talk to about my secrets or worries, Orpheus." She pretends to whisper to Orpheus" Oh Orpheus, look at that handsome man there, do you think he is handsome as well", in a rough voice," Oh yes of course your majesty, a real catch", No, that would never do" she finishes, they both continue laughing and looking around. There is then a knock at the door. A house maid enters. "Excuse me madam, but it is your bath time, shall I prepare it now." "What, it's not Friday," Princess blurts out. "Eh, we prepare you a bath daily your highness" she replies. "Of course, just joking, prepare away, we'll go in the other room. Princess and Rebecca moved into the other room as the maid opened the door to several other girls all carrying jugs of hot water and pouring them into the ornate bath in the far side of the room. Once they had finished, they stood by the bath as the first maid goes to tell Princess. She knocks and enters Rebecca's room. "Madam your bath is ready." She waits for Princess to come. "Oh, you want me now"? Princess asks. "If you wish your majesty" the maid leads her out to the bath. Upon approaching the bath, she was surrounded by maids starting to undress her. Princess crouches down and calls for Rebecca" Beccy Becky…. Help." Rebecca enters the room and laughs. "Ladies stop and step back." The maids stopped and step back. "Ladies, Princess is quite capable of dressing herself, she has been doing it for a while now, and equally she can bath herself, so please leave and return in one hour to take the bath away" Rebecca ordered. They all turn and leave the room. Rebecca then turns to Princess "I'll leave you to your privacy, see you later" Rebecca then starts to move back to her room as Princess stands and tries to take the breast plate off. "Becky, Becky, eh, can you help me, I can't get it off," she sighed, they both laughed, and Becky came back to unbuckle her cloths. "See you later" Rebecca says as she makes her way back into her room as Princess steps into the bath and lowers herself into it.

The next day high up in the mountains, Geraldo is approaching a hidden cave with the entrance covered in bracken. He pulls it away and lights a torch before entering the cave. He works his way deep into it and comes across another bundle of torches. He lights them all and throws them around the cave. It lights up and in the centre is a large stack of boxes. He goes over to them and takes out a knife and opens the first box. The lid flips of and reveals a fortune in gold bullion. He picks up a hand full and puts them in his pocket and then replaces the lid. Then he spends the next hour carrying the boxes to the entrance. Once finished he sits down and takes a long drink while rubbing his aching body. He then moves to the side of the cave and moves some more bushes, revealing an old carriage. He then loads it up and attaches his two horses. He then heads down the mountain towards the Capital.

Back at the Capital, the conference room is busy with a table headed by Princess, with Rebecca, Orpheus, Durent and a few other senior soldiers. At the far end of the conference table sits an old man who looks like a bookkeeper he is called Baldred. "So, Lord Durent, what are your views on our position" Princess asks. He stands and starts his report," Well your Majesty I have received news from several of our past Generals and senior personnel, it seems they are all rallying their men, although these soldiers are older and past their peak, but fortunately many have sons of eligible age that they have been training, but equipment is a problem. The simple fact is that to invade, you really need a numbers superiority of at least two to one. Manion can call on over fifty thousand easily and we are stretched at reaching ten." "Oh, that does not seem very hopeful" Princess explains. "With careful planning and setting up good defences on the borders, we can certainly help even it up, they must travel through passes through the mountains. Problem is we will not know which till it is too late, so must cover them all" he responds. Then there is the possibility that they attack from the sea, which would bring them straight to the city, so we must defend the borders and the coast, you see how the numbers will be stretched, especially if they attack on mass." "My God" Princess sighs. "What options do we have." Orpheus stands "There is the possibility of Mercenaries, there are many men in other countries looking for a fight and to receive a pay day." At this proposal the man at the end, Baldred stands "And how much will all this cost, the equipment, swords, shields and armour are not cheap and mercenaries, I dread to think" he asks. Princess also asks, "so Lord Durent, how much are we looking for"? He stands again and flusters as he spurts out a number "I anticipate at least 500 gold crowns for the equipment and the mercenaries depend on numbers, but I would expect 800". "And how much is in the treasury, may I ask"? Princess questions.

Baldred stands" unfortunately no funds have been added to it for many years and Manion has basically drained it. We are going to struggle to feed the men we have, let alone equip them." Princess places her head in her hands, "surely there is some answer, wasn't anything saved from Manion." I am sorry your highness, but when Manion attacked, he surrounded the city, so nothing escaped as far as I know. He replies. "It seems like we must protect the city as a priority, and we must gather any metals for the smithies. The farmers will have to donate their crops as well, unfortunately it will have to be a tax, but these are difficult times." Orpheus announces. "I will also send messages pleading for help from fellow country leaders, hopefully some will come forward." "OK I guess this meeting is closed; you all have your tasks. What can I do to help"? Princess adds. Your presence is a great help, so just carry on rallying the people, they seem to adore you". Orpheus suggests. "That was before they heard any bad news though, but I will do what I can, everyone dismiss." Princess stands and leaves, followed by Rebecca and rushes to her room. Once there she collapses on the bed. Tears appear in her eyes as she looks up to Rebecca "This is all my fault, if I hadn't sneaked into the town and made Manion aware, nothing would have happened" Princess cries. "My dear Princess, things could not just carry on, the country was dying, and did those crowds blame you, they know about Manion and have all suffered by him, they are praying that you can save them, and if not, well we will go down fighting", was Rebecca's fighting reply, she gives Princess a hug, "So let's clean that face and start". "What would I do without you Becky." Princess sighs. "Oh, you could not survive, trust me" she replies as they laugh, and Rebecca gets a bowl of water and a towel. Princess cleans her face and makes herself presentable. She stands up, shakes herself down and heads for the door, "Ok message received, let's go." They both leave.

Down in the conference room Orpheus is still present with Durent. They are looking at the map and Durent points to a few passes. "We should immediately place watch guards at these sites, just to give us an early warning. I would then send guards to here, here, and here. Locals can help build barricades, to block the passes, trenches to stop horses and carriages etc." "Good plan Durent, you get on with that, and I'll start sending pleads out to neighbouring countries, they all hate Manion" Orpheus adds. Durent rolls up the map and heads for the barracks to give out his orders.

In town Princess escorted by Rebecca and four guards wander through the streets greeting the locals and checking how the city is laid out. It is her first visit to the capital, so she has a lot to learn. She comes across a school. It has a large hall and playing fields. They enter and there is a class in progress. The children aged between ten and fifteen and doing keep fit. They all stop as she, enters. "Please do not stop" she calls out to the teacher. The male teacher immediately lowers to one knee and the boys copy him. The girls curtsy. "Please rise" she asks. She approaches them and they crowd around her. "Please sit, I need to talk to you all." They all sit and look up to her." This is all very new to me, so please excuse me if I make a mistake." Princess explains "You cannot make a mistake your highness, we are your subject, what can we do for you"? the teacher asks. "Well, I see you are all very fit and thankfully healthy, but we have hard times ahead of us, I was wandering if you could help." The children all cheer. "What exactly do you have in mind your highness, how can we help" the teacher queries. "Well, as you can see, we have a new army being built, but there has not been one for a long time, and an army marches on their stomach, so I hear, so I was wondering if we announce a school holiday, you might volunteer to help". The children again cheer "what! How!" they all shout. "Well, you young men are really fit, so I was wondering if some of you could help in the field and gather crops so everyone can eat and store supplies, it will be hard work." The boys all nod their heads in agreement. The bigger ones could help the smithies, they have a lot of work ahead of them." "I can organise them, no problem" the teacher says. A young girl puts her hand up. Princess acknowledges her. "Your majesty, what will we girls do." "You have a very important job, I need you to help in the kitchens preparing the food and again the older ones, help prepare the hospital, I am sure there will be many injured, from what I have seen of Manion's men. The Teacher stands up and gets the children into line and they all stand to attention. "I guess that is agreed then" Princess announces, "Dismiss" the children all run off to their lockers as the teacher approaches, "They will not let you down, and I think they appreciate being a part of everything." He says and thank you. "I hope so, oh I don't know your name"? "Porter" your majesty, he replies. "Very good, we must move on now, thank you." Princess turns and leaves with Rebecca and her guards. As she exits the hall, she looks at the playing fields. "This would be a good place to train the new recruits, take a note Becky of what we discussed here, hate to forget any of it," Rebecca points to her head, "Already in here, will do a report when we get back." They walk on. They approach the city entrance where guards are in place and anyone leaving or trying to enter are stopped and checked. There is a farmer with a load of vegetables and a cow tied to the back of his carriage. "Food for the City he shouts down to the guard," the guard walks around and checks the goods, "move on and thank you," the guard shouts. Then another man rolls forward it is the mountain man, Geraldo with his carriage. "Stop, what do you have there," the soldier shouts. "A gift for the Princess" he replies. "I'll have to check first." "No way" Geraldo shouts, it is private and only for the Princess," The guard reacts and pulls him down from the carriage and points a spear at him. "I said, I want to check." The guard barks, prodding Geraldo with the spear. "Stop" shouts Princess as the guard instantly stands back to attention. "He refused to...." "I know this man, he is a friend, but it is ok, you were doing your job, help him up." The guard takes Geraldo's arm and helps him up. Princess goes to Geraldo and gives him a hug. "What are you doing here, you are supposed to be in the surgery recovering" she asks. "No time for that Princess, we have work to do, can I come in." "Of course, help me up and I'll join you, Becky are you coming. No,

I'll go back with the guards, you don't need them now" Becky laughs. As Geraldo shakes the reins and the horses move on.

As Princess and Geraldo pass through the streets towards the Palace, Geraldo is amazed at the reaction of the towns people to Princess. "Looks like you have made quite an impression around here" he smiles. They approach the Palace gate, and they are opened, and Princess is met by Orpheus. "What are you doing up there" he asks, and who is this. "This is Geraldo, he is my friend from town," she replies as she climbs of the carriage. Geraldo secures the carriage and dismounts and approaches Princess. He lowers to one knee and announces, "My Princess, I have a gift for you, I have been looking after for many years." She is taken aback by his actions, "What, why…" she stutters. He goes to the back of the carriage and takes a box out and places it before her, He then opens it to the gasps of everyone. Gold bullions. "Wow, how"?? Princess tries to speak. "The kingdoms treasury was entrusted to me by the King to hide till it was time to return. This is the time. "The King, my father, you knew him." "It was my honour your highness" he replies. Orpheus orders several guards to empty the carriage and take the boxes up to the conference room. Get the bookkeeper immediately, I have some work for him," he claps his hands and turns to Princess, "We have just solved our biggest problem Princess, all is not lost, all is not lost" as he turns and follows the soldiers to the conference room. Princess turns to Geraldo, "I don't know how to thank you, how can I ever repay you." She asks. "A bath would be nice; I am sure I must smell rotten. "Off course follow me" she takes his arm and leads him to her room. She rings the bell, and six maids instantly appear. "Arrange a bath for this man and get him some new cloths, look in my father's stores." They all curtsey and advance on Geraldo who disappears beyond the groping arms of the maids. Princess laughs and turns to leave, "I'll see you later Geraldo," she laughs.

She leaves and heads to the conference room. Upon entering she sees the bookkeeper opening the boxes and passing the gold through his finger. Princess goes over to him "Is this enough for our needs" she asks, "enough, we could fund two wars, look how much is here, how did this happen" he asks. "Magic" Princess whispers. "Magic" he goes to questions her, as she places her finger to her lips. He nods to keep the secret. Orpheus comes over to her and for the first time looks relaxed. "You certainly seem to have the luck of the Gods, Princess; how did you know that man." She whispers to him "We were cell mates, don't tell anyone." She laughs and inspects some gold goblets. "How about a drink Orpheus." She points to the bottle of wine. "Oh, your Highness, why not. I'll just…" She raises her hand and pours the wine herself, "I'm not helpless Orpheus, a few days ago I was chasing chickens" she laughs, he joins in the laughing and takes the goblet and clinks her goblet which makes a glorious sound. At this moment Rebecca enters in a hurry, Princess there's a strange man in your room, he's naked and …" "ha-ha It's Geraldo, look what he brought". Rebecca looks at the boxes and is stunned. "Wow, Geraldo the mountain man, that's not who I saw." "It's Geraldo, who else would bring all this." Princess picks up a gold necklace and places it to her neck. "What do you think," she models it then throws it back and picks another one with jewels and takes it over to Rebecka and places it around her neck. "Suits you, don't you think"? "It's like my other one, don't you think" Rebecca jokes. They both laugh. At this moment there is a loud knock at the door and an elegant tall man clean shaved and looking immaculate in military regalia enters. Princess gasps after a second realising it is Geraldo. "Geraldo is that, no it can't be. Geraldo" she tries to get out of her mouth the words. He stands to attention and salutes. Your Highness, Major Geraldo Templeton at your service. She rushes over to him and wraps her arms around him. You look amazing, this is like a dream, are you really one of my soldiers." Major Templeton your highness" he replies. "What's above a Major, Major"? "General your highness." "OK then General Templeton, would you like a drink." Princess orders. "But I…." he tries to act official, but she is having none of it. "Geraldo, you are officially off duty, now, about that drink." She again asks, he relaxes" It would be a pleasure your Highness." "Princess, of duty remember" "Oh yes of course your.... Princess." She hands him a goblet of wine. He sips it and winces a smile. She laughs," I guess all those years in the mountains have changed your tastes ha-ha, she rings the bell and a maid appears, Can you get a flagon of beer and a tankard " "make that two" Orpheus interrupts. " It's been a while since we had a reason to celebrated anything" he added. The maid disappears and returns minutes later with a tray of beer and tankards. Geraldo pours two tankards and hands one to Orpheus, he then raises his tankard and makes a toast. "Here's two our Princess and our future success in battle." Everyone cheers and takes a drink. They continue inspecting the gold jewellery and Rebecca comes across a crown and places it on Princesses head, unfortunately it is the kings' crown, and it falls down to the bridge of her nose. She looks ridiculous and everyone laughs.

Chapter five

In Urania Lord Manion is inspecting his army on horseback, before him on a parade field are thousands of soldiers. They march before him and are followed by weapons for attacking the city and ports. "good "Manion announces. "My Lord, I have something special to present to you, it will make your invasion a guaranteed success" Kaaron explains. Some special soldiers come forward with tubes held upon their shoulders. They all aim at an old barn and Kaaron order "Fire." There is a massive explosive sound, and the tubes erupt into fire and the barn explodes into tiny pieces. Manion instantly stands up on his horse, "what is this, Magic"? No, my Lord just simple physics. But it should remove any barricades or force before us. "Excellent, excellent, Kaaron, lets return to the tower, and make plans." They all turn and head back to his retreat. Once back he moves over to a floor plan of his invasion. It clearly shows an invasion via two passes in the mountains and a surprise sea assault. Manion shows the plan to Kaaron. He points to the two passes. These passes reduce the size of army that can pass at any one time, but if we reduce the number to look large and fight a holding battle, the sea assault can take place and upon capturing the City we can attack the main army from behind. They will never expect this. Especially if they are commanded by a silly girl" he laughs. "A brilliant plan my Lord, we can use the new explosives on the ships as well as the passes. They will be totally confused" explains Kaaron. "How long till all the ships are ready" asks Manion. I hope within ten days, but we must keep them secret, don't want to ruin the surprise, do we"? Kaaron laughs. "Meanwhile send small skirmish attacks through the other passes, to keep them guessing" Manion orders. "Very good" Kaaron bows and exits. Manion walks onto the map and steps on the capital city.

At the port of Pargon a ship arrives. An official man departs and is escorted to the Palace. He is an ambassador of the neighbouring land of Tarmack. He approaches the Throne room where Princess sits upon her throne, now wearing a crown that fits. She is wearing a long purple gown embellished with gold braid. By her side is Orpheus, Geraldo, Durent, Rebecca and the palace guards. The man approaches and kneels on one knee. He introduces himself "Your Highness, I am Ronaldo Manchura of Espatcho. I bring greetings from my master His Royal Highness King Alphonso of Tarmack." "Please stand Lord Manchura, you are welcome to Lystonia, what news do you have for us? He pronounces" His Highness King Alphonso of Tarmack." This brings about a smirk from Princess as she looks at Rebecca who nods her attention back at the man. "As I was saying King Alphonso of Tarmack sends you greeting and wishes you success in your future dispute with Urania, Tarmack has also suffered at the hands of Lord Manion and wish you every success." "I thank King eh Alphonso for his kind thoughts, I was wondering if there was anything else he may have mentioned." The man starts again" Your Highness, King Alphonso of Tarmack want to wish you every success and" Princess lets out a little giggle covered by Orpheus coughing, "to show his support he has sent me here to show our support." "That is very nice, and your king has my thanks, was there anything else, or are you all Tarmack has to offer," she responds beginning to be frustrated. "King Alphonso of Tarmack also want to inform you that he is sending you Fifteen thousand soldiers, of which ten thousand are on horseback. As well as this he is sending five ships of food and provisions for the poor people of Lystonia." This is the Pledge of King Alphonso of Tarmack your Highness. Princess sits up, now more interested in his speech. She responds" Please tell your King Alphonso of Tarmack, that I and the people of Lystonia are very grateful for his support In this matter, when can we expect arrival of this welcomed gift"? "We have sent the ships, and they should arrive any day. The men will be a little longer, they have many miles to travel, but hopefully a week." Princess turns to Durent" is this soon enough"? "It is hard to say, we have not heard of any movement from Urania, but they are certainly ready" Durent explains. She turns back to "Lord Manchura, I thank you for this generous gift, and I would ask you to ensure that your King Alphonso of Tarmack is aware of the urgency of his men arriving as soon as possible." He again kneels and announces, "I will return to my ship immediately and inform King Alphonso of Tarmack of your request and thanks, I am sure he will be grateful for your thanks and try to reach your land as soon as possible." "That is all we can ask; I thank you for your swift action, Lord Manchura and wish you a safe journey back to Tarmack." Princess responds as Manchura backs out of the hall to his ship. Upon the doors closing Princess break out in laughter as Orpheus interrupts her laughing with "That is a very great support from our ally your Highness." "I know, I am sorry, but how many times can he name what's his name" again she laughs. Orpheus shakes his head and beckons to Rebecca to take Princess to her room to compose.

Orpheus walks over to Geraldo, "and she looks so regal", Geraldo "Give her time, she is doing amazing things, and it is all new to her, we've never been here before". "Of course, you are right, I must be patient," how are the plans going. Orpheus sighs. Geraldo responds "at a pace, new men are arriving daily, we have commandeered the school for training and the smithies are working all hours. I also have a delivery of weapons arriving by ship soon, which cost a bit, but needed. I think we will start sending men to the passes in two days, just to make room in the barracks." "Good" Orpheus responds and moves on to see other military men. Geraldo walks over to the throne and sees Princess peaking from behind the drapes, he walks over to her. She beckons him to be quiet, "Is he mad" she asks, "No, maybe frustrated, but don't worry you are doing well, I found it hard keeping a straight face and I'm military. "Oh good, can we go out to the city, I need some air" she asks. Of course, I'll get a guard together" he responds. "No just us, you and me, we don't need guards, I have you"! "But you are the Princess, it is fool hardy to not take security anything could happen" he explains. "I have my mountain man, what more do I need," she grabs him, and they rush of the back steps and down to the stables. Geraldo calls a stable hand, "Get our horses now please," "yes sire" he replies as he rushes off, shortly to return leading two prime horses. Geraldo helps Princess mount her horse and then mounts his own. They then gallop out of the stable to the city gates and into the woods beyond. Princess is leading and missing over hanging branches by inches. Geraldo shakes his head and takes chase. After a while they reach a lake. They pull up and climb down from their mounts. They lead their horses to the water and Princess begs Geraldo to join her in a swim. "Your Highness, we can't, we should not even be here, but we cannot stay away for long. She kicks of her boots and paddles into the lake and pulls off her dress and throws it onto the log by the lake edge and slowly lowers herself into the water. Geraldo pleads with her to come back but she just moves further out. Suddenly she jerks strangely and sinks below the water, her arms flailing around. Geraldo without hesitation dives into the pool and sweeps her into his arm. "Are you OK, what happened"! she laughs and puts her arms around him, "You got your uniform wet," she laughs as he throws her back into the lake and heads back to the shore soaking wet. He takes of his boots and empties them of water. Princess slowly approaches the shore and wraps her dress to cover herself. "Are you angry with me Geraldo, I was only playing." He climbs onto his horse. "We better head back" he suggests as he slowly moves off. She quickly throws her dress on and her boots and clambers on her horse and rides after him. As she catches up, he ignores her. "I was only joking Geraldo, …. Geraldo, it was a joke"! she pleads. He digs his heels into his horse and rides off towards the city. She stops for a second then shouts "Geraldo, Wait, I order you, Geraldo, wait for me." She shakes her reigns and chases of after him. Within a few minutes she has caught him up. "Geraldo, I'm sorry, I'm sorry, please say you forgive me" she pleads. He grunts and look away from her. She pulls back and advances the other side of him. "I'm sorry" she pleads again, eyes lowered. He stops, turns to her and she waits for his rebuke. He grabs her waist and pulls her toward him and kisses her passionately. She does not stop him and pulls him closer. After the long kiss ends "We better hurry back" he says as he again moves on at a gallop followed by Princess, through the city gates and into the Palace. They are met by stable hands, and they unmount. I better go and change into something dry. He walks of as she stands there watching him leave" But I…" she mutters as he disappears. She also marches of and heads straight for her room. Once there she is met by Rebecca, "Where have you been? I was worried sick" she asks. I went for a ride by the lake and fell in. "Really, you're the best swimmer I know". She claims. "Yeah, I know, I don't know what happened, Geraldo's uniforms soaking, he isn't very happy." Princess explains. Rebecca looks at her suspiciously, then how come your dress isn't wet? She looks suspiciously at Princess. "Well, that may not be exactly how it went, but he kissed me and…" "What" Rebecca shouts "You can't do that… I mean... well… tell me all about it." Rebecca drags her over to the bed and they lie down, and Princess starts to tell her what really happened. After telling all, Rebecca rang the bell and a maid appeared, Rebecca tells the maid to prepare a bath and a new outfit for the Princess. "You better look amazing when he sees you next, don't want to change his mind do we." Rebecca laughs and leaves Princess being attended by the maids.

A few hours later the conference room is laid out for a large meal. Seated at the table at its head is Princess, Rebecca to her left and Orpheus to her right. Next to him is Durent and then the bookkeeper Baldred. Next to Rebecca is Geraldo. Princess has a fine gown on and a tiara. Geraldo is in formal military uniform. Orpheus breaks the silence with "Well it's been quite an eventful day it seems"! "Oh, what do you mean" Princess asks, flashing a look to Rebecca, does he know as well. "I received a message from another ally who are offering support, maybe another ten thousand troops, I tried to tell you earlier, but I could not find you." Oh, that is excellent news, I was out in the city, and went for a ride." "I hope you took the appropriate security your highness" Orpheus states. "Oh, the best, it certainly gave me a new view of things." "Oh, what view is that"? he asks. Rebecca butts in, "You are looking extra radiant today your highness, that fresh air must have done you wonders, don't you think Colonel Templeton. She winks at Princess. "It is amazing was fresh air and sun can achieve, but yes you really think so"? She looks around the faces seeing the expectant looks on every one's faces. "It is undeniable, you are like a ray of sunshine amongst us." Geraldo claims. She responds, "Oh you… You must be toying with me she claims with a smile upon her face." "Never your Highness, I mean… I." "Only kidding" she laughs, Durent helps Geraldo by standing and making a toast. "Can I also agree with Colonel Templeton, you do indeed look radiant, here's to our princess"! he raises his glass, and everyone joins in agreeing the toast. "Please continue with your meal, enough toasts for now" Princess suggests. Everyone proceeds to lower their glasses and proceed to start eating.

Many miles away Lord Manion is in his court room receiving more bad news. Kaaron is before him telling him the latest news. "My Lord, my spies have informed me that more countries are offering support to Lystonia, this could affect our plans." Manion "what have you exactly heard." Well, it looks like San Nero is sending ten thousand men, that along with the support already offered by Tarmack of fifteen thousand and Lystonia's own army, make their numbers close to ours. We may have to rethink our plan." "We may be a little delayed, but we proceed, put word out to our allies, demand they all send fifteen thousand each, they dare not refuse." "Very good my Lord" Kaaron bows and exits. Manion raises from his throne and walks over the map on the floor. In temper he kicks the models of armies across the map. "They will be completely destroyed, and I will take all these lands" he says to his self.

Back in Lystonia the dinner has finished, and most people have left except Princess, Rebecca, and Geraldo. Princess rises from the seat and walks to the open fire and sits upon an animal skin rug in front of it. Geraldo walks over to her as Rebecca announces, "I'll eh just pop up and get your room ready Princess, See you later." She makes her quick exit as Geraldo stands above Princess, "So are you going to join me down here," she asks. "I'm not sure if I should your highness, it's ah ...." "I'm not going to order you." She pats the rug, and he lowers to her side. "I guess we should discuss earlier" Princess says. He immediately explains "I am sorry, it was a stupid impulsive thing, it won't happen again." Princess looks directly at him, "It won't, I quite liked it actually, you do know I was in a Priory for my whole life"? "Exactly, I feel I was taking advantage of you, I am sorry" he explains. "But I liked it actually, I am not sure I want it to stop." She says looking down. "But you, you are a princess." He again explains. "I am a woman also, and from the first time I saw you, I was curious about you, and trust me, you weren't looking your best, but I know I can trust you with my life, and I don't think you would ever hurt me, would you"? "No, my". She interrupts him, "we are alone now, please Princess, it is my name as well." "As you order my High...Princess." She holds his face in her hands, now can we try that kiss again, with no riding off. He pulls her towards him, and they kiss and embrace passionately. After what seems a lifetime, they separate and she looks shell shocked, "Well, that was worth waiting for" as she goes back to kiss him some more and they fall down to lie before the fire.

Up in Princess's room, Rebecca has had Princesses room prepared, with bath and bed robe. She dismisses the maids and tells them to report back in the morning, they all rush off. She vacates to her room and prepares herself for bed. As she slips into bed, she hears Princess enter her bedroom, there is the definite sound of military boots walking on the stone floor. Rebecca sits up with her sheet held up to her face. A smile across her face, she hears metal armour being dropped to the floor and the sound of splashing in the large bath. This is followed by giggles from Princess and then the sound of kissing and other noises, she is not sure of. Rebecca hides her head under her blanket and tries to sleep as she hears the creaking of princess's four poster being vigorously used. She blows her candle out and covers her ears.

The next morning Rebecca rises from her bed and creeps into Princess's room. Princess is lying on her bed with her legs walking up the wall as she is whistling a tune. Rebecca walks up to the bed post and looks down on Princess, "Good Morning, did you sleep well," she asks with a big grin on her face. "Not much sleep, but OH, what a night, I never guessed…." Was the reply. "Well, I guess you will need another bath, I'll call the maids." "I think I'll just relax for a while first, give me an hour, please." "OK, you regain your eh strength ha-ha." Rebecca gives her a kiss on her forehead and leave back to her room to get dressed herself. Several hours later Princess dressed in a long gown and head band of threaded gold enters the throne room where Orpheus is in discussions with Durent and Geraldo. They are overlooking the map of the land and pointing to different areas as possible assault areas. The number of model soldier on their side has drastically increased and everything is looking brighter. Princess walks over to them. They all stand to attention" Your Highness" they all acknowledge. "Please carry-on Gentlemen" she waves them back to their work. "Can I explain our thoughts regarding defence plans your highness." "Please do Lord Durent." "Well with the increase in our numbers and the extra time we have gained, it means we can secure the mountain passes substantially, so everyone can hold off an attack till we know for sure which ones are being used, then we transfer the unused men to those areas and force Manion back. The passes make it virtually impossible for his forces to make a wide attack, this reduces their effect and helps us". "Very good Lord Durent, any news when you expect them to advance"? Princess asks. Well, our spies have confirmed that his men are gathered beyond the mountain, but they certainly are short of numbers, so we suspect he is seeking reinforcements, or looking to the sea assault." "But we do not have a navy, how will we stop them"? Princess asks. Orpheus interrupt here and tells her" We will place a long chain across the Bay, to this we will attach many small fire boats which hopefully stop them. This along with your power which I am hoping will increase the fire attack should change their plans." "But I've only used the power once, I'm not even sure I can use it again." She explains. He reassures her" I will guide you and we will work on it over the next few days." "I have every confidence in you." Geraldo adds. "She gives a forced smile "Thanks"." Meanwhile, I think Geraldo should inspect the mountain passes to make sure the information we have is correct, he is experienced in working in that terrain, ideal for this job." Durent orders. "Whoa! Wait a minute, I do not want him to leave the City, he is needed here, I need..." Princess is interrupted by Geraldo" Your highness, this is my job, I am the right man for this, I will then return with a full report", "But what if something happens, what if…" again he interrupts " Nothing will happen to me, I have too much to come back for". I won't be long. "Excellent then" Orpheus announces as Princess walks away followed by Rebecca. Orpheus is surprised my Princess's response and turns to the men. "She is probably worried about not succeeding in her part, I'll start working with her immediately," Orpheus turns and rushes after Princess. "Princess, Princess, he calls as he rushes out the room. Durent turns to Geraldo "when will you leave"? Today I think, the sooner I am there, the better and the sooner I can return." "OK, make preparations, are you going to take a guard with you"?" No, there's enough men there and I am better working in the mountains alone, I won't be long". He excuses himself and leaves as well. Durent stares over to the map and places the fire boats across the bay. Then places Princess on the harbour wall.

Princess has rushed to her room with Rebecca. "He's going to the mountains again, what am I going to do"? "That's his job Princess, He can't just stay in the Palace, he'll end up resenting you. He won't be away long, and to be honest, he is the best man for the job". Princess sits on the side of her bed" I guess you are right, I just thought…" at this moment there is a knock at the door. It is Orpheus "Your majesty, I can see you are worried about using your power, but I assure you, you will be fine, let us go to the courtyard and do some exercises. Princess smiles "I guess so," she stands up and heads for the door. "Are you coming Rebecca"? Princess asks. "I think this is better done with just you two, I'll work on your battle dress, I've had some great ideas. Rebecca replies. Princess smiles and leaves with Orpheus.

As she enters the courtyard, she sees Geraldo leaving the palace. She calls out to him, but he does not hear her with his helmet on. He rides out as she looks dejected. "A fine officer your highness." Orpheus remarks, "Yes, don't know what we would have done without him." Orpheus picks up some torches and places them around the courtyard and lights them all. He goes over to Princess who is standing in the centre. "Right, now your highness just concentrate on the flames and imagine them growing larger. Princess starts to look at the different flames but is turning her head to see them all. Nothing is happening. She winces her eyes in concentration, but again nothing. "It's not working" she sighs. It's useless, Orpheus takes her by the shoulders standing behind her. Just concentrate on the single flame in front of you. Look deep into it and let it fill your mind. There are sparks then suddenly the fire erupts into a massive flame. She is startled and it blows out. "Excellent, excellent Orpheus shouts. He goes over to the lamp and relights it. "Again"! he shouts. Princess again concentrates and again the flame bursts into life." Now concentrate on the next one" Orpheus shouts. She looks at the next fire and it to bursts into flames. "Keep going "he shouts excitedly. As she turns around each torch erupts till the courtyard is brightly lit. all the workers around cheer. Princess then collapses to the ground. Orpheus rushes over. "Maybe that's enough for today, we will resume tomorrow your Highness, let's get you back to your room for some rest. He helps her up and they head back to her room where Rebecca is waiting. Rebecca sees the state of Princess and drops the cloth she is working on and rushes over to Princess. "What happened" she shouts. "She just over did it a bit, she'll be ok, just needs rest" Orpheus tells her. "I'm not surprised" Rebecca claims as Princess looks at her, "After all that effort." She grins at Princess. Rebecca takes her off Orpheus and he leaves as Princess sits by the fire. "Would you like a drink" she asks. "Yes, I think so, Geraldo's gone, I saw him leave. He didn't even say goodbye". Princess remarks. "He has his job to do also Princess, he'll be back, let's face it, he has a great reason to return." "I hope so" Princess sighs. Rebecca hands her a glass of wine. "He won't be long I'm sure" she adds. She picks up her glass and clinks Princesses glass, "Now tell me all about last night." Rebecca demands as she sits by Princess's feet. They break into a long discussion with lots of laughing and shocked looks on Rebecca's face.

Chapter six

A day has past and Geraldo rides into the Lystonia camp and heads for the captain's tent. He enters and the captain jumps to his feet and salutes him. "General Templeton, Captain, I believe you are expecting be." Geraldo introduces himself. "Of course, Sir, please come in and take a seat and rest from your ride. Can I get you a drink my name is Granger" The Captain says. "Thank you, I have quite a thirst. So, fill me in Captain, how are things progressing"? "Everything seems to be moving along fine. We have almost five thousand men here, and the barricade and trenches are almost finished, so they will struggle to get through us General. The captain proudly announces. "Excellent, I will inspect everything in the morning, I will then travel into the range to investigate what the enemy are up to. Geraldo tells him. "Rather you than me Sir," is the reply from the captain. "I have arranged quarters for you Sir if you wish to take a break"." Yes, I think I will rest for now, thank you." The captain calls for a soldier, "Please escort Colonel Templeton to his quarters. The soldier salutes and leads Geraldo out of the tent.

The following morning Geraldo is escorted by the captain, inspecting the troops and the field works. They have managed to dig massive trenches across the whole width of the pass, making it impossible for a horse or wagon to easily cross. "Very good captain" Geraldo remarks. "Thank you, Sir," "I think I will take a light lunch and then move into the mountains and see what I can find out." Geraldo responds, "Can you also get a pack horse of provisions ready for me, I expect to be away a few days." "I'll get on it right away Sir, meet me in my tent in 30 minutes and we can have lunch before you leave". The captain marches off as Geraldo inspects some of the artillery weapons facing the pass. He heads back to his tent to prepare for leaving.

Meanwhile back at the Palace Princess is again practicing her magic with Orpheus. Rebecca is present this time, shouting encouragement. This time Orpheus is having a large man throw the torches into the air. As he does this Princess crosses her wrists, so the bracelets join, and the torches again burst into flames. The response is much quicker this time, and she is not as tired. "Excellent Princess, at this rate we won't need an army" Orpheus lets out a rare joke. "I really doubt that fifty thousand men are a little more of a target than a few torches, but let's carry on" she adds encouragingly. "Very good your Highness Orpheus answers, let's try this." He arranges for a wall of straw bundles from the stables are built. "Are you ready your highness," he asks. "For what" before she finishes, he throws a torch over the wall. Princess instinctively prepares to fire and crosses the bracelets. The torch erupts followed by the whole wall. Rebecca claps encouragement,

"Fifty thousand, no problem" she gestures waving the flames away. "I think that's enough for today, let's go into town Becca" Princess says as Orpheus bows and waves her on. As they leave the stable boys are fighting to kill the flames of the wall. Princess turns back and crosses her arms again and the flames slowly disappear. She turns back and carries on walking, being chased by her guard who have been caught unprepared for her walk.

They enter the Town hall where there are tables of ladies all preparing food for the troops. In a corner are a group of children preparing the vegetables, peeling bags of potatoes, carrots, and other vegetables. Princess walks over to the children, "You look very busy," The children all stop what they are doing and curtsey. "Please do not stop, it looks like you are a very important part of this kitchen." A young girl speaks out" We've peels thousands of potatoes and carrots, but I've saved some for the horses". "That's a good idea" Princess encourages, well don't let me stop you, you are being so helpful". "Thank you, your Highness," they all reply. Princess and Rebecca move on and approach the smithies area. They look in without entering as it is incredibly hot. The head man comes over to her" Your highness, can I help you." "I was just looking in to see how my young men are doing." She enquires. "Very enthusiastic, they never stop, I've allowed them all to make their own sword in their free time." "That's a good idea, just don't exhaust them." "They'll be ok" he replies, as one of the boys comes over to him. "Sir, we are having trouble lighting the new furnace, it won't light, I've thrown loads of tinder in but nothing." "Maybe I can help" Princess enquires, "where is it" the boy points to the far corner of the works. There is a massive furnace with several boys trying desperately to light it. Princess walks over to it and does her magic and the furnace bursts into flames. The boys all cheer. The head smithy joins her "That's a neat trick, you couldn't come back tomorrow could you, he laughs." "Maybe" they all laugh, and Princess moves on to the playing fields were there are hundreds of young men training on parade. Most are bare chested and exercising. The Trainer comes over "Your highness, your new recruits" she looks at them as they all continue with their exercises. "Very impressive, just make sure they are ready when the time comes, I don't want to send them into action if they aren't ready." "They'll be ready your Highness, I guarantee." "Very good "she responds as she moves on. She looks out to the mountains, "I wonder how Geraldo is doing"? "I am sure he is fine Princess, he won't be away long, he has too good a reason to return." Princess playfully punches her, "schuh."

Back up in the mountains Geraldo has headed out into the pass, he turns a corner and is out of site of the soldiers. He turns to the mountain sides and heads of climbing higher and higher. From up here he can see vast areas of the pass but no sign of the enemy. He moves on further until the path is too difficult for the horses. He dismounts and ties them to a tree. He starts to climb the mountain side till he reaches a small plateau. He rests and looks down. From here he can see the enemy troops in their camp, very little preparation taking place. He sits down with his glasses and starts inspecting the enemy numbers writing down everything he sees. After some time, he hears some noise coming from above him. He ducks into a gap in the wall as two enemy soldiers pass by him. He pounces on them, knifing one and kicking the other of the mountain side. His scream can be heard through the pass to both sides. He gathers his equipment and starts to climb down. He reaches his horses and mounts them preparing to move back down the path. Meanwhile the enemy security has sounded an alarm, and a small band of soldiers are racing to where Geraldo is, he moves as fast as possible over the loose footings of the mountain side and reaches the bottom just as the soldiers come into view. They see him and head to capture him. He gallops of and heads for the camp. The enemy are catching up, but are suddenly met with a hail of arrows, they are all hit and killed or injured, one turns and heads back to his camp, while Geraldo rides past his soldiers into camp. He reaches the captains tent and dismounts. The captain comes out to welcome him back. "A bit of action I hear" the captain states. A little, nothing to worry about, I'll fill you in with what I saw". They enter the tent and Geraldo takes a seat and the captain pours two drinks. He goes behind his desk and takes his seat. "So, what did you see General"? "Well, I would say that it is very much stale mate here, they have five to ten thousand men camped beyond the pass, but there is little happening, they do not look like they are preparing to attack." "Well, that's good, isn't it"? he asks. "Well yes, but it then begs the questions, where are they going to advance, this is the obvious choice. I better move on to the next pass. Will you excuse me captain. Oh, and send them a message I am arriving imminently." "I will do immediately Sir." The captain salutes. Geraldo goes to his tent, gathers his belongings, and rides out.

Back in Urania, Lord Manion is seated on his throne with Alexander and Kaaron reporting their news. Alexander starts "My Lord, we have received over fifteen thousand extra men so far from our allies, they are being held at the port until you decide where you want them"." I assume you have kept the ships that brought them here" Manion asks. "Off course my Lord, if you decide on a sea attack, we will need them. Their captains were not happy, but they were convinced." Alexander laughs. "Very good" Manion murmurs "what news do you have Kaaron"? My lord, I have assessed the possible areas. I believe if we make two land attacks at sites C and D, then hit them from the sea, it will be the best option. I have viewed the ships and am working on a projectile that can be fired from the ships to cover the landing." Kaaron explains as he points to the sites on the map. "Excellent, so when will everything be ready"? Manion asks. I think confidently we will be ready in ten days as it will take three days at least for the ships to reach the Capital and the new men have to reach the mountain passes". "Excellent, ten days it is then." "I will start transporting the army to C and D then, my Lord" Alexander proclaims as he backs away from Manion before turning and quickly leaving. Manion rises from his throne and walks over to the map. "So how many men will the ships hold"? Initially ten thousand, supported later by another ten when the ships return.

The main Lystonian army is protecting the passes, and they are spread over several passes, so each looks like having five thousand men each. It will take them time to regroup, and we should have broken through by then with fifteen thousand bursting through C and D." Excellent, Manion encourages "Very good Sire." Kaaron agrees.

Geraldo rides into the next Lystonian camp, which happens to be area D. The camp is not as prepared as the previous one and men are still frantically digging out trenches. Geraldo rides up to the captain's tent and unmounts. He marches into the tent where the captain is behind his desk with a wench on his lap, he has a drink in his hand. Geraldo marches up to his desk and bashes his fists down on the desk. "What is going on here, out! "He shouts at the wench. The captain jumps up to attention trying to button his shirt. "Colonel, I was not expecting you… I was…" "I can see what you were doing, what is going on here, why is nothing ready here" he demands. "We had some delays, a flood and a shortage of materials and …." "And nothing, there are trees out there, aren't there, cut them down if needed." "Yes sir, immediately, I'll get on it right away.," Leave that now, show me the camp and what is actually ready." He leaves the tent, followed by the captain trying to catch him up. Geraldo looks at the men, all relaxing around the campfires and drinking. Up front by the pass are half finishes trenches and still packed equipment. "I have never seen such an unkept camp in my life Captain, you are relieved." "But…" the captain tries to explain. Where is your signal officer. The captain points to a small tent over by the other side of the camp. He marches over leaving the captain, who rushes back to his tent. At the signal tent Geraldo enters and asks the signal officer to send a message to the previous Captain from the previous camp to immediately transfer to this camp. His second in command can take over there. The signal man sends the message immediately as Geraldo heads back to the captain's tent. He barges in, "Get out and head back to the Capital, I will sort you out when I return" he shouts. "Very good Sir is the response from the captain as he grabs his belongings and starts to load a carriage. As he leaves, Geraldo goes behind his desk and sits in his seat. "Sergeant" he shouts, and an older experienced officer enters and stands to attention. "Sir." "Tell me Sergeant, what is the situation here." "I dread to inform you Sir, but it seems that only two and a half thousand men have reached us, and a lot of the equipment is missing, I have no idea where it has gone." So why are all these men lounging around, it's not a holiday camp". "The captain had strange views on who should do what and when sir" was the reply. "And you"? Geraldo looks up at him. I would have them out there digging those trenches sir," "So I do not have to ask you then, I assume." He questions. "Absolutely Sir, I'll get right on it." He salutes and marches out of the tent and a scream is heard across the camp as the Sergeant barks out orders to the men to get up and head to the trenches with tools. Geraldo heads over to the drinks table and pours himself a drink. He goes over to the map set out on another table. Nothing laid out on it. He starts placing models of soldiers and equipment on it. He looks carefully at the pass ahead and how it is wider than the previous one, with a flat entrance on the other end, perfect for the enemy. He taps his finger on the pass and thinks to himself, "this is the place." He heads back to the desk and writes a note informing the Capital of his findings. He then heads to the signal tent and hands the message to the signal officer. "Get this sent ASAP." "Very good Sir" the officer responds. Geraldo heads back to the tent and removes his jacket to relax. As he sits back the wench who was present earlier pokes her head into the tent "excuse me Sir, but could I be of service to you Sir." "I suggest you leave the camp unless you want to volunteer to help with the digging." He threatens her. "Very good Sir, I'll be off then Sir, goodbye Sir." She exits and Geraldo allows a smile on his face as he sits back and thinks of Princess.

Back at the Palace, Princess is seated on her throne as she is petitioned by numerous town people who have been waiting to see her. A man approaches her and complains that he is a baker, and the army is taking all his goods and paying pence for it.

Princess leans forward to him as asks "Tell me, if Lord Manion invaded and took over the city, how much do you think he would pay for your bread"? "He would not your highness, but…" "No buts, this is a fight for survival, and if you have to suffer a little now to live better later, I think that is fair, don't you agree"? she looks at him direct. He bows and says" well when you explain it like that your highness, please let me help you and your soldiers." "She waves him of as another man approaches and kneels before her. "Your highness, I am a simple fisherman, I fish to feed my family and to sell to the towns people. My boat has been taken for the war. I have no way to feed my family or make a living. Princess turns to Orpheus "Is this the case Orpheus." "Possibly your highness, his may have been one of the boats being used as fire ships linked to the chain. "I see" she turns to the man "I am sorry for this loss but unfortunately your boat is needed to defend the city, Orpheus, what is his boat worth" "I would think half a crown your highness" he replies. "Give him half a crown and allow his family to eat in the main hall with the army till this is all over, I assume this is acceptable to you" she asks the man. "Very fair your highness," he says as Orpheus hands him a gold coin which he immediately bites to check and backs away from Princess with a big smile on his face. Then two young children in tattered clothes approach. Princess looks at them and steps forward and bends down to them as they kneel before her. "Don't I know you, are you from my old town" "Yes, your highness, are parents were killed by the soldiers when they attacked. We have been wandering around ever since with nowhere to go. Princess takes their hands and calls Rebecca over. "Beccy please take them and get them cleaned and fed, then find them somewhere to sleep." "Very good your highness" Rebecca says as she leads the children away. Princess returns to her throne. "Are there anymore"? she asks Orpheus. "That is all for today your highness but expect more tomorrow." "Very good" she sighs as she rises and leaves the throne room and heads to her room. "

Up in her room, Princess is joined by Rebecca "Those kids were so cute, you would have thought they hadn't eaten in a week" she explains. "Maybe they hadn't" Princess responds. "I think it may be safer for them to take them back to the Priory, there's a chance they will know others and it is certainly safer than being here if Manion invades." "I arrange transport for them tomorrow then" Rebecca replies, do you want to see what I've been working on"? Rebecca asks. "Oh what"? Rebecca rushes to her room and brings back an outfit, like an all in one with a pattern like flames. "What do you think" she asks." Oh, very bright, not exactly Suttle." Rebecca inspects it at arm's length "do you think, you'll have your armour over it as well." "Oh yes, well do you want me to try it on"? "Well, I was hoping you would, just to check the fit." She shows a jar of pins. Princess takes of her gown and Rebecca helps her get into the outfit. Once on, Princess looks at the mirror and moves to show it off. "What do you think"? asks Rebecca. "It fits OK, let's add the armour." Is the response. Rebecca picks up the breastplate and carries it over to princess and helps her put it on. Again, Princess looks at the mirror. "You know, it's not bad, certainly more comfortable than chainmail ha-ha" she states." I'm glad you like it" Rebecca adds as she takes out her pins and shortens the sleeves. "Perfect she claims as she starts to unbuckle the breast plate. "I'll just fix the sleeves and we are done" she says. "Thanks Becky, it's very nice," hopefully I won't be to near to the enemy to need the chain mail." She hopes.

Back at the mountain camp Geraldo is sitting behind the captain's old desk when Captain Granger enters. He stands and salutes. "Relax Captain, glad you got here so fast, I am afraid you have a lot of work to do here." "It will be an honour Sir," he responds. "Let's walk, Geraldo leads him out of the tent to inspect the camp. The captain sees the relaxed atmosphere of the men and the lack of work happening. They reach the trenches and there are just three men doing anything. "You see the problem Captain" Geraldo explains. "My god Sir, where to start, I guess we get the sergeants together first and then call for a parade to see what we actually have here." "Good idea, you have my full support to sort it out, unfortunately I have to move on to the next pass, but I will return in a couple of days, good luck" Geraldo explains as he walks over to the tent and packs his belongings, Captain Granger calls the Sergeants to attention and starts balking out orders at them. Geraldo mounts his horse and gallops out of the camp.

The next morning at the Capital, a large army arrives from Tarmack. They stop at the city gates. Princess dressed in her battle uniform rides out supported by Durent and her guards. She stops before the army and the General rides from them towards her. "General Borden of Tarmack your Highness, may I introduce you to the soldiers of Tarmack with the blessing of King Alphonso of Tarmack." She lets out a slight smile but hold it. "Thank you General, please introduce me to your men." The two join and Borden leads her across the front line of the troops, and over to the cavalry. As she passes by the men salute and the men on horse present their swords. They make their way back to Durent and the three of them return into the city. Upon them disappearing, a braided soldier barks out a command and the lines of troop relax and move on to set up camp by the wagons held at the back. Princess and her entourage enter the Palace, dismount, and make their way to the conference room. Orpheus is waiting there with Rebecca who hands out drinks as they all stand by the map. Durent opens the conversation with "So here is the battle stage, we see that they may try a sea invasion, but more likely to come through the mountain passes. Borden views the map, waves his hand over the map and points to the passes. "These are easily defended; I believe the sea is the point of attack." Possible, but we cannot get it wrong, so we are going to have to defend all points. Durent responds. "We have a top man up in the mountains to gain information, he should be back soon, hopefully" Princess cuts in. Borden reacts" That will be a great help, information is the key to this, it looks like we have the men. Durent" I agree"! General we feel it is probably better to have your men defend the coast and city and our men the passes". Orpheus states. Borden agrees" Yes that makes sense, the less we have to travel the more rested and fit my men will be". "That's agreed then" Durent responds. Princess announces, "let's move to the table and eat." "General Borden, please sit next to me" Princess requests. They take their seats and maids come into the room carrying trays of food. Another fills their goblets with fine wine and Orpheus makes a toast. "We welcome you and your men General Borden." They all raise their goblets and Borden responds" Thank you for your warm welcome, it is an honour to meet your highness and we are proud to offer our services to defend your city." Princess acknowledges this "Thank you for your kind words General, I am most grateful, now please enjoy your meal." They all start choosing their food and start eating.

Meanwhile Geraldo is again up in the mountain spying on Manion's troops. He is now at site C. Below him, he sees fifteen thousand men all preparing for a move out to the front. He quietly creeps back to his lines and enters the C camp. He approaches the captain and warns him that there is a large army heading his way and to prepare his men. The captain calls in his officers who all rush in, he explains the situation to them and explains what Geraldo has said to him. He dismisses them and they all rush of to prepare their men. Geraldo shakes the captains' hand, wishes him luck, and leaves for the city.

Next morning Princess wakes up and sees the maids already in her room running her bath and preparing her clothes. Rebecca enters the room and waves the maids off. She goes over to Princess and notices a bruise on her back. She pokes it and Princess winces in pain. "What's this" she asks. "Oh, I fell over yesterday while training, it's nothing." "Doesn't look nothing, lie on the bed and I'll massage it with oil. Princess removes her nightdress and lies on the bed. Rebecca pours oil down her back and Princess sighs and relaxes; her eyes closed. Rebecca starts massaging her. "Is that to hard" she asks. "No, you can push harder," "Ok Rebecca replies as a much harder pressure moves up Princesses back and down again. Princess lets out a deep breath as she feels a kiss in her lower back. She is startled and looks around and sees Geraldo kneeling over her, oh, "carry on" she laughs as he kisses her back again and keep going, moving up to her neck and kisses her ear. She turns over and wraps her arms around him and gives him a passionate kiss. "I missed you" she whispers. "Me too, that's why I rushed back." But now we have work. He picks her up and carries her over to the bath and carefully lowers her into it. "Are you going to join me" she asks. No, I have a lot of information to report, I will see you when you come down, don't be long" he explains. "Yes Sir "she salutes him and then ducks under the water. He leaves and Rebecca returns. As Princess rises from the water. She laughs seeing Rebecca where Geraldo stood, she says" That's a clever trick the disappearing and reappearing with him. "Its magic is the response." Princess stands and Rebecca wrap's her in a towel as she steps out of the bath.

Down in the conference room, Geraldo meets Orpheus, Durent and Borden. "Welcome back General" Orpheus explains and introduces him to General Borden. "Nice to meet you General, glad you made it here" They all move over to the map and Geraldo points out that he expects fifteen thousand at both C and D and less than five at the other passes. I suggest we reduce A, B, and E to two and a half thousand and boost C and D to at least ten thousand. The defences are strong, so that should be enough to hold them. What's happening at the sea front". Orpheus explains the situation as" Well we have laid a massive chain along the length of the beach and port. This has boats attached to keep the chain afloat and are filled with straw and oil to create a fire break. With Princess exploding these, it should stop any invasion here. "Good, and how many men have you General Borden." "We have fifteen thousand ready to defend the beach." That seems a lot. May I suggest we move five thousand of them to a midway point between the city and the passes to support any front that weakens" "That's a good idea General, I will transfer them immediately, can you show me where you want them. Geraldo points at a plateau midway with a town in its centre. "If you move here, there are plenty of stores there for your men and water." "Excellent, I'll get right on it." The General leaves to arrange the placement with his men. Princess and Rebecca enter the room and are welcomed by everyone. "Morning gentlemen" Princess greets them. "What are the plans for today? I think we should inspect the sea front and see how the chain works." "Ok, well shall we leave"? Geraldo responds.

They all reach the beach and soldiers are lining up catapults facing the sea. There must be twenty-five of them, all with a small mountain of round balls to eject. Geraldo nods" Very impressive, have they been calibrated yet." "I am not sure, let me ask" Borden responds, and he rides over to one of the catapults soldiers. After a brief chat, Borden rides back to the group. "Yes, they seem happy with things, they are going to do a trial fire to show us." He raises his arm and lowers it and the catapult bursts into action. They all look and then disappointment shows over everyone face as the ball does not even reach the chain, let alone beyond it. "Oh, ah let me sort this out, give me a few minutes". He rides over to the same catapult and screams abuse at the soldiers for embarrassing him. They rush to load another ball and change the angle of the catapult. He shouts out "fire"! The catapult again burst into action and this time the ball flies well over the chain to hopefully where the waiting leading ships will be. He cheers and rides back to the group. Geraldo welcomes him back "Much better, but I suggest you check all the others, just in case." "I will do, if you will excuse me, I will personally oversee this matter" Borden states as he bows to Princess and rides back to the line of catapults. The group move of to where the troops are camped on the beach front. They are actively preparing their weapons and building spiked walls to stop a possible invasion. They are very efficient. Geraldo comments "This is much better; they seem to know what they are doing." Princess looks to Orpheus, "where will I be." "I think centre stage makes sense, then there are plenty of men at your sides, to cover any sneak attacks from the flanks." "You will also have your own guard of men I will hand pick" Geraldo adds. "I won't need them Princess responds, "I'll have you by my side". "Eh your Highness" He starts to reply. She looks worried as whenever he calls her "Your Highness," it is news she will not like. "You will be here with me won't you"? "I have to be with our men covering the passes with Durent, I can't be here." "Why can't, Durent handle it on his own, he's well experienced" she rebukes. There are too many passes for one man, so we will have to split them, I will take A, B and C, and he will take the others. "There is no doubt they will advance from there." He tries to explain. "Great, do what you want," she digs her heels in and gallops of back to the palace, followed by Rebecca and then the others.

She gallops through the palace gates, dismounts, and storms into the Palace and up to her room and slams the door. A few minutes later there is a small knock at the door and Rebecca pokes her head through the open gap. "Is it safe to come in"? she asks. "Yeah, come in Beccy, it's not you." Princess tells her, "Why does he always have to go away, it's so unfair"! "It's his job and he is doing it for you as well, you both have responsibilities here, you are here and him there, it won't be for long". "Well, what if he is injured, or killed, what then"! she responds. Calmly, Rebecca explains, "there is more of a risk with you than him, you are going to be out front and centre doing your thing, he'll be behind thousands of men, shouting orders, and then he will hurry back, he'll be fine. "I guess you're right, sorry, we better go down and make the peace" Princess admits. "Very regal of you your Highness." Rebecca jokes as the two of them leave the room.

They enter the throne room and Princess goes up to Geraldo, "I'm sorry for my outburst, I understand your position." "Thank you, Your Highness, I would rather be with you, but I have to go, but I promise to return as soon as possible, after it is all over" he replies. "Friends" Princess adds. "friends" he agrees. He leads her to her throne, and she takes her seat. Orpheus approaches with news from a messenger. He is reading the report as he approaches. "Your Highness, it appears that a large force of ships left Urania yesterday heading straight for us, possibly 250 ships with fifteen thousand men on board. They should arrive tomorrow, which means that the passes will be attacked tomorrow as well. Durent and Geraldo immediately jump into action. They both bow to Princess and make their exits. As they leave General Borden enters and kneels before Princess. "I assume you have also received the news; I have placed my men on immediate alert, and we are preparing for the attack tomorrow morning at low tide. "Very good General, is there anything else you need"? "Nothing, we came self-sufficient, for this, so I will await you on the beach front tomorrow, I will stay in camp tonight." He responds. Princess stands to acknowledge his words and he rises, turns, and leaves. "Well, I guess this is it, what's going to happen to the people within the city" Princess asks Orpheus. "They will be safe within the walls, protected by the City Guard. The hospital is fully prepared and ready, so I suggest we have a good meal and an early night. Get as much sleep as possible." Orpheus suggests." I'll organise the dinner for 7PM, ok". Rebecca asks. Princess nods. "I suggest when you get back, we do a city walk about and reassure everyone, they will know something is happening when the soldiers start preparing." "I'll be as quick as I can." Rebecca shouts as she runs out of the room. Orpheus approaches Princess, "I wish we had more time for your training, but you just have to be confident in what you can do, your father was magnificent when using his power in battle, it was unfortunate a stray arrow hit him in the eye." "Urgh"! Princess responds, I wish you hadn't told me that". "Don't worry you will be well out of arrow reach." He responds reassuringly as Rebecca runs back into the room. "Ok we are off, I think I better take my guard this time, are you joining us"? Princess asks. "I don't think so, it is you they want to see, not some old man, and I have a lot of messages to send to alert everyone." He bows and leaves as Princess calls her guard, and she leaves followed by Rebecca and the guard. They head out of the Palace and a crowd has gathers looking for reassurance. Princess stands on a nearby wall and calls out to the people.

"Please do not worry, we are well prepared for this invasion and are confident of repulsing the invaders, stay in your houses unless you are needed in support." "Bless you" a lady calls out as a shout breaks out" Princess, Princess, Princess...." "Move back to your homes and care for your families. We will celebrate in the Town centre after our success" Princess announces. They all cheer and separate as princess jumps down and walks on. She heads to the Smithies corner were everyone is working frantically. She enters the main building and is welcomed by the head Smithy. He bows and approaches her. "How are things progressing here," she asks. "We are busy, but the army is basically fully equipped, I have a gift for you your Highness, if you will accept it." He adds. A young boy steps forward with a long box. He kneels down and holds the box out to her. The Smithy opens the lid and presents Princess with a magnificent sword. "It is both strong and light, and I hope you never need it, your Highness ". She takes the sword from it and waves it in the air. "It is beautiful, thank you, Hopefully, it will only be used for awards after victory." "I pray you are correct your highness" he finishes. Rebecca straps the scarab around her waist and Princess lowers the sword into it. "Thank you and everyone keep up the good work." They all cheer as she moves on. She approaches the hospital and enters. There are rows of beds lined up all empty and ready for the wounded. The nurses are rushing around preparing equipment tables etc. The Matron comes over and curtseys to Princess. "Welcome your Highness, we are ready for what comes our way." She explains. "So, I see, I hope the children have been useful, "well they have certainly kept us amused as they practiced putting on bandages. They all ended up tied up" She laughs, "but they certainly are eager to help." "Just try and keep them away from too much blood." Princess asks. "They are being restricted to helping the treated men with drinks and company" she replies. "Good, it looks ready for action, but I hope it won't be needed." "That would be ideal, but unlikely your Highness" she sighs. "I know, well I wish you luck" and the Princess moves on. As she steps outside the hospital a squad of men rush pass to mount the battlements. She steps back looking to see if anything is happening. Everything is quiet so she moves on. Rebecca approaches her. "Maybe we should get back to the Palace Princess." She asks. "Very good, let's get back" Princess confirms. They turn and head back to the Palace.

Up by the Passes Durent and Geraldo have reached their camps. Geraldo greets Captain Granger. "How are things going Captain." "We are ready Sir, the men are dug in, do you wish to inspect." "No, I am sure you know what you are doing." As they are talking a messenger enters the tent and stands to attention." Message arrived from the Capital Sir," he hands it to the captain. He passes it on to Geraldo who opens it and reads it. "It seems Manion's ships left for the city yesterday and should arrive tomorrow, so we can assume they will attack here in the morning. Better alert your men" Geraldo orders. "Very good Sir" Captain Granger leaves the tent and Geraldo looks at the sitemap. He picks up a ship attacking the Capital and throws it across the room. The captain re-enters. And Geraldo regains his composure. "Everyone's prepared Sir, I have sent scouts out into the pass to see if there is any movement." Granger informs. "Very good Captain, I think I need a drink now, do you mind" Geraldo asks. "Help yourself Sir" he beacons as Geraldo pours a glass, "And you"." No thanks, I need a clear head and I am not a big drinker." Granger explains. Geraldo takes a seat as the captain sits behind his desk. "I guess they will do a full assault in the morning, probably 5am". Geraldo explains. "We are expecting fifteen thousand through here and D, each, that's quite a number, but at least they will be thinned out by the mountain walls, not much room for movement." "We should be able to hold them back, unless they practice climbing over their dead." "Yeah, I hope you are right." Granger adds. Once the smaller passes have been cleared, they can support us if we need extra help" Geraldo explains. Well, here's hoping they think the same as us". Geraldo lifts his glass as Granger lifts an imaginary one.

The next morning at 4am, unexpectedly Manion's troops attack AB and E with massive forces over running each camp within the hour. No word reached C and D as at 6am another strong force attacks them. They are battled to a standstill with arrows coming down from the mountain sides and catapult balls hitting the campsite. Geraldo is up front and cutting any Manion troops that break through as suddenly both C and D are hit by the large forces from the other passes attacking from the sides. This is a shock to the troops, who have little defence from these directions and the battle is brutal, the Lystonian troops vastly outnumbered. Geraldo and Granger fight hand to hand until Granger receives an arrow in his chest, he falls to the floor and is dragged back to a safe area by Geraldo. He leaves him there and rushes back to the battle desperately trying to put some order in his troops position. They pull over any wagons for cover and to build quick obstacles, but the battle seems lost. After two hours of battle the remnants of the Lystonian army retreat, battered and bruised, thousands left dead and bleeding. The Manion troops triumphantly cheer as Lord Manion rides through the C pass in triumph. He halts his men to regroup and Geraldo and his remaining men, maybe one thousand, stumbles back through the woods towards the city.

At this time Orpheus receives a message of the disaster and the news of the few Lystonian men retreating back to the city. Princess gasps and immediately asks, "What about General Templeton, is he safe." She pleads." I have no news of him your Highness." "We should rush to his aid immediately, order the troops." At this moment, a messenger enters the room and bows. He proclaims, "Enemy ships have been sited your highness, we are under attack." "I am afraid General Templeton, and his troops will have to survive, we must head to the beach immediately" Orpheus explains. "I guess so" Princess replies. They rush out of the room and head to the beach at a gallop. Princess enters her tent and Rebecca helps her with her armour. Orpheus views the oncoming ships with his spy glass. "There are several hundred ships as expected your Highness, we should make our way down to the beach. She grabs her sword and marches out, through the soldiers, she moves to the sea front. The soldiers behind her and the catapults firing their balls which are now alight. Orpheus signals the bow men to light their arrows and fire at the boats attached to the chain. After a few misses, a few hit target and small fires start. Nothing to worry the enemy with. "This is your moment your highness" Orpheus announces. Princess steps forward and crosses her arms to ignite the small fires on the boats. There is no effect. She turns to Orpheus, what's wrong, nothing's happening". At this moment, the leading ships open fire with a new weapon which fires projectiles over the chain and into the troops where they explode. This is Kaaron's secret weapon. The explosions happen up and down the beach as soldiers scatter for their lives. Another round is fired and an explosion hits near Princess and she is knocked off her feet. Orpheus shouts "Try again, light the flames, light the flames"! Princess rises and again crosses her arms to ignite the boats. "They are too far away" she shouts to Orpheus. She starts to wade into the water to get nearer and tries again. No effect, as the explosions are increasing and the Tarmack soldiers move out of range leaving the Princess alone in the water. Again, she crosses her arms to no effect. She reaches up to the sky and prays, "God help me." There is a loud crackle as a wind blows. She places her hands into the water and raises them up. The sky turns dark, and the sea rises to build a gigantic wave which she motions away from the shore and towards the enemy ship. The wave by now over one hundred feet high crashes down on the ships smashing them to pieces and thousands of men are left screaming as they are forced under the sea. The sea calms as the devastation is seen for the first time. Only a hand full of ships survive and there are bodies and ship parts floating in the water. Princess turns and heads to the shore where she collapses to the ground. Rebecca rushes to her and rests her head in her lap, the water lapping around her reviving Princess a little. "You did it, I don't know how, but you did it. Orpheus comes over "Well done Your highness. I guess you inherited your mother's powers as well, incredible. Some soldiers rush to Princess and carry her to her tent. Rebecca gives her a drink and takes the breast plate of her. "Are you alright"? she asks. "I'm ok, just exhausted, what's the news. She can hear the cheering outside the tent as the soldiers celebrate and the city people rush to the beach to see the devastation. Everyone is cheering and dancing and kids are picking up souvenirs from the ships like weapons and flags. "What's the news on Geraldo "Princess asks. "No news on him but what is left of our troops are making a hasty retreat, back to the city or captured. I doubt they will make it without help, it will be a massacre." Princess sits up "We must ride to them, send this army"." But you are exhausted your Highness, you need rest." Orpheus pleaded." We must prepare the city for attack from Manion's men from the pass, he won't be happy losing his fleet". he added. "I am fine, get me my horse and prepare the men to ride forward immediately." "But your majesty, the men are a lost cause, he tried to explain again." Orpheus am I the Ruler here or not." She shouts as she stands up. She replaces her sword in its sheath and awaits his response. "Very good your Highness, I will inform General Borden. He exits the tent and Princess again collapses down. Rebecca catches her. "You're not ready and will be worse after a long horse ride." "I can't just sit here while there are men counting on me, not to mention Geraldo. At this point General Borden enters the camp and asks what she is thinking. "Your highness my men have just fault a massive battle, they can't possible march off now, we should defend the City." Again, Princess rises, now clearly losing her patience. What battle did your men have, how many of the enemy did they confront, they never reached shore, thanks to me"! she shouted at him, prepare your men and do as you are ordered. General Borden backs down "Very well your highness, but in the open field, we will be hopelessly outnumbered and without artillery." She throws him a look to kill, and he nods and backs out of the tent. As he leaves Orpheus enters. "I guess you are not listening, so go and I will prepare the city with the few troops we have left. I'll move the catapults inside the city wall". "Thank you, and you stay with him here Rebecca, prepare for many wounded." "No, I have to go with you" Rebecca pleaded. "You are needed here Becky, please don't fight me on this." She nodded agreement and went to help Princess with the breast plate. Don't bother with that, it is heavy and will slow me down. Let's move, where is my horse. They step outside and a groom is holding her horse. She climbs up and heads to the front of the mounted troops. She waves forward and gallops off followed by hundreds of troops, followed by wagons and foot soldiers. Rebecca watches Princess leave and heads back to the Palace. All around her are cheering city folk, but she has a concerned look on her face. She is joined by Orpheus.

Back at the retreating soldiers from the pass, there is a rabble of men clambering through the forest as fast as possible, many now without their weapons. The back group slowly being caught and cut down by the Manion soldiers on horseback chasing them. Meanwhile Manion is in the Lystonian camp, now his. He laughs and drinks Granger's drink as his soldiers drag in a wounded Officer. They raise his head, and it is Captain Granger, still alive after being hidden my Geraldo. "How many men are left in the city" Manion shouts at him. "I don't know" he said, I only know that they have been attacked, but no news of the result, there was fifteen thousand." "Well, that is unlikely now" Manion laughs. At this moment, a messenger enters and hands Manion a message. He throws his drink across the room, the whole fleet lost, how"!" I guess the little girl bested you" Granger laughs as Manion takes out his knife and cuts his throat. He marches out and shouts to his army heads. Mount up, we head for the capital now. He mounts his horse and rides off, followed by his army, frantically trying to mount up. It is a clear race now, who will reach the retreating men first, Manion or Princess.

Princess is riding hard stretching ahead of her troops, oblivious of any danger she may be in. The retreating troops are continuing to run towards the city, praying for a miracle. She comes across a clearing and halts her horse, the clearance stretches over two hundred yards to the edge of the forest. She slowly moves forward as her troops catch up to her and create a line behind her several men deep. They slowly move forward together as a few stragglers appear from the forest. She halts as more and more appear. They see her and start running as fast as they can, first a dozen, then hundreds until they have all cleared the forest and are getting closer to Princess and her army as Manion's men also start to appear. They stop and start to line up against Princess. More and more of them appear as they soon out number Princesses men. They then start to move forward as they lower their spears ready to charge. Princess raises her hand to stop her men then moves forward alone. Ahead of her is no fire or water and her men look in confusion as she stops and dismounts her horse. She reaches up to the sky and then kneels and places her hands on the ground. Again, the sky darkens and there is a crash of thunder as the forest behind the Manion troops intertwine to block their exit as they see the trap and start to rush forward. Princess then again raises her arms and then forcibly hits the ground and the ground before her opens as an earthquake tears a massive gap in the ground and the attacking men crash into the deep whole. Pushed forward by the forestry behind them. Then just as quickly as it appears, the land seals up swallowing the men enclosed and then starts to move to create a fifty-foot-high wall of earth to block any further armies from Manion. Princess's men all cheer as she again collapses to the ground. Behind the wall Manion appears stunned by what he sees. He says nothing and slowly turns to return to the camp. Princess's men rush to her to help as General Borden orders his men to surround them and capture the Princess. He throws a bar down to a guard and tells him to tie her hands to either end to sperate them and reduce any risk. She is then placed into a wagon, and they all slowly march back to the city, the Lystonian men unarmed and guarded.

They proceed to the city as the city folk are celebrating the beach battle unaware of what has happened in the forest. Rebecca is frantically worried looking from the parapets towards the mountains. She suddenly sees the front of the Tarmack army and assumes everything went well and rushes down to the gates to welcome them. General Borden proudly heads his men as he passes Rebecca who looks confused. "Where is the Princess" she calls up to him," She is behind us, she is safe" he answers. She waits to see the Princess as more and more soldiers pass her. Borden reaches the Palace, and his troops start to surround the town centre and enter the Palace. Suddenly Rebecca sees Princess in the wagon chained up. She shouts out" what's going on", as a guard hits her over the head and throws her also into the wagon. Princess tries to help her, but it is impossible. The cheering crowds are starting to murmur and look confused as they also see their army men all tied and surrounded by Tarmack soldiers. Foot soldiers hold them back as Princesses wagon passes through the gate and into the palace. Princess is dragged to the throne room where Ronaldo Manchura is seated upon the throne. Princess is placed on her knees before him and is joined by Orpheus. Ronaldo stands and introduces himself again to Princess. "Your Highness, I, Ronaldo Manchura on behalf of his Highness King Alphonso of Tarmack, claim this land as a subject of Tarmack. You will not be killed, but you will be secured as I am aware of what power it appears you have, very impressive, very impressive indeed, but they do not match the brilliance of Ronaldo Manchurian, who planned this peaceful invasion, he raises his hand to the gods. Princess looks up, "Peaceful, my army is destroyed, nearly all dead." She rebukes. "Your Highness, that was not by His Highness King Alphonso of Tarmack, that was by Lord Manion and his rabble. We just assisted you till you were defenceless and here I am. Sitting on your throne" he laughs. "You won't get away with this, you are a pathetic creature." Princess tells him. "Sticks and stones, I am here, and you are there and helpless, I think I am fine, take her away and chain her up so she can't try any more tricks." He points to Orpheus "Take him as well and put him next to her, they can be company" he laughs. Princess and Orpheus are dragged away as Rebecca is brought forward, she has gained consciousness and is forced to kneel before Ronaldo. "Are my dear Rebecca, so sweet and helpful to your dear Princess, maybe you can serve me." "I would rather join Princess if you don't mind." She retorts. "Rubbish, you will be my servant and keep me amused, you can do that for me can't you." He responds. "Never, you will never be forgiven for what you have done." She replies. "Rubbish "he says as he waves in his guards leading several children all chained together. Rebecca recognises some of them. "Don't hurt them, they are innocent" she pleads. "Well, are we coming to an agreement then" he replies as she nods her head agreeing. "Good, then unchain her and remove the children, they can work in the kitchens." He orders. A guard unchains Rebecca. Now come and sit at my feet. She stands and walks over to him and sits at his feet. "See it is easy, isn't it." "What about Princess, what are you going to do to her"? Are that depending on so many things, but nothing for the moment, it depends on how she behaves, and you of course and what King Alphonso of Tarmack wishes, not to mention on what Lord Manion decides to do.

Down in the dungeon Princess's wrists are chained to a separation bar and another around her neck, chains her to the wall. On the floor is Orpheus, hands and feet chained. Orpheus, "are you OK"? Princess asks. "Oh, a headache, they hit me pretty hard, but I'm OK, and you"? I'm Ok, not hurt just so sorry for what's happened, so many men killed, and what about Geraldo"? "I never saw him, so he either escaped or is captured, or died on the battlefield, I'm sorry" was Orpheus's reply. A tear falls from Princess's eye, then a rat runs across her feet, and she screams but cannot do anything due to the bar, she shakes the chains, as Orpheus picks the rat up and throws it out of the window. "What are we going to do, they even took my bracelets, it's hopeless" she screams. "Not necessarily Your Highness, those bracelets were only an aid to help you concentrate, but the power is within you, we just have to help you learn." "Within me, but how"? "Your highness, your power comes from your family, and it seems you have inherited all their powers in one, so things are not helpless, we just have to be careful." "Ok where do we start." "Well, if we can get you to ignite your powers without the bracelets, we can't do much from here, but if they take us out, it is a different situation." Orpheus explains. "Right so where do we start"? Look out of the window up at the sky, now think of rain." Princess looks out and concentrates but nothing happens. "It's hopeless." "Not necessarily your Highness, remember when you forced the sea, your hands weren't crossed, you were just emotional, think of something like then. Princess thinks of Geraldo and whether he is dead or not. Outside the sky darkens and thunderclaps and it starts to rain heavily. And rain enters the cell through the open window. Before the rain hits the ground, she stops it, and it swirls into a gentle trickle, and it pours into Orpheus's mouth. "Amazing your Highness, amazing" Orpheus exclaims. Princess relaxes and the water falls to the floor and the rain parts. "I understand now, we must just be patient. Princess says. "Thanks for the drink Your Highness" Orpheus sighs.

In the forest, trapped behind the wall Princess built and surrounded by Manion's men, Geraldo, creeps through the undergrowth through the forest to the wall. There is a small number of men guarding it, but they are relaxed as there is no way past it. They are sitting around a fire and joking and drinking. One soldier raises his glass "here's to the Princess, she saved us risking our lives on another invasion" They all laugh. "Yeah, I don't want to face her again, guess she is celebrating back at the city." They all agree, unaware that Princess is in fact a prisoner herself. Geraldo makes his was along the edge of the forest, making his way to the edge of the wall. Where it stops the forest is extra thick and unpassable. Geraldo looks up at the wall now out of site of the soldiers and takes out his knife. He cuts some branches from a tree and cuts them to foot length pieces and sharpens them. He then takes of his boots and places a stick against one of the soles. He rips off his sleeve and tears it into shreds and proceeds to tie the stick to the boot leaving a four-inch protrusion. He then does the same to the other boot and puts both back on his feet. He then holds a stick in each hand and approaches the Wall. He sticks in the left-hand stick into the wall and then kicks the wall two feet up the wall and pulls himself up before using his right hand to reach higher, followed by his left foot and slowly makes his way up the wall.

Back at the City a magnificent ship approaches. It is King Alphonso. Waiting at the dock is Ronaldo. The ship docks and a band play there is a group of un-enthusiastic city folk crowded to welcome him. The King disembarks the ship and Ronaldo kneels before him. "Your Highness, I present to you the city." "Very good, Lord Manchura, please proceed to the city" the King acknowledges. Ronaldo leads him to horses waiting and they ride towards the city gate followed by the Kings entourage. The city folk have been forced to stand by the roadsides to wave Tarmack flags and cheer. They pass the folk and ride into the Palace grounds. Here they dismount and head indoors for the throne room. King Alphonso marches into the room and up to the Throne where Rebecca is sitting. He sits on the throne and looks down at her. "How is your dear Princess my dear"? He asks. "I have not seen her your Highness; I hope she is being treated well." "Well shall we see, guards, fetch me the Princess" he commands. Two guards rush of as Ronaldo approaches the throne. "We have had to take action to prevent her using her powers" he informs the King. He stands to the side of the King, looking down on Rebecca. Then the door opens, and the guards drag princess in with her hands still chained to the bar. She is forced to the ground before King Alphonso. Rebecca instinctively rushes to help her but is stopped by a guard. Ronaldo wags a finger at her, and she sits back. King Alphonso leans forward and looks at Princess straight in the face. "Are these chains necessary Lord Manchura"? he asks. "Definitely, her power seems to work when her arms are crossed, so this way she is relatively harmless" Alphonso responds. "A shame but better safe than sorry" to the Princess "I would like to thank you for all your help in defeating Lord Manion and handing me your country at no loss to ourselves, truly magical ha-ha." He sits back laughing. He waves Princess away as the guards pick her up. "Take her away, I think I should bath and rest after my journey." Very good your Highness, please follow me", He clicks his fingers at Rebecca. You come with us". They exit.

Meanwhile Geraldo have climbed the wall and reached the base of the other side. He fixes his boots and removes his uniform, then heads for the city. As he walks along the road, he sees Lystonian weapons and uniforms thrown away. He assumes from the soldiers captured, yet he is unaware of what is happening in the city. After a few miles, he reaches an Inn and enters. All the locals are very subdued and there are a few Tarmack soldiers enjoying themselves abusing their positions as conquerors. Geraldo approaches the bar and asks the bar man for a drink. He looks over to the soldiers, "what's with them" he asks the bar man. They are celebrating their successful takeover of Lystonia, the armies destroyed, and I dread to think what has happened to the Princess. "My god, I never knew" he claims. "Where have you been hiding" the bar man asks disrespectfully. "I was trapped behind the wall, I have to get to the city, do you have a horse I can use." "Yeah, we collected plenty after the battle, they're behind the Inn, help yourself, although don't know what you can do there" he questions. "Thanks," Geraldo throws some coins on the bar and leaves in a hurry as one of the soldiers calls out for more beer. Geraldo finds a horse and rides of towards the city.

In Princesses room, the maids have run a bath and Ronaldo orders them out. He then turns to Rebecca "You will look after his Highness and do as he say." He orders her, then excuses himself to the King and leaves. The king sits on the side of the bed and calls to her" here girl, help me undress." He sticks his leg out so she can take his boot of and then the other. He stands up and holds his arms out. She starts to undo his shirt button and takes it off. He looks down and smiles. She hesitates and then undoes his belt holding his trousers and lowers them. He laughs and steps out of them. He steps over to the bath in a vest and underwear. She stands by the bed. "Here girl I can't get in like this. She goes over and pulls his vest of and then steps behind him and lowers his underwear. He steps into the bath and lies back. "Wash my back girl "he asks as he leans forward. She steps behind him with some soap and a loafer. She starts to wash his back and he offers his arms next. She moves around and washes his arms. He lies back then suddenly a leg appears sticking out the bath. He smiles at her. She carefully washes his foot and wipes the loafer up his leg, he lets out a sigh, "you done this before ha-ha," she nods no. He then sticks up the other leg and to proceeds to clean this. He then grins and stand up revealing himself to her, He looks down "continue" he orders. She hesitates but proceeds to finish his cleaning. After he shouts, "Towel," she rushes over to the towel and wraps it around him as he steps out. "Dry me," she rubs his back and arms. "And my legs, kneel" he says as she kneels in front of him and dries his legs stopping at the thighs. He laughs and walks over to the bed. He laughs as he lies back "undress and join me girl." He demands. She steps forward and slowly undoes her dress and lowers it to the floor and stands in her petticoat. He looks at her and she slips it off her shoulders and it falls to the floor. "Very nice, get here now girl" She steps forward and climbs onto the bed, and he pulls her towards him. He takes her arms and holds them behind her back and kisses her neck and then forcibly on the mouth. She is emotionless, as he takes her breast in his hand squeezing it and lowering his head to kiss and suck. He then throws her onto the bed on her stomach and spreads her legs. "Please don't" she mutters, as he laughs. He kneels behind her and forces himself inside her. She cries out but is ignored regardless of her moans of pain. He shows no mercy and forces himself on her throughout the night.

Down in the cells Princess is again chained to the wall. She has told Orpheus, "King Alphonso of Tarmack has arrived, he seemed very pleased with all our help." "He is a rat" Orpheus responds, "and a coward"." I saw Rebecca, she seems safe, is by the throne but safe, at least she is not suffering or locked up." She tells him. "Thank God for that, things could have been very different" he responds. She shakes her chains, "I just wish I could get out of these" she cries. "Patience Your Highness, your time will come" he calms her.

Approaching the City, Geraldo dismounts his horse messes up his hair and rubs dirt into his face and hands. He walks along the road to the city gates and is stopped by the guard. "Halt what do you want here" he asks. "I live here sir, I have just returned from a journey, what's happening here." The guard laughs, there's been a few changes he laughs" as he waves Geraldo through. "Thank you, sir, I need to see my wife and kids." He walks on and disappears up the road and heads towards the smithies area. He enters and sees the chief smithy. He is instantly recognised and is pulled aside out of view. "What happened" he asked. The smithy tells him, The Princess was magnificent and created a tidal wave which destroyed the whole invasion fleet" Geraldo looks shocked, "then she rode off to help you and from what I hear saved our men and created a massive wall to stop Manion's men from chasing" "yes I saw the wall, I wondered where that came from". "But then, the Tarmack army turned on her and she was taken prisoner." "She is still alive then." He pleads. "I believe so sir" the smithy says reassuringly. "Thank God how are we going to save her" he asks. "That's your department I'm afraid sir, but if I can help in any way, just ask." "I'll need a place to hide while I plan" Geraldo asks. No problem I have a storeroom and there's a few of our men hiding there already". "Great" Geraldo adds as the smithy leads him away to the barn. Upon entering he looks around and sees the remnant of the army, around twenty men, some injured. Most seem to be the palace guard. They welcome him and they exchange stories.

The next morning the King wakes and climbs out of the bed, Rebecca is lying her head in the pillow, she is obviously in trauma and pain, she does not move. The King shakes her. "Help me get dressed girl, I have things to do, I can't lie around here all-day" he laughs. She turns and climbs out of the bed and grabs her petticoat and puts it on. There is blood on the bed and down her legs. She limps over to the King, not saying a word. She proceeds to dress him and when he is ready, he marches out. "I will see you downstairs girl" were his leaving words." She regains her composure, goes to a bowl of water and she washes herself down and finishes dressing and leaves the room. She does not however go to the throne room but heads for the cells. She approaches them and is stopped by the guards. "What do you want here "the guard asks. "I am to check on the Princess, make sure you are not mistreating her and see if she needs anything." "She is fine, no need to see her" the guard rebukes. "Oh, I'll tell King Alphonso you disobeyed his order to let me in," "Oh no, it's OK here let me open up. He unlocks the door and opens it. Rebecca sees Princess chained to the wall and Orpheus lying on the ground. She is shocked at the position princess is in. She turns to the guard. "Why is she still chained up, the King ordered her released, how can she be comfortable like that, you wait till I tell King Alphonso," She screams at the guard. "But I never received an order to unchain her, of course I can do that, I am sorry, please do not tell His Highness" He rushes over to Princess and releases her neck and stops at the wrists, "Are you sure, Lord Manchura was adamant about the wrists, he asks. "Oh well if you want to obey Lord Manchura over the King, you do that, I'll be off", she turns to leave as the guard frantically starts to unchain Princesses wrists and then the guard bends over to unchain Orpheus, he looks up at Rebecca, "him as well" She nods and he undoes Orpheus's chains as the guard turns triumphant the bar securing Princess swings across his face knocking him unconscious across the room. "Princess are you OK" Rebecca cries as she hugs her, I was so worried. "I am fine, thanks to you, chain him up and gag him. We must escape." The princess adds. "That's not going to be easy, I never thought that far ahead in my plan" Rebecca laughs. They hug again and help Orpheus up. They make their way out of the cell and down the corridor away from the main part of the palace. They come to a storeroom and enter it. Inside there are hardware stores and some food. Up on the wall is a window looking out to the stables. "There's are escape, just have to work out how" Rebecca states. "Leave that to me" Princess replies. She goes over to the wall with the window and places her hands on it. She concentrates and there is a rumble, and the room shakes, then the wall starts to crumble and a whole is created. Rebecca looks shocked at this. "Hurry we have to go." All three scurry out as an alarm is blown. "Damn! Princess shouts, head for the stables. They all run and barge through the doors to be met by the stable boys. They stop in their tracks not knowing what the boys will do. They are quickly reassured as the boys tell them to be quiet and lead them out the back to the smithies workshop. Here they meet the head smithy who kneels to the Princess, he beckons them to follow him. He takes them also out the back to the barn and opens the door. The first-person Princess sees is Geraldo. She rushes over to him, and they kiss. He holds her and asks, "How did you escape" She points to Rebecca, "My secret weapon" Rebecca comes over and they all hug. Orpheus steps forward and raises his arms as if to join in but realises it is inappropriate, He comments. This is very nice, but we have to get out of the city, how can we do this." I have a wagon that passes to and throw through the city gate daily" the smithy states." We can hide you in that." All of us" Geraldo asks. "It may take two trips, but it can be done, we are constantly sending equipment to the troops down by the port." "Ok we leave tomorrow at first light, till then we hold up here." Orders Geraldo but we better find somewhere to hide in case they come and search here also. The smithy grabs him and asks him to help lift an anvil which is on a large round stone. Once off, the smithy slides the stone aside to reveal steps down to a room. "Climb down here, you won't be found here." They all rush down the steps into the room as the smithy hands them some torches and then slides the stone back across the steps and they are in darkness. Geraldo lights the torches as they hear the smithy grunting as he lifts the anvil and places it on top of the stone. He then leaves.

Elsewhere around the palace the guards are frantically searching for the Princess. The cell guard is brought before King

Alphonso. And thrown on his knees. The King stands up and screams at him" What have you done you fool." The guard sputters out "Your Highness, the girl told me you ordered the release of the chains and then it all went dark." The King turns and orders the guards, take him away and chain him up till I decide what to do with him. The guards drag him away. "Where can they be" he asks. "It is their City your Highness, so they will have support and knowledge," Ronaldo responds, but we will check every house and barn, till we find them, they will not escape." He adds. "They better not King Alphonso responds. He storms of to his room forgetting Rebecca is also gone. The city houses are all searched by the Tarmack soldiers, bursting into every house, and causing chaos, turning furniture over and throwing things around the houses. but to no avail. They also checked the barn where Princess is hiding, and one actually sat on the stone as the other soldiers looked around. They left and Princess and the group wait till nightfall. The smithy returns and removes the anvil and slides the stone, the door opens, and they climb out. Geraldo speaks up, "We must get through the city gate. There will be even more soldiers guarding it now, we need a diversion. The smithy suggests "How about a fire nearby so they are nearest to it." "Great idea" Geraldo says, "and if there are any still there, I will deal with them." Ok let's move. The smithy asks them to wait for his signal. The group creep along the side lanes towards the gate and hide till the call of "Fire"! A few minutes later it starts, and several town people are shouting "fire" and most of the guards' rush to check leaving just two on the gate. Geraldo leads the group and creeps up to the first guard who was looking to where the fire was. He creeps behind him and draws his knife and cuts his throat. The other guard hears a commotion and looks over as Geraldo throws the knife deep into the man's chest and he falls to the ground dead. Geraldo beacons for the other to come out and follow him, they head down to the port and find a small boat that is just big enough for them all. They all board and one of the men unties the boat and they lower the sail. As they push away from shore, they are seen by other guards who alert the others and as they sail away from the port, the shore side is full of soldiers waving their sword for nothing. The boat continues until the city is out of site. Princess looks at Geraldo and asks, "So where are we going to go." "Well, I fear the only place we can try is Norland, they are not allies but they are not enemies either. "Ok, do you want any wind," she laughs. "No thanks, you go and rest." She smiles and goes and lies next to Rebecca. They cover themselves in a blanket and try and sleep. Orpheus joins Geraldo, "She's quite a woman, her Highness." "Yeah amazing." He replies. "You do realise that she will have to marry into another royal family to keep the peace etc." Geraldo does not like the idea of this but responds with "That will be her decision, not a group of politicians." "Somethings are inevitable I am afraid" Orpheus rebukes. He then walks away and sits in the middle of the boat.

The next morning, the group is woken up by the boat being tossed around by the sea. "Tie yourselves down, it's getting rough." "Hang on "Princess shouts and she leans over the side and places her hand in the water. The storm immediately calms, and the boat becomes stable. "That's a neat trick" Geraldo laughs as Rebecca brings him a drink as he has been up all night steering the boat. "How much longer do you think it will take to get there" Rebecca asks. "I'm not sure Geraldo replies, but can you get someone to take over from me so I can get some sleep." "Oh, can I" she says excitedly. "Well, I can't see why not, just watch the compass and keep heading east, we should reach somewhere." He responds, hands her the wheel and leaves to find somewhere to rest.

Back in Lystonia, King Alphonso is screaming at everyone. "You are all incompetent; you have let a very dangerous weapon escape. What is the news from the Uranian border." Ronaldo speaks up, "there is no news your Highness, they haven't even tried to breach the wall. They probably do not even know that we have captured Lystonia from under them". "Well hopefully it will remain like that, but we better prepare a defence wall, just in case." Very good your Highness, I will get right on it". Ronaldo turns away and marches off, followed by a few senior officers. King Alphonso then turns to a maid, "get me a drink wench" he barks, and she rushes of. Shortly after she returns with a tray with a bottle and goblet. With trembling hands, she pours the drink and steps forward to hand it to the king. He grabs it from her, and she backs away. He sits back and looks around the throne room. It still has Lystonian flags hanging. "Take them flags down and put up Tarmack flags." There is frantic action as servants pull down the Lystonia flags and start looking for Tarmack flags.

Back in the Uranian camp Manion is sitting on his throne talking to Kaaran "what is the news on the border"? he asks. "It is very strange my Lord, it is very quiet and there seems to be no guards guarding it at all"! "That's not normal, they should be reinforcing, they must be super confident with that witch of theirs." He argues. I am waiting for information from some spies I send in earlier, that will give us a clearer idea." "Let me know when they arrive" Manion orders. "Very good my Lord," is the response as Kaaran turns and leaves the tent.

Back in Lystonia, the servants have found Tarmack flags and are dressing the room as Renaldo re-enters the room. He looks around, "That looks a lot better your Highness, I have sent men to build the defences," he reports. "Very good King Alphonso replies, "They won't stay still for long" he explains. Ronaldo steps forward, "My Lord, may I suggest we send for more reinforcements, just in case, we did not lose many men before, but Manion still has a substantial force, compared to ours." "Yes, very good, make it happen. Ronaldo again rushes of to send a message to their home base.

Back on the boat, Geraldo wakes and moves over to where Princess is standing forward looking ahead for the shore front. He moves close and puts his arms around her. "Won't be long now" he reassures her. "Yeah, I'm just a little worried about what we will be met with." "You are a Princess; they should greet you with honours" he reassures her. A Princess of a beaten land, no honour there." She responds. "Just wait till they see what you are capable off, that should convince them." He tells her. "But why should they help"? She asks. Well, they are a country on the limits of our land mass. To trade they have to use their ships or travel through Tarmack, and their relationship is not great, they barely tolerate each other". "I hope you are right" she replies as she turns and hugs him. He lifts her chin and kisses her on the lips. She closes her eyes as Rebecca calls out "Land"! Princess immediately opens her eyes and looks out to see land appearing. "Where now" she asks. "We'll have to track the coast until we find a port" Geraldo says "come on let's join Rebecca. Geraldo shouts out to the few remaining men. Prepare your equipment men, we have to make an impression when we land". The men frantically gather up their uniforms and start putting them on and adding their armour and swords. An hour passes and then there is a shout out" Port ahead Sir" the man reports. Geraldo takes the wheel and heads straight for it. It is a small port, which is ideal as they should not meet any confrontation. They approach the port side, and a rope is thrown out and the boat is pulled in and tied up. The men climb out and stand to attention. Geraldo helps Princess and Rebecca off the boat as Orpheus climbs out himself as an elderly gentleman approaches them. He bows and introduces himself. Welcome strangers, my name is Summerton, I am the mayor of this small town, may I ask who I am addressing. Geraldo steps forward and presents Princess still looking drab from her stay in the cell. "This is her Highness, Princess from Lystonia, we have travelled a long way through a storm, so please excuse our appearance." Summerton steps forward, offers his arm to Princess, please let me show you to the town hall, there you can refresh and clean up. "It would be a pleasure Mr Summerton" Princess smiles as she takes his arm. They lead of followed by Geraldo, Rebecca, Orpheus, and the Guard. They walk the short walk to the hall as town folk approach to see the strangers. Princess waves at them as she passes, while they just have quizzed looks on their faces. They reach the hall and enter. Summerton claps his hands, and two maids rush out and curtsey before him. "Please take her highness and aid to the guests' quarters and help them clean up. I will arrange some food for you all. "Thank you" Princess says, and she leaves being led by the maids. Summerton approaches Geraldo, your men can rest in the stables till the food is ready, give them a chance to clean up. Meanwhile can I offer you and your associate a drink" Summerton points to a table with a jug of beer. "Thank you, this is the Princesses advisor, Orpheus, we both have a thirst after that trip." They pour three drinks and Summerton invites him to sit down. "So, tell me Mr. eh? Summerton asks. "Templeton Colonel Geraldo Templeton. "And I should address you as"? "Geraldo is fine, thank you." He responds. "So, as I was about to ask, what is your story Geraldo"? "Well, a lot has happened in a very short time, her Highness was only found after being missing from birth, and it turns out she has the powers of her family, she is really quite amazing. Lystonia was attacked by Lord Manion and received the support of King Alphonso of Tarmack. The Lystonian army was used to defend the Manion border while the Tarmack army defended the city from a sea attack. In one fowl swoop she single handed destroyed 250 of Manion's fleet and thousands of men were lost. Meanwhile the Lystonian army had been overrun and were pulling back as the Princess rushed to our aid. Here she controlled the forest to stop the Uranian army and then managed to build a massive mud wall must be 50 feet high. The day was saved, when the Tarmack army turned on us and captured the Princess stopping her using her powers. I was still behind enemy lines at this moment and only met up with her after she escaped the prison and here, we are, we need to get to Norlands capital to meet the King and ask for his assistance." Geraldo finishes. "Well, that is quite a story, but after a night's rest, I would be honoured to lead you to the city" Summerton offers. "We are very grateful" Geraldo responds, and they clink glasses. The table is being prepared for dinner and all the soldiers enter dressed without their armour. They are welcomed and sit at the end of the table and are each given glasses of beer. They are in fine mood as princess and Rebecca enter the room. Princess is dresses in an elegant dress and is escorted by a young lady of similar age. Summerton and Geraldo all rise, joined by the soldiers and Orpheus and all stand to attention as Princess approaches Summerton. Princess" Thank you Mr Summerton, this young lady has been a great help and offered me this beautiful dress". "Ah please let me introduce you to my daughter Patricia." Patricia curtseys, "Your Highness." Princess takes her hand and thanks her, "Thank you, you have been most kind." Summerton interrupt and invites everyone to take their seats. He sits at the head of the table with Princess to his right and Geraldo to his left. Patricia is next to him, then Orpheus and Rebecca next to Princess. The ladies are poured wine and Summerton open the conversation. "It appears you have had quite an adventure your Highness, I am eager to see these amazing powers of yours" "I hope they will not be needed Mr Summerton" She replies. "So, what will you ask of our King." Summerton asks. Orpheus replies, "Well we hope he will offer his support in reclaiming our land." This takes Mr Summerton aback, "Oh, we are not a country known for its fighting prowess Orpheus, you are expecting us to take on not only our neighbour King Alphonso but Lord Manion as well"! "I know it is a lot" Princess speaks out, "but we have plenty to offer, you know are land was a prosperous land before Manion invaded and with the right plan we can certainly achieve success." "Well, I wish you every success, your Highness, please enjoy your food." Summerton points to the food. They all tuck in. As the atmosphere relaxes Patricia speak up "Princess, can you show us an example of your power. "Oh, I eh, why not are you cold, she points to the fireplace which is unlit, and it bursts into flame. Summerton is shocked by this. "My, I see what you meant by power, how big a fire can you create"? Joking, Princess replies, I could burn this building down, but don't worry I can also make it rain and put it out ha-ha". She laughs as Patricia claps her hands. "That's amazing, I wish I could do that." Geraldo tries to calm her with, "Unfortunately it also places a target on your back." Princess looks behind her. "I'll survive" she says. "Well, I think it's amazing, regardless" Patricia claims. They carry on eating and drinking and when they finish the ladies excuse themselves from the room and make their way to the guest room to chat more.

The next morning the soldiers have been given horses and are mounted while waiting for Princess. There is a delay as Patricia is begging her father if she can join them on their trip to the city. He is refusing but Princess asks him on her behalf, "You know she would be a great help to myself whilst there, if you would not mind" she asks. "Oh well if you request it your Highness, I suppose she can join us." Patricia jumps in the air and gives him a kiss and rushes to get her things. She returns quickly and they all leave the building to mount their horses. Summerton leads off with Princess by his side as the group exit the town.

After a long day riding, they are approaching the Capital of Norland. They ride up to the City Gates and stop. A guard comes out and asks their reason for being here. Soldier shouts, "Please state your reason for being here"? Summerton leans down to him and explains who he has brought to the city. The soldier turns and re-enters the city. They all wait until he reappears accompanied by a guard on horseback. The Soldier calls out "Your Highness is welcome; this guard will escort you to His Highness. The horse guard takes the lead, and they follow him into the city. They enter the castle where the King of Norland resides. They reach the entrance and dismount. They are welcomed by some guards and a man in fully court regalia. His name is Lord Thomson. He greets them, Your Highness, you are very welcome here in Norland. Please follow me to His Highness King Stephan. He offers Princess his arm which she accepts, and they walk into the castle followed by Orpheus, Geraldo, Rebecca, Summerton, and Patricia. The soldiers are led away to rest their horses and themselves.

Upon entering the Throne room, the group are met by a large hall with courtiers standing on either side of the room. At the end is a large throne where King Stefan sits. The large throne is needed as he is an enormous overweight man. Sitting next to him on a smaller seat is Prince Edward, aged around sixteen and also grossly overweight. They are surrounded by maids all holding either drinks or trays of food. The group walk up to the throne and the men all kneel and the lady's curtsey. King Stefan attempt to stand to welcome them but gives up. "Welcome your Highness" he gasps, struggling to breath. Princess steps forward "Thank you for welcoming us, your Highness. You have a lovely country." "You are welcome your highness, what brings you to my country"? Princess looks around at the surrounding courtiers. "Maybe we can talk in private your Highness, it is a delicate matter" she explains. "I am sorry your Highness, very well, let us first arrange accommodation for you and then we will talk once you are rested." The King responds. He waves to one courtier to lead the group away. All except Summerton. The King calls out, "Clear the room." Everyone instantly disappears into the shadows and the King beckons for Summerton to approach him. "So, tell me, what will they be requesting from me"? Summerton grimaces as he explains, "Your Highness, they have a story that I believe you will want to hear, but what they intend to ask is considerable" "I expected that, they do not arrive un-announced if there is not a major problem. "She is very pretty" Prince Edward remarks. "Good enough for a Prince" King Stefan laughs.

Back in Lystonia, King Alphonso is welcoming another fleet, full of soldiers. He sits on a chair underneath an open tent. He is excited and clapping as each ship lands and disembarks. Waiting by the port side are numerous wagons of items stolen from the palace and any gold they have found. This will be reloaded on a ship and sent back to Tarmack.

Over at the mountain camp Manion is discussing the invasion with his senior officers and Kaaron. Kaaron opens the meeting "My Lord, we have started to clear the wall, it is very solid, but we intend to place my explosives into it and blow it apart. Then we can proceed to the capital. It appears that troops have arrive to prepare a defence, so the quicker we act the better". Lord Manion asks, "What numbers will we be facing." Kaaron replies, well we know they lost around twenty thousand plus on the mountain, which would have been virtually all the Lystonian army. That would leave only those from other allies. If they are still here." "Excellent, then prepare for an advance on the city, how long do you need to breach the wall Kaaron" Manion asks. "We can breach it early tomorrow, lets wake them up at five "Kaaron laughs. "Very good, gentlemen prepare your troops." Manion orders and the Officers all leave the tent.

Back at Norland, the hall has been prepared with a long dining table with thirty chairs running the length and an extra-large one for King Stephan at the Head. He is standing drinking a wine talking to his son as Princess and her group enter. King Stephan welcomes them and introduces them to some of the courtiers joining them before they all sit. King Stephan at the head with Princess to his right and Prince Edward to his left. The sides then list on the right Orpheus, Rebecca, and Summerton along with some courtiers. On the Left next to Edward is Geraldo, Patricia, and other courtiers. The King raises his glass," I welcome Your Highness to our humble land, and hope that your future is a safe and pleasant one." Everyone raises their glasses and cheer to Princess. Princess responds, "Thank you your Highness, you are truly a generous host, and you have a lovely land." He smiles at her, "Well that's the courteous bit over, so tell me Your Highness, why are you really here"? Princess smiles at him, "Your highness, I am sure you have heard of what happened in my land and our situation, so I won't waste time explaining what happened, but will be honest with you." "That's good, direct to the point" Stephan responds, he leans towards her. "Well, we were tricked by King Alphonso, but he is not strong, and I am sure that Manion will proceed with his invasion and vanquish Alphonso." "Probably" Stephan agrees. "So, I am asking for your support to retake Lystonia after my enemies have weakened each other." "Oh" Stephan queries, "but why would I risk my people for an issue that is nothing to do with us" he adds. Princess responds with "Your highness, you would receive the gratitude of Lystonia and become a major friend, and it would certainly weaken Tarmack, who I know has been a thorn in your side for many years." "Not enough to risk a war though" he claims. "Maybe, so what would you want in return for your support"? Stephan looks up and then at his son. "Well, our two lands have not exactly been close in the past, so maybe if we were closer, it might help convince me." "Of course, your Highness, we would become great friends" she claims laying her hand on his. "I do not think friendship is enough to risk the lives of our brave men" he says taking his hand away, "But maybe if we were closer, like maybe family, we would have an excellent reason to fight by your side." He grins and looks at Orpheus and then Geraldo. "Well, how can that happen" Princess asks looking confused. Orpheus who understands the situation interrupt, "I think his Highness is thinking of a bond between the Two families, Lystonia and Norland, like a royal marriage. "What"! Princess says surprised." Between whom"? "I suspect his Highness is suggesting a bond between yourself and himself." "What"! she stands surprised. King Stephan also stands towering over her and laughs, "No, I am not that cruel to force myself on such a young lady as you." He claims. Relieved Princess relaxes and retakes her seat, "Oh I am sorry your highness, I was mistaken, I apologise." No apology needed your Highness, I was suggesting a handsome heir, Prince Edward." Princess looks over to Edward who is preening himself. Orpheus again interludes to kill the atmosphere, "I believe that the Princess would need a little time to get to know his highness before making such an important decision, your highness, but a few days courting would not be amiss, would it my Princess. King Stephan claps his hands and announces "Very good, we will announce the engagement of Prince Edward to Your Highness Princess, and they can marry in four days. Then we can talk about retaking Lystonia and bring it back into the family. Eat up everyone this is a time to celebrate." He waves to the servants to serve more drinks as Geraldo stands, "excuse me your Highness, but I must go and check on my men." The king waves him off and he marches off. Princess watches him as he leaves, knowing he is fuming. Orpheus changes the attention, "maybe Patricia can act as chaperone to the young couple". "Excellent idea, you will be staying for the wedding Summerton, won't you. "I would be honoured, and I am sure

Patricia is a perfect choice." Princess tries to speak out "But." she is interrupted. "Then it is settled, you have made a proud father very happy your Highness." She smiles, and stands, with all the excitement I am feeling a little overwhelmed, she states, I think I will retire to my room, Rebecca can you assist me." "Ah the excitement of it all, I understand, so have sweet dreams and you can meet Prince Edward tomorrow morning and he can show you around the city." "Thank you, your highness, Edward, Good night." She turns and leaves the room with Rebecca following behind her. "More wine King Stephan orders, and the courtesans all cheer.

Princess rushes into her room and falls on her bed crying, Rebecca sits next to her placing her hand on her back. "I can't marry that creature, he's horrendous, I love Geraldo" Princess pleads. "I know Princess, trust me I am sure that is the reason why he left, but unfortunately this is how heads of countries work. Building on joining families. At least you're not being offered Manion or King Alphonso of Tarmack she laughs, trying to break the tension. Princess turns and looks at her, tears running down her face "But he is so fat," I can't. I'd rather go back to the cells. "That could be arranged Rebecca laughs and gives Princess a hug. "Just meet him, he might have a great character," Princess looks at her questioningly. Rebecca shrugs "Well he could," they both laugh. "I'll stay with you tonight, keep you company and keep any visitors away. "I'll burn anyone who comes in" Princess says.

Down in the stables Geraldo is losing his temper and throwing things around. He grabs his horse and rides out. His men do not try to stop him, knowing he is best left alone and not knowing what has happened. Orpheus enters the stables and asks where Geraldo is. "He just rode out Sir, he was not exactly happy. We thought it was better to let him be." "Very wise" Orpheus states, let me know when he returns, if he returns." He turns and leaves. The soldiers look at each other confused. One speaks up "Well this is not our problem let's find a bar and relax." They all agree and head out to the town. Everyone has left the Throne room except King Stefan and Prince Edwards. "Well, that went better than I expected Stephan laughs." "She is gorgeous father; I can't wait to be alone with her he laughs." "Well, be careful, this is a great opportunity to gain both Tarmack and Lystonia at little cost, I may even get a grandchild." He laughs and calls for another drink. The maid pours him one and then as she hands it to him, he grabs her and places her on his lap. "This is how you treat a woman son; he grabs her body and gropes her kissing her neck. He then suddenly stops. He thinks "Of course you will have to be a little more careful," he smiles, "you don't want to be burnt do you." "It would be worth it "Edward replies. The king then throws the girl at Edwards. Here go and practice on her. Edwards takes the girl by her arms and drags her away. The girl pleading to be released. "Later" Edwards shouts as they leave the room heading to his bedroom. Stephan sits back looks up and smiles.

The next Morning there is a massive explosion along the length of the wall. Tons of rubble fly into the air and fall on the trenches made by the Tarmack soldiers. Many are buried alive. Manion's men then charge across cutting down the Tarmack survivors' and there is a massive battle of hand-to-hand combat. The Manion side push the Tarmack army back until they collapse and retreat in an unorderly manner rushing to the protection of the city. Manion walks over the dead bodies of the battle and orders that his men hold and rest. "Let them run, we know where they are going." He looks for Kaaran. Eventually Kaaran reaches him. "How long will it take till you can get your cannons here." They are in the pass, so if you can get the men to clear a path through these bodies, we can be ready to move on in two hours. Well, the men need to rest, so we will proceed in four hours, and you meanwhile bring your equipment forward to the wall." "Very good my Lord," Kaaran turns and walks back to the encampment. Manion lifts his sword and wipes the blood of it. He walks forward to the main road and looks towards the city. An officer comes up to him." Send a scouting force ahead to see what we are facing and report back." "Very good" the officer replies and calls together a squad of men on horseback and they ride off.

Meanwhile next morning Princess rises and dresses. She turns to Rebecca "Don't leave me alone with him." "I won't Rebecca confirms as they leave the room and head for the throne room. Here King Stefan and Prince Edward are waiting. Edward is excited when he sees princess. "You look beautiful" he says. "Thank you, your Highness." "I've arranged for us to take a trip to a beautiful lake, I hope you will like it." He tells her. "I am sure we will." She turns to Rebecca, "Are we ready"? "Yes, your Highness, I'll bring everything we will need." "That won't be necessary" Edward interrupts, "I've arranged everything for the two of us." "It would not be right for her Highness not to be chaperoned." The king stands to control the situation. "Rubbish, they are grown up and both Royal, so they know how to behave," let the sweethearts have time to get to know each other." "But, your Highness, I need my maid," Princess pleads. "Nonsense, she can prepare for your return" King Stefan instructs. "Of course, your highness," Rebecca curtseys and looks to Princess. The look of anger on Princess's face is plain to see, but Prince Edwards is oblivious to it. "Excellent, then let's leave for a wonderful day" he suggests. He takes princess's arm and leads her out of the throne room and to the stables. Princess mounts her horse as a step is brought for Edward to help him climb on his mount. Princess looks at him with revulsion. He takes the reigns, and they head out of the city into the woods. Rebecca watches them leave from the throne room window. Orpheus arrives and approaches Rebecca. "Is Geraldo around" he asks. "I haven't seen him since last night, have you checked whether he is with his men." "I'm sure he will turn up, let him know I need to see him, if you see him." He asks.

Upon reaching a delightful lake the couple pull up by a tent prepared by the palace maids. There is plenty of food and drink. Princess dismounts and heads into the tent. Eventually Edward manages to dismount, and he joins her. He asks her "Would you like a drink, Princess." "Yes, a large one please" She responds as a smile comes across his face. "Excellent, I thought we could go for a relaxing swim." "Oh, I don't swim" she lies. "Don't worry, I'll teach you, drink up." He downs his drink and waits for Princess. She sips hers slowly. He starts getting impatient and starts undoing his shirt buttons. Princess looks away as do the maids. One sniggers and he explodes. "Get out all of you." The maids rush out. "Now hurry up Princess and undress, he sits down and removes his boots and undoes his trousers standing there waiting. "I am shy, your highness, I have not brought a swimsuit." "Nonsense, you don't need one, I'll look away" He laughs and looks out of the tent towards the lake. Princess flustered, undoes her dress, and slips it off. "You get in first" she asks. He laughs and runs into the lake creating a big splash with an unsuccessful dive. Princess steps out in her underclothes, I white simple top and breaches. She steps towards the lake and steps in and rushes to lower herself to her neck to hide herself. Edwards bursts from under the water like a whale and swims over to her. "Don't be afraid, I've got you, I'm like a fish" he remarks. She smiles and gives him her hand. He pulls her towards him and notices her clothes. "What is this, you don't need them, we are to be married." "Then you should wait till the wedding night, shouldn't you" she explains. "But I'm a Prince, we can do what we want." Princess releases herself from his clutches and tells him. "In Lystonia, we do not see each other naked till after the wedding night." Edward looks around, "are we in Lystonia, or Norland"? he asks. "So, stop being shy and lets swim." He swims of and calls her to him. He is in a shallower area. She swims after him and stands up. Unaware that she is standing there with her wet clothes which are virtually see through. Edward looks at her. "Beautiful, even better than I prayed for." She looks at her clothes and ducts down under the water. Edwards, laughs "I've seen everything now, so no point being shy." He goes over to her and grabs her waist. "Now let's start those swimming lessons." Her places his arm behind her backs and then takes his other hand to push her onto her back. Before she can stop him, he is giving instructions. "Now kick your legs, I'll support you." In a panic she collapses and sinks under the water. As she reappears, she puts out her arms to stop him, "I do not need lessons, I am cold and want to get dry." "Very good your Highness, let's go and get warm. He takes her hand and leads her out. He climbs out of the lake as she reverts her eyes at his naked body. He laughs as she tries to hide hers. They enter the tent, and he grabs a towel and raps it around her. "We better get those wet clothes of you, don't you think"? "Yes, please turn the other way" she orders. He turns away from her grabbing a towel for himself and wraps it around his waist. As she removes her wet clothes, he sneaks a peek and is caught by Princess. "Edward, which is not honourable." She scolds him. "But we are going to get married, I need to see what I'm getting for all our help." "This is impossible," she storms out of the tent and goes over to a large fire that is before the tent. A maid rushes over to her and gives her another towel, and another brings her dress. Three maids form a screen around her as she dresses and gets warm. Edward appears at the tent entrance, still naked. "Princess come and assist me sweetheart." She crouches down on the ground out of site. "Princess, I'm waiting." He calls impatiently. He then goes into the tent. A male servant arrives and enters the tent" Can I assist you your Highness"? "Did I call for you. No, get out"! The servant runs out as Princess stands at the tent entrance. "I'd like to get back now your Highness; I think it is going to rain." "Nonsense he shouts it's a sunny day." Princess has her arms behind her back and waves her hands as the sky darkens and rain pours down. Princess pleads. "Impossible we can't ride in this weather, we will have to wait in the tent, come and sit with me here." She looks up and sighs then goes over to sit with him. "I think I need another drink if you don't mind." She asks. "Excellent idea, then we can discuss our wedding and night" he laughs. He pours her drink which she instantly downs. He smiles and pours another. He then takes her hand. "So, what do you wish to wear and colour"? "Oh, I want a great white gown with pearls, and a parade around the city so everyone can see us, and all the Lords of your country here to show their pleasure in our wedding. With lots of gifts. And I want some of my friends to join us. "That will take some time won't it." He asks. "Well, you did ask, and you wouldn't want to disappoint me would you." Princess has finally worked out a way of dealing with him. "Anything you wish my Princess" She gives him a big smile and wraps her arms around her. Once her arms are around him, she waves her hands, and the rain stops and the sun bursts out. "Oh, look the rains stopped, lets rush back to the castle and tell everyone what we have decided, I'm so excited." "Right away" Edwards says as Princess laughs, "I think you better get dressed first though." He looks down at his naked body, "Oh one minute" He rushes to climb into his outfit and calls out for their horses. The horses are brought and Edward orders, "Everyone back to the castle, we have a wedding to prepare." He then leads Princess out of the tent and over to her horse and helps her mount it. She grabs her reigns, "Race you back to the castle" she screams and gallops off and Edward frantically tries to mount his calling out "I'm right behind you" as she disappears into the woods. He follows shortly after. Princess rides into the castle entrance and dismounts and is met by Rebecca" How did it go" she asks! Oh, we have a wedding to arrange, a great big wedding." She rushes into the castle followed by a perplexed Rebecca. Shortly after Edwards arrives exhausted and dismounts and stumbles into the castle. In the throne room, King Stephan is sitting on his throne with Princess sitting in Edwards. They are laughing and talking. Prince Edward enters the room to hear The King confirming "So you decided on a grand wedding, it will take some time, but if that is what you want." Edwards looks a little confused, "Oh yes, we thought it would be for the best. Princess excuses herself" Will you excuse me your Highness, I am exhausted from all the swimming, and I have plans to make." "Off course your Highness." "Oh, I'll join you Princess, we can work on it together" Edward suggests. "Oh no this is the bride's job, let me surprise you." She explains "Oh yes of course, see you at dinner" he concedes. She dances of followed by Rebecca. They enter her room and Princess locks the door behind her. "You cunny devil" Rebecca accuses Princess. "Well, I had to slow him down somehow, no way am I marrying him in three days." They both laugh. "Well let's start making the biggest most elaborate wedding list we can imagine.

Back at Manion's camp his men are lined up to advance on the city. Manion heads the line of troops with Kaaran and Alexander by his side. The line stretches well over two miles. Possibly twenty thousand men is approaching. In the city the Gates have been closed and men are manning the turrets with archers. Outside in three groups are Tarmack soldiers, with horsemen on either side. They wait to see how big of a force is going to face them. King Alphonso is looking out from the battlements with Ronaldo. "How long till they reach here" he asks. "Very soon is the response as the first of Manion's men appear in the opening and move to the far right of the field. They are joined by more and more men until one massive group of men face the Tarmack army. Tarmack is vastly outnumbered. "This is when we could do with the Princess's help" Ronaldo remarks. King Alphonso grimaces.

Suddenly a man rides out from Manion's troops carrying a white flag. He heads to the gate to appeal to the King. Upon reaching the gate he calls out. "Lord Manion offers you mercy if you surrender and march back to Tarmack, without your weapons." The King bluffs, "You know what we did to your fleet and at the wall. Turn around and leave our land and you can leave in peace." "So be it" the messenger shouts, you will all die." He turns and rides back to Manion, throwing the white flag on the floor as he leaves. Once he rides through the troops to Manion the troops start to slowly march forward. Till they are some two hundred yards away when a hail of arrows fly into the sky and fall on the Manion army. Many men fall, but not enough to make a difference and they speed up their advance to a charge. Again, the arrows fly with a similar result. Manion's men are yards from the front line and the sound of armour clashing is deafening. The Tarmack army hold their line for a short while, but the sheer weight of the oncoming army starts to buckle it. The Tarmack horsemen try and support but are quickly chased of by Manion's horsemen. It is a vicious battle with one obvious winner. It is over within the hour and the survivors of the Tarmack army retreat to the port. Lord Manion regroups his men to surround the city. Then Kaaran brings forward his weapons. A line of cannons lines up facing the city gate and walls. Lord Manion prepares to send another messenger as Manion discusses the siege with Kaaran. "How long till your weapons are ready." "My Lord, if I can have an hour to make sure everything is set up correctly, we can proceed." "Good" Manion replies, he turns to the messenger" tell them they have four hours to surrender." "Very good my Lord," the messenger replies as he rides of waving another white flag. Kaaran looks at Manion, "My Lord, why give them so long." "Our men have fault twice already today and marched a distance, so they need a rest, meanwhile those behind the walls will be panicking. Manion explains. Kaaran nods in agreement to Manion's thoughts. Manion turns to Alexander "take what men you need and clear the port." "Very good" Alexander replies and rides of to the port followed by his cavalry.

Back at Norland Princess and Rebecca enter the Throne room for dinner. Present are the same people as before minus Geraldo. King Stephan is sitting in his seat and stands to welcome Princess. Everyone else joins him and Princess and Rebecca take their seats. King Stephan opens the conversation by announce "Her Highness Princess of Lystonia and Prince Edward have agreed to marriage and plans are in hand for it to take place soon." Everyone claps and the King raises his glass, "Too the happy couple." Everyone raises their glasses and cheer. "So, your Highness, are you going to give any clues as to what you plan are." Everyone turns towards Princess. "Well, it is early days, but it will be a white wedding with a ball to celebrate. I think Prince Edward and Myself should do a parade around the city, so everyone can see us and join in the celebrations, I would like to invite all the Lords and Ladies of your land and any left in mine, so messages will have to be sent out, and I am drawing up a list of requests for the quests, if this is agreeable to your highness". "Nothing is too much for my son's wedding," we will start preparing tomorrow." Again, everyone cheers, and Edward has the biggest smile on his face. Edwards places his hand on Princess's. "So, tell me more and when, I can't wait"! "Well, naturally we have to get all the invites out, mine will have to take longer as it is so far away, but I really want my people here as well." "Off course, that's not a problem, I can wait for the wedding, but not for you." He squeezes her hand. "You know anything worth having is worth waiting for, aren't I worth it"? she asks. "Oh. off course, I just thought, He responds surprised. "Yes, I was brought up in a priory, I was left there at birth, so I have been brought up very religiously." "I was not suggesting anything, you know"." Off course not, I know you are a complete gentleman." Rebecca almost chokes on her drink at this. Princess looks at her "Bless you, my child." Rebecca clears here throat "Thank you your Highness." Rebecca replies and throws Princess a smile. Orpheus breaks the conversation to ask King Stephan "Your Highness, is there any news from Lystonia. The King winces "Well I didn't want to ruin the occasion, but it seems that Lord Manion has invaded, and broken through the wall and is currently surrounding the Capital. "Oh my God, we must take action, what good is a Princess without her land," She grabs King Stephen's hand, we will take action immediately, won't we." Prince Edward on cue buts in, "Of course we will take action, I will personally lead our army for you, my Princess." "You are so thoughtful, my Prince. He smiles as his father looks at his son knowing he has been trapped into action. "Very well then, I guess the quicker we attack, the less time they will have to prepare"." I wonder who we will be facing" Princess asks. "Well going be history, my money is definitely on Lord Manion, he is ruthless." Stephan says. "Call the generals and we will meet in the conference room in one hour." "Excellent your Highness, we will meet you there." Orpheus stands and leaves the table as does Princess and Rebecca. Princess rushes over to Orpheus and whispers in his ear, "Where is Geraldo, we need him here." "I know your Highness, I will try and find him, he was very unhappy at the wedding news." Princess goes back to the dinner table and leans down to Edward; will you be at the meeting"? "Of course,"

He replies. "OK, I'll see you there, will you excuse us. Everyone stands up as Princess and Rebecca leave.

They enter their room. "Well, that went better than I expected." Princess explains. "I don't know how you can keep a straight face" Rebecca laughs. "Well, we have our delay, hopefully something will happen in battle and the marriage won't proceed." "That's a bit harsh" Rebecca tells her. "Well, you didn't think I would agree to marry that idiot without a get out clause, did you"? "No, but wishing him harm is a little…" "Would you marry him"? "Oh no never." "Well, there's your answer, I hope Geraldo is OK."

Back at Lystonia's Capital, Manion's men are preparing to attack. Manion and Kaaran come out of their tent and walk forward. Lord Manion calls to his men, "It has been a long day but one more push and we will have victory." His men all cheer as he orders Kaaran, "proceed"! Kaaran signals his team operating his weapons. They all light the wicks and together there is an amazing explosion as the walls and buildings inside are hit with the weapons. Numerous holes are made in the walls and several buildings have collapsed. There is a great cheer from Manion's men, as Karan's teams reload. After a couple of minutes, they all signal they are ready and Kaaran signals to fire. Again, the explosions blast out and the walls are again hit and this time also the main gate is heavily damaged, but still holding. "Aim them all at the gate." Kaaran orders, and when ready signals to "fire." They all fire and the city gate is destroyed with the surrounding walls. Lord Manion orders "charge and his men rush forward, the horsemen leading, quickly reach the gates and ride through the guards protecting the city entrance. The horsemen cut down some and ride on as Manion's footmen reach the entrance and proceed to hand-to-hand combat. The Tarmack men are over run and retreat to the Palace. The gate is closed, and the Palace is surrounded by Manion's men. Everyone halts and waits for Manion and Kaaran to arrive. Manion arrive as his men attach chains to the gates and the other ends to horses. They await

Manion's command. Manion raises his arm, and the horsemen pull the gates of their hinges. The soldiers rush through killing any Tarmack men as they come across them, it is a massacre. They reach the Throne room and barge in. King Alphonso is on his throne, a line of men in front of him. Double the number of Manion's men face them and they await Manion. He arrives and walks up to Alphonso's men. "You wish to die for this weakling" Manion points at Alphonso. His men take a step forward and Alphonso's men start to drop their swords. Alphonso stands up as his men part and kneel. Lord Manion walks forward and draws his sword then without a word swings and cuts of Alphonso's head in a single blow. Alphonso's men remove Alphonso's body and Lord Manion steps forward and sits on the throne. His men then gather up Alphonso's men and again place them on their knees before Lord Manion. "Where is the Princess" he shouts. One man speaks out, "My Lord, she escaped several days ago, no one knows where she is." Manion nods to his men and they cut down the Tarmack men. Lord Manion sits back on the throne. "Send out men to find the Princess, she must be somewhere"? Lord Manion orders.

In Norland, the war meeting is taking place. King Stephan is marking points of access. Obviously, we will send the main force through Tarmack, as most of their army is in Lystonia. We will also send forces by sea carrying the heavy equipment. How do you wish to travel your Highness looking at Princess" I will go by land, hopefully I can gain any Lystonian troops still in hiding to join us, Princess explains. "Very good. I will therefore go by sea and meet you at the Capital. Prince Edward will obviously travel with you for protection" he responds. "Of course, I will protect him" she responds." King Stephan looks at her, "He will protect you your Highness" he barks. "Oh, off course, my mistake, I am so used to being alone" she responds. Prince Edward steps up to her and raps his arms around her, "Don't you worry, you are in safe hands." Edward tells her. "So, when will we leave" Princess asks. The forward troops can leave tomorrow. Stephan announces. "Good I will travel with them then" she claims, "and of course Prince Edward will join me, won't you"! "We will lead from the front," Edward says. Orpheus interrupt "I will travel with King Stephan and the troops that came with us will travel with you as personal guard." "Very good" Princess agrees. "I suggest everyone has an early night as we will have an early start," King Stephan suggests. They all agree and leave for their rooms. As Princess is leaving, she pulls Orpheus aside "Any news on Geraldo"? "Nothing your highness, sorry" he replies. "Ok good night then." She leaves.

The next morning King Stephan sees off his troops led by Prince Edward and Princess. They are no more than a few miles from the Castle when they come across a man on horseback. As they get nearer, Princess's heart speeds up as she realises it is Geraldo. He calmly trots up the them and bows his head to Princess. "I believe my services are needed here your Highness; he suggests. "You would have been greatly missed if you had been late" she smiles. He lines up behind her. They proceed on their march.

Meanwhile back in Lystonia, Lord Manion is inspecting his army who are still outside the city. He is with Alexander. "Any news on that Princess" he asks, "Nothing, she certainly is not in the city, so I guess she has fled overseas." Alexander informs. "Good, as long as she is not here, good ridden." Manion responds. "What defences are in place down by the port"? Manion asks. We have recreated the chain and boats that they used, only we have used Kaaran's powder. "Good idea, that will surprise them." Manion responds. "I would also like to move some men down to the border between Tarmack and here, just till we know what is going on in Tarmack and find out where the Princess is," Alexander asks. "Good idea, proceed." Is Manion's response. They head back to the Palace.

Princess and her soldiers reach the border of Tarmack. Ahead of them in an opening is a small army of Tarmack soldiers. They are lined up to face Princess and her men even though out numbered. An Officer of the Tarmack soldiers' rides forwards twenty metres and stops. Prince Edwards orders his men to face the enemy. There is an atmosphere ready to explode. Princess stands centre and Edwards joins her with Geraldo. Edward turns to Geraldo for advice, "Shall we attack or let them come to us"? "I would stand and let them come to us," was Geraldo's advice. "Just hold here for I moment, I want to talk to them." Princess interrupt and without waiting rides out to the single soldier. She told him, she was Her Highness Princess of Lystonia. He takes out his sword and raises it in the sky. Geraldo prepares to ride towards them to rescue her when the man brings his sword to his chin and bows. All the troops behind him kneel and shout out "Princess"! The sole soldier rides alongside Princess and asks her to inspect the guard. He tells her that they know what King Alphonso did and they swear allegiance to her, along with this guard there are another eight thousand men waiting to join nearer the Capital. She rides along the line and when she reaches the end she rides back to her men. "What happened"! Prince Edwards asks. "They have sworn allegiance to me it seems and there's another eight thousand waiting to join us," she responds. "Amazing you have just taken a whole country and not lost a life," Geraldo Says. "You mean allegiance to King Stephan, don't you"? Edward asks. "Do you want to ask them" Geraldo asks. "Ah no, we are all on the same side, aren't we"? "Exactly" Geraldo replies "I suggest we make camp here so we can meet the new troops." "Agreed" Edward responds as Geraldo looks with contempt.

Hours later there is a massive camp built and the two armies are bonding and having fun. Princess, Edward, and Geraldo walk among the troops and are impressed with the comradery. Around one fire two massive men from each side challenge each other and wrestle cheered on by their own sides. After meet and greeting many men, they head back to their tent. Princess announces she is tired and is going to her tent to sleep. She wishes Edward and Geraldo good night as she leaves followed by Rebecca. As they head for their tent Rebecca asks, "So will they be fighting to see who will visit you later." "No, I have put two massive guards on my tent to keep everyone away," Princess laughs. They enter their tent and watch as two of the biggest men ever stand outside.

Back at Lystonia's capital, Lord Manion is sitting on his throne as a messenger rushes in. He kneels before Manion. "My Lord, I have news of Her Highness, Princess" he announces. "Speak up" Manion orders. "She is in Norland looking to build a new army to reclaim her land," he claims. Manion laughs, "So let her try, we have more men and experience, and Norland is not exactly a major force"! "But she is already picking up more men as she passes through Tarmack, I understand around ten thousand already, and there must be men left in hiding in Lystonia"? the messenger questions. "Hiding is the word here, they have lost once already and run, who needs men like them, my men either fight or die, but none run" Manion states. Kaaron steps forward, "My Lord, I do not think we should ignore this news, at least set up a defensive line." "Maybe, Alexander can handle this matter, and don't let her escape again"! is Manion's response as he stands and walks off to the voice of Alexander replying, "Very good my Lord". He then also leaves the room. Kaaron looks at the map on a table nearby and checks out the entrances from Tarmack. He presses his finger on an obvious opening and then sticks a knife in front of the entrance.

In the morning Alexander and Kaaron are viewing the opening that has been pointed out as most obvious attack route. Alexander points out where a defence wall will be built and a trench. "Yes, that worked so well last time," Kaaron sarcastically states. "These are tried and tested defences" Alexander claims in his defence. "What do you suggest," he asks. Well, they will come through this forest in line, so let's keep them like this as long as possible and take them out as they proceed. Do not place a defence wall in front of them, but either side, so they cannot spread out. Then have your men behind these defences. Then when enough have entered the trap, you cut them all down. "An interesting idea, they certainly won't expect it". Alexander acknowledges. "Lets' try it." He decides. He calls in his officers and explains the idea. After explaining it they all head out to prepare the trap. Kaaron and Alexander head back to the palace to update Manion.

Back in Tarmack, Princess and her army are proceeding and meet the Tarmack army waiting for her. Before her is row after row of men all standing to attention. Princess rides forward and moves through the rows. She stops and calls out to them "Men of Tarmack, I am humbled by your support here and accept your allegiance to me." The men all cheer. She rides back to Geraldo, Rebecca, and Edward. Rebecca states" She is becoming quite a politician isn't she"? "Amazing" Geraldo replies. "She will make a good wife to support me" Edward remarks to comical looks from Geraldo and Rebecca. They both agree with smiles on their face. Princess rides back to them, let's move on while it is still light. Geraldo orders everyone to proceed. The line of troops is getting longer and longer.

Meanwhile on board his ship, King Stephan is leading his armada towards Lystonia's Capital. He is looking out from the steering wheel being steered by the captain. "How long till we reach Lystonia" Stephan asks. "Within two days your Highness, but we do not want to arrive before the land forces arrive. We will stand just beyond the horizon, till we know they have arrived." He answers. "Very good Captain, proceed." Stephan orders. He leaves to go to his cabin.

In the Lystonian Throne room Alexander is explaining their trap to Manion. "Very good, just hope the Princess is not leading the army, wouldn't want it to all end too quick," Manion laughs. Kaaron adds "I'm hoping she is right at the back, then we can dispose of as many men as we want." He laughs. "You have never seen her power but look around at what happened to our fleet and men, you are making a mistake underestimating her." Alexander claims. "Rubbish, we know what to expect now, no ships." Manion claims. "And an escape strategy" Alexander interrupts. "You worry too much, just because she has best you, how many times, two!" Kaaron taunts." Enough, we mustn't fight amongst ourselves", Manion suggests. "Drink and look forward to our victory, we already have added two countries to our empire, and I have another surprise for you, there are thirty thousand more men coming from Mondova, should be here any day." Alexander is surprised, "Monrovian's, wow! They are vicious horsemen" "Exactly, they won't expect that" Manion confirms. They all raise their glasses to drink.

Princess and her army are a few miles short of the border and set up camp. Geraldo sends out scouts to see what to expect ahead. They pitch up their tents and the men prepare their weapons for the coming battle. Prince Edward is boasting of the coming battle they are about to have. Imagine how the people of Norland will react when I return the conqueror of the Great Lord Manion! "I'm sure they will be cheering really loud for the conquering hero." Geraldo smiles, looking at Princess and Rebecca. Rebecca chips in "They won't know where to cheer first, King Stephan, Prince Edward or maybe even Princess." Princess gives them a questioning look," I am sure they will be really proud of you darling," she tells him as she gives him an embrace and kisses his cheek. As this Is happening the scouts rush back and give their report to Geraldo. He heads to the map and calls everyone over. He points to where Manion's men are setting up their trap. Geraldo explains that the path to Lystonia, is the only route available to us and they are surrounded by deep forests. "It seems they have built defences on the flanks to keep us in line ready to attack in force and taking us out with just a small line available to attack." "How wide is the opening and how long"? Princess asks. "It looks like it is about 15 metres wide and one hundred metres long, so only 15 horses or 25 men wide. It's a killing field". "Well what can we do, go back to Norland" Prince Edward asks"." And disappoint those cheering crowds, I don't think so" Princess rebukes. She looks at the map and points to two points either side of the path before the opening. "If we can send some of our men through the forest either side and come out behind their men, then we can trick them into thinking we are advancing and hit them from behind." "Great idea my dear but it would take weeks to clear a path through that forest," Edward tells her condescendingly. "You leave that to me" she replies. "Follow me." She walks out of the tent followed by Geraldo, Edward and Rebecca and a few senior officers and heads to the think forest. Upon reaching it, she kneels before the forest growth and places her hands on the ground. Initially nothing happens then suddenly there is movement within the forest. Trees begin to sway, and branches intertwine, and trees and bushes uproot and are carried aside by the other trees. She stands and as she moves forward the path opens before her. After a few metres she stops and turns to the astonished group behind her. "Will this do"? she asks. "This is why I have sworn my lifetime allegiance to you my Princess" Geraldo claims and takes her hand and leads her back to the tent. They all stand around the map and Geraldo instructs, "If we send the Tarmack army down the right path and an equal number of Norland soldiers down the left, the rest can slowly advance till we attack, they won't expect this." Rebecca asks, Your Highness, how long do you think it will take you to clear the two paths, they will need to be quite wide and long." "I really don't know, but we can't proceed until they are made, that is for sure, also I don't know what it will take out of me." Rebecca then takes over, "In that case I insist that she gets as much rest now gentlemen, so that is enough for tonight, you can all leave." "Of course, excuse us your Highness." Geraldo accepts but Prince Edward tries to suggest something else" I was hoping we could spend some time together tonight and," "I don't think so" Rebecca cuts him off. She ushers the men out of the tent and her and princess fall back on the couch laughing. The next day a messenger rushes into the throne room where Lord Manion is awaiting news. He approaches the throne and kneels. Manion, "report." "My Lord, it appears that a substantial force has reached the border and then just stopped. There seems no reason, we are all on standby in position." Kaaron suggests "They obviously have sent scouts who explained their position and they have no answer to our plan, maybe they will turn and go home," he laughs. "I doubt it, it is not easy to turn an army back without even trying to fight, they must be up to something." Manion explains. "Well, there is no way through the forest except the path so that just leaves a sea invasion, and that is not easy, especially with our defences." Kaaron claims. "Send men into the path and see what happens" Manion orders. "Very good my Lord. Alexander says and leaves. Kaaron reminds Manion that the new troops should arrive tomorrow, that should secure the sea approach even more. "They must be up to something" Manion exclaims. "We will have to wait for Alexander's return I fear," Kaaron suggests. Manion shrugs and slouches into the throne.

The next day Princess is escorted by Rebecca and Geraldo to an area some 150 metres from the front opening. Before them are several hundred men guarding the pass. Princess turns to her right and kneels to touch the ground. As expected, the ground moves and the trees and bushes begin to move aside to create a wide pass large enough to pass the men through in number. She goes forward approximately 50 metres before falling to the floor exhausted. Rebecca rushes to her and holds her. She is given a drink and Rebecca tells her to stop and rest. "How far have we gone"? Princess asks. "That's about fifty metres, we need another 50 then turn left then another 150, can you manage all this Princess"? Geraldo asks concerned. "I have to" Princess replies, just give me a moment." Well, this fifty has taken 2 hours and we have another 200. That's another 8 hours, you can't possible manage that, and that's just this path". "I have to" Princess replies. Rebecca grabs a stick and draws the two lines they are cutting through the forest "Eh! can I make a suggestion, can't we cut the corner, from here cut through to fifty metres from the opening that would save a bit" Rebecca suggests. "It would, but it is still a long way," Geraldo explains. "Ok, then we go on, cut through and prey I can keep going" Princess confirms. She climbs to her feet and continues the path. 25 metres later she again stops. "I can't, it's too much." She sits down head bowed. Rebecca puts her arms around her, "sweetheart, I know it's hard, but you have to continue, everyone is depending on you, we can't send the men straight into that trap." "I know, help me up." Princess acknowledges. She continues with the path although going dramatically slower. Rebecca turns to Geraldo, I'm going back to the camp, she is going to need to eat and drink, I won't be long". She climbs on her horse and rides off.

Meanwhile Manion's scouts have entered the path and been immediately confronted by the guards. They rush back to Manion. Upon reaching the Palace, they approach Manion. "My Lord, they are camped less than a mile from the border. There does not seem to be any action taking place, just a few guards protecting the approach, I see no way they can advance"! "This does not make sense," how can we get them to come out and fight"? Manion asks. "I'm really not sure, maybe get someone to go and challenge them," Kaaron suggests. "I can't see that happening somehow, what about setting light to the forest and burn them out"? "That's something to consider," Kaaron replies. "I'll investigate the consequences.

Back in Tarmack, Princess has continued and progressed over 100 metres. Rebecca arrives back with a wagon with food and drink and a number of men with axes. "I brought some help, they can tidy the edges for you, but for now, stop and eat, refresh yourself. Princess immediately stops and collapses by the side of the wagon and is helped by Rebecca. Geraldo takes the men over to where Princess was working and gets them to clear the ground, so it is easier for the army to walk over. Within minutes these men were sweating and tired. One of them asked how Princess had managed to create such a large path? "That's what she does Geraldo laughs, just think yourself lucky she is on our side" he laughs. Princess is refreshed and stands to continue work. The men step aside and look astonished as Princess continues to open the path. She is up to the initial speed and proceeding with the path as the men encouraged her. The path stops a few metres from the opening, so the Manion troops do not see it. They all then return to the camp, ready for a busy day tomorrow.

In Lystonia Kaaron is explaining to Manion his idea to fire the forest and either capture the enemy in a circle of fire or force them back to Norland. "If we place the shore battlements in front of the forest, we can fire my explosives all around them." "Excellent, move them then and we can start thinking of going back to Urania, looks like we won't need the extra troops, but we will see" Manion says. "Excellent my Lord, I will start moving them there tomorrow. Then hopefully we can proceed the day after. Now it seems it is a race to who can prepare first and get the first attack in.

The next day Princess and here team start working on the second path, it seems she is getting stronger the more she uses her powers, and she finishes within six hours. During this time Kaaron has also finished moving his equipment from the beach to the forest. Everything is set for battle tomorrow. As Princess rests and eats, Geraldo has moved all the soldiers who will come from the two paths into place under the cover of darkness.

The next morning Lord Manion, Kaaron, and Alexander along with extra soldiers have travelled to their camp at the forest entrance. Princess has refreshed and rides ahead of her army accompanied by Prince Edward. They reach the opening and stop. Princess looks over at the view of Manion's men and the Kaaron weapons. Princess turns to Edward "They have brought reinforcements and catapults; we need to fall back. His response is "Nonsense" he raises his sword and shouts "Charge"! He gallops forward followed by his men and are quickly fired upon by the flank archers of Manion. Kaaron orders the firing of the catapults which are all lit and are round jugs filled with oil. The first barrage is fired and fall on the advancing Norland soldiers before bursting into flames. Princess, who has not advanced climbs of her horse and raises her arms to the sky. The clouds darken and rain pours down, dowsing the fires and soaking the men. She then starts walking forward as the armies from the paths burst out and attack the archers from behind. Princess reaches the front and again raises her arms and points to a single catapult and lightning bursts down hitting the catapult and destroying it and killing the operators. She repeats this again and again until all the catapults are destroyed, and she turns on the army in front of her who have not moved but looked shocked. The path armies have destroyed the flank archers and are now moving forward. Princess reaches forward to the enemy rows and fire bursts out from her body, a human flame thrower, the front rows are all aflame and men are dying before her. This along with the flank armies now crashing into the sides of the main troops, forces them back. Prince Edward, who has been knocked of his horse and was face down in the mud looks up, seeing what Princess is achieving. He staggers to climb to his feet and again raises his sword and orders his men forward. He rushes past Princess with his men behind him, as Princess stops her fire bolts. Manion's men start to turn in panic and run back to the city, chasing after Lord Manion, Kaaron, and Alexander. As their army runs it is chased by the Norland cavalry who cut down many, whilst other Manion men are throwing their weapons away to save weight or simply surrendering. Those that surrender are quickly surrounded as Princess's troops regrouped under Geraldo's instructions. The cavalry returns to the base having gone beyond a safe distance. The remaining Manion army continue their run back to the city seeking the protection of the city walls. Geraldo orders the Manion men be stripped of all weapons and armour and are then marched back to their previous camp and held, surrounded by Norland troops. The fight has been dragged out from them. Princess walks up to Edward, "why did you charge, we were not ready, and many men died because of you"? "But we won, this is a great victory" he replies. "No thanks to you"! she shouts, she points to the many dead Norland soldiers, "Their deaths are on you." she adds. "But we won"! he replies oblivious of his actions. Princess walks away to Geraldo, when she reaches him, she looks back at Edward "He's an idiot, keep him away from me." Geraldo smiles, "Very good your Highness."

Rebecca reaches them and wraps her arms around Princess, she looks over her inspecting her, "You are ok, aren't you"? "I'm fine thanks," Princess reassures her. "Are you crazy just walking forward, what if you had been hit" Rebecca shouts. "I had no choice, we rushed the advance, but it all worked out" Princess explained. "Well don't do that again" Rebecca tells her off and looks at Geraldo, "Don't leave her side again"! she barks at him." Yes, Sir" he salutes and smiles. Princess sits on what is left of a catapult and asks, "So what do we do now"? Geraldo replies, I suggest we rest for a few hours then proceed to the city, they won't be ready now, so it should be reasonably safe, and if the fleet is there, they can then land safely with us protecting the beach". "Very good, I'll leave it to you." Prince Edward wonders over, "So what are we going to do now, Attack them again"? "Ask Geraldo, he knows." She lies back and rests as Rebecca places a blanket over her. Geraldo has moved off to see the officers to explain the plan. Prince Edwards runs after him. "Geraldo, Geraldo, what are we going to do next." Geraldo keeps walking till he reaches the officers, and they all take a seat so he can explain. Prince Edwards stands behind them listening.

Geraldo starts by explaining that the army will split in two, one two defend the beach so the rest of the Norland men can land whilst the other one creates a blockade around the city gate to stop them from leaving or receiving reinforcements. I suggest the Tarmack men hold the gate whilst the horsemen defend the approaches. The Norland troops defend the beach and welcome the King. Edward raises his hand, "eh who will lead which troops"." Well, it makes sense that you lead your men and welcome your father, I'll handle the gate and Durent lead the horsemen". Edward seems pleased with this decision. "Where will Princess be, may I suggest welcoming my father with me." "She is too valuable to be used as a welcome garland, she will have a floating role so she can support any troops in trouble, men prepare your troops for departure in two hours." They all stand and leave to prepare their forces. All except Edward who heads back to

Princess. He peeks his head in the tent, "you awake sweetheart"? As if by magic Rebecca appears, "No she is fast asleep and will remain that way, don't you have an army to prepare." "I just thought," she interrupts him "Don't think, just follow orders like everyone else and let her rest." She closes the tent. "But I thought…" he gives up and walks over to his troops. In the tent Princess opens her eyes, "Has he gone"? she asks. "Yes, I think he's quite scared of me" she laughs. "Good, just don't scare Geraldo off," they both laugh.

Within the city walls Manion's men are preparing the defences and repairing the gates and the battlements are full of archers. In the throne room, Manion is on his throne with Alexander. "What do you suggest, we aren't used to defending, do we open the gates and fight them or wait to see what they come up with. I think we sit and wait it out, they were kind enough to supply the city with plenty of stores and food, so we might as wait for the reinforcements to arrive, that is when we hit them. Kaaron enters hearing this suggestion, "good idea and it will give me time to prepare some more explosives. "Then it's decided" Manion confirms. "I'll inform those who need to know." Alexander confirms as Manion asks "I don't suppose there is any way we can capture this Princess, make her work for us, we would be unstoppable." "I guess that capturing her would not be impossible but keeping her and forcing her to work for us, I fear is impossible" Alexander explains. "Just an idea, then she must die" Manion responds.

Time has come for the army to advance on the city. This time there are two armies, one attacking the city, the Tarmack men led by Geraldo and the Norland men led by Edward head for the beach. Geraldo is delighted to not see an army waiting to confront them. "Great, we can set up and build defences, lead your men direct to the beach Prince Edward." He heads direct to the city and stops some 500 metres from the city wall and his men spread out to cover the city entrance. Durent carries on with the horsemen to cover the road to Urania. They all set up camp and the city is most definitely under siege. Geraldo sets up the main tent as Princess arrives. Edward has a smaller tent down by the beach as does Durent. Princess rides direct to Geraldo. She enters his tent and gives him a hug and kiss. He holds her shoulders, "careful sweetheart, you know that the idiot will be here as soon as he hears you have arrived." "I was hoping that he would be occupied with his fathers' arrival" Princess says. As they are chatting there is a horn blowing. King Stephan is arriving. Prince Edward is waiting by the dock as the Kings ship ties up. Princess and Geraldo also turn up and wait for the King and Orpheus to disembark. Orpheus catches up to Geraldo and takes his arm. "Where did you appear from"? "You didn't think I would leave her here alone did you," Geraldo replies. "Guess not, well she seems a lot happier." Orpheus adds. "You've missed all the excitement, there is no limits to her power, truly amazing." Geraldo informs him. King Stephan lounges on a couch as Edward tells him how he won the battle at the pass to the amazement of the others. King Stephen asks, "I see you have even more men than when you left." "Yes, the remnants of the Tarmack army joined us almost immediately and swore allegiance. They have been very useful." Geraldo informs him. "I must make a point of meeting them so they can meet there new King" Stephan suggests. "Well, I am sure they have been impressed in how Prince Edward charged into battle, fearless was one description" Geraldo confirms. Princess whispers to Rebecca, "Not what I called him" they laugh. Prince Edward announces he has arranged a dinner to celebrate us all being together. So come back in an hour. Princess, Rebecca, Geraldo, and Orpheus all leave instantly and head to Geraldo's tent. "I hope someone has thought of a way to lose them two losers," Princess asks. "Anything can happen during a battle, especially when you are an idiot" Geraldo reassures her. "I hope so" she sighs. Geraldo hands everyone drinks and toasts their meeting up again. Orpheus asks," So tell me of these new powers you mentioned, what exactly happened at the last battle.

103

Geraldo explains how Princess cleared the two paths so the armies could come up behind the enemy, and how she put out the fires caused by Kaaron's weapons, and after Edward charging off stupidly, she saved him with lighting bursts exploding the catapults and then burning the whole front of the army, forcing them to turn and run, even Manion. Orpheus looks surprised" and how physically are you feeling your Highness"? "Oh, I was really tired early on, especially cutting through the paths, but the battles were relatively easy and not too taxing." "Well, it looks like the rest of us aren't needed now" Orpheus laughs and places his hands on her shoulders. "I am so proud of you." "Rebecca deserves a lot of the credit; she has really looked after me." "I have no doubt of that, you two were always like sisters" he replies. "So, there's only one real problem we have to sort out, it's about 16 years old and weighs a ton, Rebecca explains before laughing with Princess. They all discuss the last few weeks and Orpheus tells of his journey with King Stephan. "Guess we better join them for dinner" your Prince will be missing you" Geraldo suggests with a grin on his face. "Yeah thanks" is Princess's response and they all head back to join King Stephan and Edward. As they are entering the tent, they see Edward waving his sword around, trying to explain how he won the war. The others all stand at the entrance looking at him as he notices them and stops, slowly putting his sword away. King Stephan calls out "Come in, don't lounge about outside, tell me more of this battle, it sounds fascinating, I'm surprised that Manion turned and ran just from a charging army"? Princess looks at Edward, "Oh we can tell you that later, let's eat and relax before tomorrow." "Very well" Stephan agrees. They all sit, and the food is served.

The next morning there are men rushing around preparing for battle. Manion has sent his men out of the city to form up in front of the city gates. Before them is the substantial forces of the Norland and Tarmack army. The horsemen are still covering the path, so unlikely to participate in the initial battle. Geraldo stands before the Tarmack army and Prince Edward on horseback is in front of the Norland one. Behind them all, on horseback is King Stephan, Princess, Orpheus, and Rebecca. King Stephan raises his arm to signal a slow march forward. The men slowly move off, to which there is no response from the Uranian army. Once the army are within two hundred metres of the city wall, Kaaran orders his cannons which he had kept back for the parapets to open fire. Explosions erupt before the advancing army, but not reaching them yet. They proceed as the cannons fire again, this time on target and the explosions hit the advancing men, both Tarmack and Norland. King Stephan orders a charge and the men run forward, still being hit by the cannon. The cannon fire is accurate and being very effective, with many men falling dead or terribly injured. The army does not however stop and run on. This is when the Manion army start to move forward to meet them, the cannon stop having done their work and the archers on the parapets take over. Thousands of arrows fly into the sky falling on the advancing armies. Again, many men fall, and Princess wonders if they will even reach the city." We must do something" she says. King Stephan stays still and just says, "this is war, men will die."

Meanwhile at the pass, the army Manion had expected has arrived and tore into the Norland horsemen, decimating them with little difficulty, they are vicious and certainly not a regimented army but more barbaric. This battle is very short, with the Norland men falling or turning and running. The Manion reinforcements, gallop on and reach the opening before the city. Without hesitation they charge into the Norland troops pushing them back. Princess is shocked at this. "Who are they, they are not Uranian." "Mercenaries probably, I didn't expect this." The hand-to-hand battle is vicious and the Norland army is losing far too many to protect the Tarmack's flank. Being attacked on foot and horseback is too much and Edward is still shouting at them to charge, although he is being ignored. Then a rider with a curved sword attacks him and with a single blow removed Edwards head, his body falls forward on his horse which runs off. The Norland army turn and run-in retreat, back to the King. He himself, turns his

105

horse, having seen his son fall, and heads towards the beach for an escape if necessary. With the Norland men in retreat, the Manion men who beat them, turn in to attack Geraldo and his men, they are outnumbered and out gunned. Princess looks at the chaos around the battlefield, " I don't know what to do, they are too mixed up". Rebecca suggests "Can you stop the new men reaching Geraldo and give him a chance to retreat." "I'll try" Princess says and rides forward. The fresh troops have not yet reached Geraldo and she sends a burst of flames the length of the field to separate them. This stops the horsemen as their horses stop at the fire before them. This gives Geraldo's men a little confidence and they battle on. As the fires dies, Princess climbs of her horse and touches the ground like before and builds another wall of mud and stones. She then climbs back on her horse and heads towards Geraldo to help him. As she rides, she raises her hand to the sky and the sky darkens and thunder and lightning hit the city wall. She then creates a break fire between the city and the Manion men fighting Geraldo. With the Tarmack men encouraged by Geraldo's fighting words and seeing the wall and fires, they fight even harder and the Manion men, now trapped lose all fight and try to run back but can't and then slowly stop and surrender. Princess reaches Geraldo and wraps her arms around him, "are you ok" she asks, "never mind me, what about you," I'm fine let's get to the beach. As she rides with him for the beach, she is joined by Rebecca and Orpheus, who is speechless by what he has just seen. They reach the beach only to see King Stephan on his ship sailing away to freedom. "Oh no you don't Princess shouts. She again raises her arms and lightning flashes down causing the ship to explode. "The weddings off"! she adds. Rebecca jumps in the air celebrating as Geraldo picks up Princess and carries her into the tent. You wait here and rest while I go and check the men.

He marches out and looks at his battered but cheerful men. Sitting along the beach are hundreds of Manion's men, now stripped of their weapons. Geraldo sets up guards to stop any more attacks from the city, which is unlikely at present. Meanwhile the

Norland troops who had survived start wondering into the camp. Geraldo welcomes them and tells them to rest. They look out to sea and see King Stephan's ship sinking but seem unconcerned. They start to mix with the Tarmack men, and they all rest around numerous campfires. Eventually singing starts up.

In the castle, Manion is furious as he has lost half of his men. Alexander walks up to him, "My Lord, we have lost many men, but no more than they have, and we now have the extra cavalry." "What good are they against that witch" Manion scream as Kaaran joins them, "May I make a suggestion, my Lord, you know when a large army does not works, it is possible a single man can succeed". Manion's manner changes, "Explain"! "Well, I suggest we send in an expert to kill just her, then they have no hero and no hope, they will then fall easily." "Excellent, arrange it as soon as possible." "It will have to be done at night, so we must keep them tied down till tomorrow night, we can make a diversion by blowing up her new wall, like we did before." "Make it happen" Manion orders, much happier than he was earlier. Kaaran disappears to make more explosives and to arrange the murder.

Back in the tent, everyone is more relaxed having survived a vicious battle. They are all eating and drinking and discussing the coming days. "So do we fight on or re treat to fight another day" Orpheus asks. "I would suggest keep fighting, Manion is weak now, if you let him get back to his land, he can rebuild and return." Princess answers. "I agree." Geraldo adds," We lost a lot of men, but no more than them, and where would we go." "Yes, I guess you are right," well at least let us relax tomorrow, they can't leave without us knowing, maybe we can convince some of the captured men to join us"? "I will approach them tomorrow when they see what you can do in the light of day." Great, then let's eat up and get some rest. "Very good your Highness, I will see you tomorrow," Orpheus responds. He exits the tent and Geraldo takes this as a hint, "Oh I'll leave you as well, your highness." "I'm not that tired, silly" she laughs. He looks at her and moves nearer to her. Rebecca takes the hint "Well maybe I should make my exit here then" she laughs and leaves, closing the tent behind her. Geraldo leans over and kisses Princess passionately as she waves her hands, and the fires all go out in the tent.

The next morning Princess is woken up by Rebecca. Geraldo is gone. "Morning Princess" Rebecca says as Princess looks around, "where's Geraldo"? "He's down by the beach checking the prisoners. No rest for the wicked" Rebecca answers. "Are you ready for breakfast"? "Oh yes please, I have quite an appetite" Princess relies. Rebecca looks at her "I'm not surprised," she grins "that was quite a battle yesterday." "Funny" Princess laughs back.

Down on the beach Geraldo is joined by Orpheus talking to the Manion men. "The Princess is giving you two choices to choose from, one that you stay captive and will be taken back to Tarmack, or you can join her in our battle for Lystonia. The Uranian men look at each other then slowly some start to stand, "I choose Princess" they shout as others join in. maybe seventy five percent of them decide to join Princess. The others are led away and head for the Tarmack path under Norland guards. Orpheus turns to Geraldo, "she is a natural leader, and what she did yesterday was just unbelievable." "I tried to tell you" Geraldo confirms. "Yes, but until you see it, you can't imagine, and that wall, the lightning, you have to protect her, if we lose her, it is over." "I know, I won't leave her side." At this point Rebecca comes down to them. Geraldo, Princess want to see you, she has a problem." "Very good, excuse me Orpheus." Orpheus was just about to say he would join him as Rebecca cuts in, I'll stay here with you, and you can explain what is happening to the prisoners". They sit down and Orpheus begins to explain that many of Manion's men have joined them. She sits there looking interested as Geraldo enters Princess's tent. "Your Highness," Geraldo announces himself. "what's the problem"? Princess is sitting at a table with two plates. "Nothing, I thought you might be hungry after all that effort yesterday," she asks smiling. "Well, it was quite a day, I must admit, I am a little hungry." "Thought so, take a seat and relax" she orders. He removes his armour and joins her. She leans over and gives him a kiss, "Good Morning"! He smiles back at her.

Inside the castle, Kaaron approaches Lord Manion and informs him that he has prepared more explosives and found a man to kill Princess tonight. Manion is delighted as Alexander enters the throne room. He approaches Manion. "My Lord, we are ready to destroy the wall, it is important to get the horsemen out of the city. They can do nothing behind the wall." "Yes, I am aware of that, start work on destroying the wall, but we will not release the horsemen until it is darker as a diversion for the assassin". "Very good" my Lord. I will arrange them to leave and head on the road to our land for a couple of miles and wait there for when they are needed." "Continue" Manion orders and Alexander turns and leaves. "So, it is all down to your assassin it seems." Manion suggests. "I have every confidence in him, and there are so many men from different countries in their camp, it will be easy to infiltrate." "Well let's move to the wall and watch the wall come down" Manion grins. They leave the room. Alexander has placed a small straw wall in front of the gate and set light to it to create a smoke screen. A small team of men then head for the wall and start sticking the explosives into the wall. As the clock strikes, they light their fuses and run back to the gate. Within seconds there is a massive explosion and the wall bursts into small pieces covering the area before it. Geraldo rushes out of the tent and calls to arms. The men head to the front, to see no action coming from the castle and the wall gone. "Hold here" Geraldo orders. He rides along the castle wall and to the path to Uranian to see if any men are escaping, but to his surprise there is nothing. He rides back to his men." Stand down but put up more defences back to the path." They all relax as more men arrive to carry the spiked fencing along to the path. Geraldo heads back to the tent.

He re -enters it and reports. "Seems they did not like your wall Princess." He jokes. "There's plenty where that came from" she responds. Geraldo approaches her, "I would like to bring the fleet into shore just in case it is needed to retreat, I have no idea what their next plan will be." "You are in command Geraldo, do what you think best, shall I put up another wall"? "That won't be necessary this time, the numbers are a lot less." He explains. "Very good." She agrees as Geraldo leave to call for the ships. The rest of the day is eerily silent with Manion's men watching from the parapets and Princess's men sat around fires waiting. Princess, Rebecca, Geraldo, and Orpheus are relaxing having a drink as there is a loud horn blowing. The city gates burst open, and the horsemen rush out and head back to Uranian. Geraldo and Orpheus rush out of the tent to check what is happening. Princess calls to Rebecca to help with her armour. Princess is standing with her back to the tent opening and Rebecca is rushing to buckle up the chest plate. Suddenly Rebecca falls to the floor next to her. Princess turns and sees a tall dark man before her. Before she can react, he draws his long dagger and stabs her clean through her breast plate and out her back. She falls to her knees and then falls on her face. The man disappears as quietly as he arrived, disappearing into the dark.

Outside, all clear is sounded as Geraldo and Orpheus head back to the tent as they hear a horrendous scream. They run to the tent to see Rebecca holding the limp body of Princess in her arms, the dagger still in her body blood covering both of them. Geraldo rushes to them and picks Princess up and carries her over to the bed. He takes his knife out and cuts the straps of the breast plate. He then realises he cannot remove it as it is held firmly in place by the dagger. Orpheus tells him to remove the dagger. He holds it in his hands and slowly withdraws it. There is no reaction from Princess as he throws the beast plate away. Rebecca leans over princess to check her heart and breathing. "There's hardly any breath and the heartbeat is so slow." She gets up and grabs a jug of water and some cloths, she takes Geraldo's Knife and rips of

Princesses tops and washes the wounds, both front and back. "Go and find a doctor quick" she tells Orpheus. He rushes out as Rebeca cuts up clothes and holds them against each would front and back and adds pressure. "What shall I do," Geraldo asks her. "Get the ships ready, this battle is over, we have to get her to a city to recover. Geraldo leaves as a doctor arrives with Orpheus. Geraldo heads to his officers and gives out instructions. He plans to set up campfire around the camp but not near the beach. They will rush to get Princess out whilst the troops slowly board the other ships while a few remain till the end making noise and singing, to cover to retreat. The doctor gives Princess some herbal ointments and bandages her wounds. Geraldo then picks her up and carries her along with Rebecca, Orpheus and the Princess guard and they board the ship. Geraldo orders the captain of the ship to set off for Norland. He then jumps off the ship to cover the retreat with his men. Rebecca tries to stop him, but Orpheus stops her, "He has his job to do, let him go." Rebecca stops and heads back to Princess, who is still motionless and white. She kneels next to her and starts to pray. Orpheus joins her and they pray together. The ship heads of alone, leaving the beach behind them. Geraldo watches from the shore until the ship disappears over the horizon. He then moves to his men and help them board the ships and encourage the other to make more noise.

From the castle wall, Lord Manion, Alexander, and Kaaran, watch the camp below. Kaaran laughs "It seems they are having a sing song, wonder what they are celebrating"? Alexander asks Manion, "Shouldn't we attack now Lord, it is obvious she is dead, and they are leaving." "No let them have their little play, they are nothing now. We will wait till tomorrow and head back to Uranian to regroup, they are no longer a concern, we will return later." "Very good my Lord." "Congratulations both of you, you both played your part. Now we will expand to four countries when we return." He lets out a loud laugh and heads back into the castle. They follow.

The next morning the city gates open and Lord Manion accompanied by Alexander and some horsemen ride out to view the beach and port. It is empty of men, ships and equipment and tied to a post is the breast plate of Princess still covered in blood and the hole plain to see. Manion rides over to it and rips it of the post and raises it to the sky. "Here is my prize" he laughs. Alexander rides to him. Manion turns to him," send a message to the horsemen that we are triumphant, and they should head home, I will be in touch in the near future." "Yes sire" Alexander agrees and rides off to deliver the message. Karan has arranged a celebration guard to line the road as Manion returns to the city holding up the breast plate of Princess. The city folk who have come out are crying at the loss of the Princess and aware of the knowledge they are still in servitude. Manion rides triumphant through the streets and enters the Palace. The people rush out of the gate to view the carnage outside, on the beach and port and fall to their knees in despair.

Meanwhile on Princesses ship Rebecca is washing princesses face. She is still unconscious as the doctor enters to check on her. He examines the wounds and checks her pulse. "How is she" Rebecca asks. "Well, she should definitely be dead, is my conclusion, but it seems that this young lady is anything but normal, we just have to wait and pray, it is up to her and whatever is keeping her alive." He leaves. Rebecca rests her head on Princess and cries. Orpheus enters and hold her shoulders. "You should go topside and get some air and food; I can't have both of you sick on me." She looks up and he takes her hand. "I can't leave her "Rebecca explains. "I have a lady here to keep an eye on her, let's get you up top now. She nods her head and they both leave the cabin.

Back with the fleet is Geraldo. He is standing by the captain of his ship. "Can't we go any faster, I need to get back as soon as possible." "We can only go as fast as the wind will allow us sire." Geraldo shrugs and moves down to his men all sitting and looking despondent. He is not in the mood to rally them and heads to his cabin.

In the Lystonian Capital, Manion's army are all lined up outside the city, waiting for him to arrive and lead them home. The palace gate opens, and Lord Manion rides out followed by Alexander and Kaaran and his personal guard. They ride out through the city gates and heads to the front of his men, and they proceed towards Urania. Left behind is a small garrison of men to keep order. The city folk have all stayed inside their homes as the garrison men lock the city gates.

Chapter seven

Three days have passed, and princess's ship is approaching Norland. Rebecca has been by her side constantly and is looking tired and worried. Rebecca has her head resting on the side of Princesses bed crying and talking to a non-responsive body. "And if you don't get better, I do not know what I am going to tell Geraldo, he will probably send me back to the Priory to pray for forgiveness." As she continues her rant a hand rests on her head. It is Princesses, she jumps up, you're back. She gives princess a massive hug and calls for the doctor. "Where are we, Princess asks"? "We're on our way back to Norland, I've been so worried about you"? "So, I see, you look terrible" Princess laughs and then winces as laughing pulls her wounds. "I don't care, you are alive"! The doctor enters, he takes Princesses wrist and checks her pulse. "How are you feeling Your Highness." "Weak, and tired and my chest hurts." Rebecca picks up a long dagger "Look this went right through you," she explains. Princess winces, "right through." "Yeah, you have a couple of holes, but the doctor says, if you wake up, they will heal." "I hope so, can I have some water, I won't leak will I," she jokes and winces from pain again. Rebecca leans over and helps her drink some water. "Where's Geraldo, what happened to the army." "We had to leave Lystonia in a hurry, Geraldo stayed behind to sort the army out, we won't know anything till we reach land." "Oh, I hope he is OK"!

Princess sighs. "He will be, I'll go and get you something to eat," Rebecca says. "Just a soup" nothing heavy." Princess asks. Rebecca leaves as the doctor checks Princess's wounds and rebandages them. As he finishes, Rebecca returns with a tray holding a bowl of soup and fruit juice. "Here try this," she places the tray on Princesses lap and Princess tries to pick up the spoon but winces in pain. "Ouch, I can't lift my arm." "Let me help" Rebecca takes the spoon and feeds Princess the soup. The doctor makes his leave as Orpheus arrives. "How are we doing" he asks. "Feel like someone stabbed a knife right through me" Princess replies, making sure not to laugh. "We will reach land any moment now, so just rest, and recover" he exits. Princess looks at Rebecca, you look like you need a good rest as well, you know it's crazy, we went through all those battles, and I got injured in my tent". Rebecca laughs and I got a big bump on my head as well. They both laugh even though it hurts. Rebecca takes the tray away as they hear the shout of Land ahead. "We're here Princess, I'll get your things ready." Princess just lies there motionless. She can hear the ship touch the dock and the men prepare the ship for disembarking. Two massive men knock on the cabin door and enter. They are carrying a stretcher. "Careful with her, she is very sore" Rebecca tells them. They carefully lift Princess off the bed and onto the stretcher and Rebecca covers her in a blanket. They lift her up and start to carry her on deck and across the boarding planks to a waiting wagon. There waiting is Summerton. "Welcome back your Highness, I hope you are feeling better." "Nice to see you Mr Summerton, I am a little better. Would you like to stay at my home or go straight to the Palace" he asks. "I think the Palace if that is OK." "Certainly, your Highness, I'll tell the guard and of course accompany you, Patricia can't wait to see you either. "I look forward to seeing her too." The men carry her to a wagon and place her carefully on cushions laid out to comfort her, Rebecca jumps in with her. "I'll go by horseback, I think" Orpheus suggests. The party move off and head towards the Castle slowly. The trip is uneventful as her arrival has been kept quiet. After hours of travelling, they reach the Castle and enter. Princess is carefully carried up to the Kings room which has been prepared for her. There are a group of maids with big smiles on their faces as she enters the room. They all curtsey to her as one uncovers the blankets, and the men lift her onto the bed. The blanket is then placed over her. Rebeca asks one of the maids to get her some water. She rushes of and returns with a jug and glass. She pours the water and hands it to Rebecca who helps Princess drink.

Down in the throne room, Orpheus is seated with Summerton explaining what has happened. "I had heard some rumours from some of our men who had escaped and returned to the city. They told of Edwards death and King Stephen's abandonment of his army and what the Princess did." "OH" Orpheus sighs, not knowing what the reaction to this news would be. "The men talked about how strong and courageous her Highness was and how all the men gave her allegiance, I assure you, there is no risk to her here, in fact the city folk are delighted at the outcome, ask the maids." "Thank goodness," we really were not sure what to expect. She is the Crown of Norland now as well as Lystonia, and from what I hear the same goes for Tarmack." "Well can I suggest a drink to celebrate our new Queen. They both go over to the table and pour themselves two large drinks as the door bursts open to their surprise, Orpheus instinctively ducks for cover as Geraldo enters the room. "Where is Princess, Orpheus," "Oh Geraldo, thank God you are OK and here," Let me take you to her, you are just what she needs. He leads him to Princess's room and stops at the door. He knocks and awaits a call. "Enter, Orpheus steps back as Geraldo peeks around the door to see Princess in her bed. He rushes forward as both Princess and Rebecca scream. He rushes to Princess's side and gives her a hug and kiss. "You made it, I was so worried, I hadn't heard anything about you" she tells him. I have broken every rule to get here quick as possible, how are you." "Sore, but so much better know, Rebecca has been an angel." "Of course, you two are like sisters, thank you so much Rebecca" Geraldo tells her. "Well, if it is all right with you Princess, I will leave you in his competent hands, and I'll go and have a bath, I must look horrendous." Princess turns to Rebecca "Sweetheart, go and rest, and have anything you want, I'll see you later." Rebecca hurries the maids out of the room and they all head to Princesses old room where Rebecca now stays, and they prepare a bath for her. Back in Princesses room, Geraldo is holding her hand and telling her what has happened since the assassination attempt. He tells her he left her breast plate behind to make Manion think she was dead, so he would not rush to reinvade. Hopefully, it will work. "He better stay away, or I will destroy him" she tells him. Well, we have a lot of work ahead of us, so you make sure you hurry up and get well. "I will, but for now, I think I should rest." "OK my darling, I will go and clean up and see you later." He kisses her forehead, calls for a maid to stay with her and leaves. He makes his way to his room and bathes.

Back in Urania Lord Manion is seated on his throne awaiting updates on his enemies. Alexander approaches him. "Lord Manion beckons him to come forward and report. "My Lord, the armies have all headed back to Norland, but no news on the Princess, so she is assumed dead." "Excellent, then concentrate on training new recruits, when they are ready, we will reinvade across the continent," Manion orders. "Very good my Lord." He salutes and leaves. Kaaran enters and joins Manion. I have heard of another person with similar powers to the Princess, I feel we should do everything to find them and have them work for us"." Where is this person" Manion asks. I hear they live in Portland, north of here." "Then go there and take plenty of men to support you. "Very good my Lord, I will leave in the morning." Manion calls over a maid to pour some drinks. They raise their glasses and enjoy their drinks.

The next morning Kaaran stands at the city gates before two hundred men and awaits Lord Manion blessing. He arrives and rides up to the front of the men. He wishes Kaaran a successful journey and to return with his prise. Kaaran leads of followed by his men. As these men leave, Alexander returns with one hundred men in casual clothes, gathered up to join the army. He rides up to

Manion. "My Lord, I have booked up these men, but fear we will need plenty more, I may have to go further afield." "Ok, make your leave Alexander and return with many more men for us." Manion says. "I will my Lord, I will just restock my wagons and be on my way." "So be it." Lord Manion waves him off and turns and returns to his castle.

Back in Norland, Orpheus and Geraldo are seated in the throne room as the doors open and Princess, supported by Rebecca enter the room. Geraldo rushes up to her and takes her arm and leads her to her throne. "How are you feeling your Highness," he asks. "Well, I am feeling better, but I have been told to take it slowly." "Take all the time you need" he replies. Orpheus steps forward, "My Highness, I feel as you are now able to sit here, I believe we should invite all the Lords of this and Tarmack to offer allegiance to you." "Surely it is too early for this" Geraldo insists. "Maybe, but it will take time to announce her majesties wellbeing and to invite them here, so now is not too early." "I agree Orpheus, just do not invite any of them her for a few days, I would not want to relapse when they are here." "Very good your Highness." Orpheus leaves to arrange invites. Geraldo moves next to Princess, "what would you like to do today then my Highness." Well, I would like to get some fresh air." She replies. "How about a carriage ride around the city to see the people." "That would be a great idea. Leave it to me, I will return shortly, Rebecca can you make sure she is dressed warm and has a blanket." Rebecca nods to him and leaves as does Geraldo. Princess sits on her throne as all present stand and just watch her. She points to a gentleman. "Please will you step forward and introduce yourself to me." He steps forward and kneels, "Your Highness, my name is Lord Caruthers, I come from the highlands. I swear my allegiance to you." Well thank you for that my Lord, but at this moment, I was just trying to meet you all." He stands bows and steps back. She points to another man who repeats this parade. All repeating allegiance to her. Finally, Rebecca returns with a blanket and a coat for her. She sees a man on his knees before her. He stands, bows, and returns to the side as Rebecca approaches Princess. "Seems you have been busy your Highness," she asks. "Well, I had to do something, the silence was killing, shall we proceed to the carriage". I think we should wait for Geraldo, don't you". Rebecca suggests. Just as she finishes her words Geraldo enters and approaches Princess. Your Highness If I can escort you." She offers him her hand and rises. They leave the room followed by Rebecca and the other courtiers, down the stairs and to the awaiting carriage. Behind them are twenty horsemen.

Geraldo helps her into the carriage and Rebecca sits next to her and covers them both in a blanket. Geraldo sits opposite. He calls out to the driver to move out. The carriage moves of followed by the horsemen into the city. As they pass by the city folk they bow and curtsey to Princess and when they reach a crowd, they all cheer. Princess looks out and waves at them and remarks "It does not look like they are missing their King much, does it." "I think the word has got around, and he was not exactly popular anyway. The army certainly do not miss him". "Good, should make things easier." They continue on their journey as the crowd starts to follow them. "We better head back to the castle" Geraldo suggests. He orders the Coach driver to proceed back to the castle. They head through the gates and Princess is helped out of the carriage and back into the castle. Upon reaching the throne room, she hears that a crowd has appeared outside the gate. Rebecca suggests that Princess should appear on the balcony so they can see she is well. Princess agrees and the doors to the balcony open and Princess supported by Geraldo, walk forward. The crowd instantly let out a cheer and call her name, Princess, Princess. She does not make a speech but waves to them before being helped back in doors. As she is out of site her legs buckle and Geraldo catches her. "That's enough for today, he picks her up and carries her back to her room where Rebecca prepares her for bed. Geraldo waits outside and returns when Rebecca opens the door. He wishes Princess a good night and gives her a kiss. "Now rest and do as Rebecca says, ok"! "Ok, see you tomorrow." He gives Rebeca a kiss on the cheek and leaves. Rebecca tucks her in and sits by her side. She looks at Princess seriously and asks, "I have to ask, but do you really prefer Geraldo to Prince Edward"? They both burst into laughter and Rebecca kisses her forehead and leaves.

The next day Orpheus and Geraldo are in the throne room as Princess and Rebecca enter. Everyone bows and curtseys, as she takes the throne. Orpheus steps forward, your highness, I was thinking, you will have all the lords of the land coming, so it makes sense to make this a coronation ceremony, technically you have not been crowned in any." "Oops she says, was it necessary." "Well yes your highness and it will certainly get the three countries behind you," he responds. "You do now I cannot wear three crowns at once." "Yes, we can have a special one made; it will be unique." Orpheus explains. "So, be it, might as well get everything out of the way, does that mean any Lords from Lystonia will be attending"? "Yes, your highness." Is his response. "Very good, I'll leave it to you then." She commands. Geraldo steps forward. "Your highness, won't this alert Lord Manion of your wellbeing"? "He'll know by then, so the more united the armies and people are the better," is her response.

Back in Lystonia, the soldiers left behind are abusing the city folk and the city is becoming run down and a place of despair. The people are again taxed and abused with no one for them to turn too. When they appeal, they are reminded that their dear Princess is dead, and her army defeated. They are unaware of the truth at this time. In the school where Princess visited, the children are down and suffering. The teacher is desperately trying to encourage them but fighting a losing battle. The city has had its life sucked out of it, and hardly worth reinvading.

In Urania, Lord Manion continues his reign of tyranny. The local folk are down beaten and suffer whilst the army enjoy the rewards of battle, even when they have lost. Manion is awaiting news from Kaaran and Alexander. It seems that all is quiet in all lands while things are rebuilt and regrouped. Orpheus has sent messages to all the Lords of the lands as Geraldo is training new recruits. It appears everything is heading for another major war.

Chapter eight

A month has passed, and the time has come for the coronation. Ships have been arriving carrying Lord and Ladies and gifts for the Princess. The city is full of visitors and tradesmen selling food, gifts, and mementos. The throne room is decorated with flags from all three countries. Princess is in her room being prepared. Her hair and makeup are being prepared and hanging on a stand is a stunning gown. The maids are fussing around as Rebecca keeps control of everything, ice cool. Princess is motionless and just stairs into the mirror. "You look beautiful your Highness, Rebecca comments. "I'm exhausted already, and it hasn't even started yet, I was less scared going into battle, is her response. "You'll be fine, and I'll be right there with you." Rebecca encouragingly hugs her. "I wish I could see Geraldo, he's always busy lately" Princess complains. "He is building you an army, and he is probably in his room at this moment, looking at a similar mirror, making sure he looks the part as well."

Down in the Throne room, the Lords and Ladies are gathering and a small group of young children, Princess has asked to attend. The room is surrounded by magnificent soldiers dressed in their best uniforms. Orpheus is being busy checking everything, and the archbishop, who will make the coronation speech is checking his words. As the time approaches, Rebecca helps Princess into the gown, which is an enormous weight. "Well, I can't run away in this" Princess jokes. Rebecca leads her out of the room followed by her maids and down the stairs. At the bottom waiting is Geraldo, looking magnificent in his best uniform. Also waiting are six royal guards. The guards lead the way to the entrance of the throne room followed by Geraldo holding his sword out front.

120

Behind him comes Princess with a long train which Rebecca is holding and the maids behind. They stop at the door and Geraldo Bangs the door with the Sword handle. The trumpets blast and everyone inside stand as the doors open. The guards enter and stop just passed the entrance and Geraldo slowly leads followed by Princess, and the entourage. As they proceed down the aisle the Lords and Ladies either bow or curtsey. The military orchestra play as they finally reach the end where there is a stall. The Princess kneels on it as Geraldo stands behind her, Rebecca to her left. The archbishop steps forward and starts his speech. He announces that today brings three great nations together and asks Princess if she is willing to accept her place as the head of the countries. She acknowledges a simple "Yes"! There is a great cheer, as Gerald steps forward and offers his arm and leads her to take her place on the throne. She takes his arm, rises, and walks forward, turns, and sits. Geraldo stands to her right. The archbishop comes forward and announces that with this crown, Her Highness Princess will become Queen of Lystonia, Tarmack and Norland. The Lords all Kneel allegiance as the lady's curtsey low as the crown is places upon Princesses head. The trumpets blast out again and everyone cheers. The noise subsides, and Geraldo helps Princess rise and follows her as she walks down the aisle through the doors and onto the open balcony. Outside there are thousands of people all cheering and singing in the streets. The Princess walks to the front of the balcony and waves to the crowd alone, Again the crowd erupt in noise, then Princess is joined by Geraldo, Rebecca, Orpheus, Archbishop and other Lords and Ladies of choice. There is a party atmosphere as Princess again waves and kisses the crowd. The children who watched then join Princess and wave to the crowd as well. The people behind Princess then start to move back into the room leaving princess alone and again she gives a last wave to the crowd and turns to leave. Not wanting her to go they cheer even more and chant her name over and over again. She disappears but in encouraged by Rebecca to go back out. She does this and again the crowd explode in celebration and cheers. She gives a last wave and retreats into the room. As this has been happening, all the seats that had filled the room have miraculously disappeared and there is music playing. Geraldo leads Princess back to the Throne, and she takes her seat. The music starts and everyone starts to dance. Princess is sitting on her throne listening to the music and watching everyone enjoy themselves. Rebecca sees her tapping her feet. "Your highness, would you like to dance"? "Dance, I can hardly move in this dress." "I thought about that when I designed it" Rebecca tells her. She clicks her fingers, and a team of maids rush up and surround Princess. Rebecca helps her stand, and she feels hands touching her from all sides. Within seconds, the outer gown and main skirt have disappeared, and she is wearing a full length but much more manageable gown. "All you need now is a partner." Geraldo steps forward, "It would be an honour." He offers his hand and the couple step down to the dance floor. Knowing that Princess would probably not know too much about how this works he takes the lead, holds her behind her back and takes her hand. The dance floor clears and the music restarts and he carry's her across the floor in a poetry of motion. The crowd watching applause and then start joining in. An officer walks up to Rebecca, excuse me madam, but could I have the pleasure of this dance. She is shocked but readily agrees. He guides her down to the floor and they enjoy the dance along with Princess and Geraldo. The evening is going well as the doors to the Throne room burst open and Alexander, along with a handful of men burst into the room. The music stops and everyone steps back to the sides. Princess does not flinch. She stands before him. Alexander walks up close to her, forcing Geraldo to also step closer. Princess stops him. Why are you interrupting our celebration, may I ask. I bring a gift from Lord Manion. He turns to the doors and all the children from the school in Lystonia are dragged in, in chains, battered and bruised. They fall on the floor before her. "He also gives you a message. He will meet you in 30 days at the gates of Lystonia's capital to settle this dispute. Princess looks at the children and raises her hands and flames burst out and engulf all Alexanders men. He cowers down. She steps up to him and tells him" This is the second time I have let you go, there won't be a third, you go back to your Lord and tell him that they are the last children he will ever harm. I will be waiting for him in 30 days. Alexander turns and quickly leaves. Princess and Rebecca kneel down to the children and comfort them and Call to the guards, "Get these chains off"! The soldiers struggle to release them. Princess takes the chain of the first girl and holds it in her hands. The room becomes cold as the chain becomes iced up. Princess calls to Geraldo. "Hit it now." He takes out his sword and strikes the chain to the shock of the child, but it shatters. She holds the chains of the other and the soldiers step forward and repeat the action. Rebecca calls over the maids and tells them to take the children away and clean and feed them. The children are whisked away as Princess walks back to her throne. She takes her seat. Everyone moves forward towards her. "Well, you saw what we have ahead of us, so prepare for battle, we will leave in 25 days, Princess announces. Everyone cheers as she stands and storms out of the room, followed by Geraldo, Rebecca, and Orpheus.

She rushes to her room and sits in front of the fire. Rebecca collects four glasses and pours everyone a drink. Princess looks up, "will we be ready"? Geraldo sits beside her. "We have to be" he tells her encouragingly. Orpheus speaks up, "Manion must have regrouped pretty quick, but even so, he must be up to something. Geraldo tells Orpheus, "You will have to send messages to all the landowners to send their men from all countries." "Yes, I will tomorrow morning." "What do you want me to do"? Princess asks. Orpheus reassures her, "You do enough, I'm still stunned by how you keep surprising me. Can we send men to the Lystonia Uranian border, to stop any early intrusions," she asks. "Not at this time, we need to move on force, there are too many passes, I suggest we place a large garrison in the Capital city and stop them there"! "Ok, whatever you suggest" she replies. Orpheus hands his drink back "I better go and check I have enough ink and paper to send all these messages, please excuse me." Me bows and leaves the room. Princess holds Geraldo "We have to beat Manion this time, no more chances," she tells him. "We will or die trying." He replies. "Well on that, I think I will take my leave also. Rebecca stands up and gives Princess and Geraldo a kiss and leaves for her room. "Well, I guess that just leaves us, can you give me a hand getting out of this dress, seems I've lost all my helpers," she laughs. "Thought you would never ask" was his quick reply as he places his arms around her back and starts to undo the dozens of buttons. After struggling a while, he whispers, "This dress is safer than your armour" they laugh as the dress falls to the floor. He then picks her up and carries her to the bed.

Next morning, Princess is again in the throne room greeting people. She turns to Rebecca, "how are the children." "They feel a lot happier being here with you. They have been cleaned, fed and dresses." Good can you send for them. Rebecca goes to a maid and instructs her. "What are you going to do with them," Rebecca asks. "I guess I will ask them," she replies. A few moments later the children are led into the room and stood before Princess. She ushers them towards her and asks them to sit. "How are you, my little soldiers." They all express relief and happy to see her alive. "Tell me, we have to decide what to do with you, I see two options, one, I am sending a small army to your home to guard it till we arrive in 25 days, and you can leave with them, or you can stay here with me and we can travel together to the City". They all cheer to stay with her. One little girl puts her hand up. Princess points to her. "Your Highness, we can help like we did before." "You are my bravest soldiers" Princess smiles at them, ok, Rebecca is your Captain, so you will do as she says, OK"! They all agree and look to Rebecca. "Right, well let's all go down to the kitchen and see what help they need, you boys wait here, till I return, seeing as you are trained smithies now." The boys sit with smiles on their faces.

Geraldo steps forward, "your Highness, I suggest that I visit Tarmack and check on the army there, Norlands is settled, and they know what they have to prepare" he tells her. "I agree and if possible, try and see what is happening in Lystonia." "I will do. My Princess." "But don't be long," she smiles. "You won't miss me" he laughs. "You better hope I do "she laughs back. He turns and leaves. Suddenly Princess is sitting on her throne and realises how her life has changed, and a personal life is now impossible. Rebecca returns and the boys stand. "Right, you lads, let's go find the smithies." "I'll come" Princess suddenly suggests. Rebecca was going to stop her, but felt she needed to get out of the Throne room. "OK, we better find someone who knows the way." A servant steps forward. "Your Highness, I was brought up in the area, I would be honoured to escort you." "Very Good" Princess replies and he leads her out, followed by the others. The room is full of courtiers looking around and nothing to do.

Down on the street, Princess is met by her guard, and they make their way to the smithy area. As before Princess enters and is welcomed by a shocked Smithy. "Your Highness, I am honoured, what can I do for you"? "Well, I know you have a lot of work ahead of you, with all the new weapons we will need, I have some very enthusiastic young men here, who helped in Lystonia before, and I thought you could use there help and it would keep them occupied till we head back to Lystonia". "Well let's see what they can do shall we"? he responds and hands one of the boy a hammer. "Try working this" he says. He takes a red-hot piece of iron out of the flame and places it on the anvil. The boy steps forward, takes hold of the iron and starts to pound it, turning every few hits. "Well, he has certainly been taught something, it will be a pleasure to have them, and they are much needed, I might add." "Excellent, treat them well and make sure they are returned to the castle each night."

Meanwhile Orpheus has entered the Throne room looking for Princess. He is told she took some boys into town as she re-enters and takes her throne. Orpheus steps forward, "Your highness, I have organised messages across the land and am hopeful of more men joining us." "I hope so, we lost so many last time." "But so did they your Highness"! She shrugs. "25 days is not long; can you ensure there are enough supplies" she asks.

"Already working on it your highness." There will be two ships leaving tomorrow for the capital and they will wait offshore, till it is safe, they have plenty of food and other supplies, is there anything else I can do for you." "I am just worried about the people in the Capital, can you find out what is going on there." "I will send a spy to find out your Highness." "Very good, thank you." He turns and leaves. Princess turns to Rebecca, "So what shall I do now"? Rebecca responds, just be yourself, and do not overdo it, I think it is important that the people see you and maybe we can visit some of the other towns here". Great idea, can we leave tomorrow." "I can't see why not, the children are occupied, Geraldo has gone, and Orpheus is busy being busy, so seems a great time to get away." Princess turns to a maid. "Can you arrange lunch; I am a little hungry." "Very good your Highness" she replies and heads to the kitchen. The table is prepared for her and Rebecca and Orpheus, all the Courtiers have been dismissed.

Thirty minutes later the food arrives, and the maids are joined by two little girls who are carrying a tray. On the tray are some biscuits shaped like a princess. The Head maid introduces the children. "Your highness, the children have made you some special biscuits. The little girl lifts the tray to Princess, who graciously takes one and offers one to Rebecca. They both take a bite. "Eh this is delicious, she takes another, well I do not want to ruin my meal, so can you take them to my room for later, thank you so much." The girls have massive smiles on their faces and rush of to the bedroom. "They are so sweet, when you consider what they were like only hours ago." "I know, they are so strong, were we ever like that." "You were." Rebecca laughs.

Geraldo and a small force cross the border into Tarmack, there they are met again by some men. They introduce themselves and state they have been waiting for his appearance, they will escort him to the city. They ride on and the officer explains what has been happening in Tarmack since the coronation. Generally, everyone is delighted with the removal of King Alphonso, although he does have a relative up north Tarmack who is

126

claiming the crown. "I see Geraldo Responds, we will see". They eventually reach the city and march through the gate. The people are lining the roads but disappointed that Princess is not here. They ride into the castle and dismount then move inside. There Geraldo meets all the senior officers and is shown a map of Tarmack. He is shown where the pretender to the crown is situated. "How many men does he have"? he asks. "He probably has a thousand available, but whether they are all loyal to him is another thing" the officer informs him. "OK well let's sort what we can here, and then decide what to do with him"! They sit around a long table and the officers inform him of men numbers and equipment. They have been leading a recruitment drive and it has been encouraging, but time is against them. "Concentrate on the recruitment and training and prepare a force of two thousand to travel to the pretender at end of week. They then enjoy some drinks and talk about the battle of Lystonia, the ex-King and of course the powers of Princess.

Chapter Nine

In Urania, Lord Manion has been busy hiring mercenaries, preparing for the coming battle. He certainly is not as confident as he was last time, but years of battle have given him an arrogance. He is watching two men fighting hand to hand before him for his entertainment as Kaaran enters unexpected, accompanied by a poor looking young man. He approaches Manion as Manion waves the fighter off. "My Lord, I believe I have found what we were looking for." Kaaran explains. He pulls the man forward. "I believe he has similar powers, just untrained." "Well, you have a few weeks to do that, I want to see what he can do"? Manion orders. Kaaran pulls the man forward and points to a table. "Hit that" he shouts. The man slowly raises his arms and closes his eyes. Slowly a glow appears in his hand and a thin flame burst forward and covering the table. It is not however destroyed.

"That's not going to stop an army" Manion shouts. Kaaran responds, "nor could the Princess till she had too." "I'll give him a week to impress me" Manion grunts. Kaaran grabs the man's arms and drags him away. Manion calls the fighters back and they start again, but Manion is now in a bad mood and jumps forward and attacks both men, raining blows down on them until they are both unconscious. He then returns to his throne as the men are dragged away.

A week passes and Kaaran brings the man back to show his progress. There is a bale of hay placed at the end of the hall. He turns to Manion, "my Lord, please let me show the progress in a week. The man turns and faces the bale and raises his arms. There is a flicker in his hands and then it erupts, and a burst of flames covers the hay, and it disappears before everyone's eyes. Manion sits up a lot happier now. "So, what is his name"? "Richard, my Lord." "We'll call him destroyer, keep working on him, hopefully he will only become more powerful." "Thank you, my Lord," Kaaran leads the man out. Manion sits back on his throne with a smile on his face.

In Tarmack Geraldo has been busy raising an army and support. Everyone is eager to help as they know if they do not that Tarmack would be Manion's next port of call. It is here that Geraldo receives a report on the Lystonian capital. It seems that only some fifty of Manion's men are securing it, they are running wild in the city, and everyone is in panic. He decides to act without checking with Princess and gathers a small army of men, around 250. They make their way out of the city and head for Lystonia.

In Norland, everything is progressing well, and the ships leave port. Princess is settled in court life and confidently making plans. The army has increased to sixty thousand, which is more than she ever dreamed of, and the smithies are handing out armour and weapons on a daily basis. Princess still regularly visits them and to check on the boys helping. She is sitting on her throne as a messenger arrives. It is a message from Geraldo informing her of his intent to recapture Lystonia's Capital and release the people from tyranny. She hands the message to Rebecca who reads it and looks at the concerned look on Princesses face. "I am sure there is no need to worry, there is no way he would do this if there was any risk. We heard there was only a small garrison left behind." "I know, but, well you know, I worry, why couldn't he wait"? "I am sure he had his reasons, but on the bright side if we can take the city early, we can leave sooner as well." This idea cheers Princess up. "That's true, let's leave two weeks earlier." That may be pushing it, but maybe some of us can go and the rest join later." OK, that's what we will do".

Days later, just out of site of the city, Geraldo is spying on the garrison and the comings and goings. He calls his officers. "We must obtain some wagons and dress men up like farmers and get them behind the walls, security is not high as there's not many, and they are mostly drunk." The officers agree and send men out to the local farmers to get the wagons and goods to look legitimate. They hide their weapons under the wagon, so even if the goods are checked they won't be found. Over the next day they send wagons in, none of which are checked, and they have a dozen men behind the wall. Their aim is to take the gate so Geraldo and the rest can charge in. They wait till early morning and the men inside creep towards the six men guarding the closed gate on the inside. They take out each one quietly with daggers and open the gates. Within moments Geraldo and his men ride in and head for the Palace. They easily get pass the guards at the gate and there is a short but decisive fight. Geraldo runs on ahead with a small support and into the Throne room. There he finds the officer sitting on the throne. Geraldo walks up to him. That is not your seat. The man stands and draws his sword and lunges at Geraldo who slips the sword and brings his own down on the man, killing him instantly, the other soldiers still standing all surrender and are led away. Geraldo takes the seat and calls for a messenger. He tells the man to send a messenger to Princess to let her, the city is taken. He then goes to rise as a group of frantic folk rush into the room.

They rush towards the throne and plead to him on news of their children. The relief on their faces when he tells them that they are all well and guests of the Princess and that she is bringing them home soon. They all thank him and start telling of the horrors of Manion's men. He reassures them that the Princess will return in days and the city will be safe from now on. He then tells them to go home and prepare for her arrival. They all bless him and leave. One of his officers enters and informs him the city is secure, the gates closed, and men are manning the parapets. "Good, tomorrow we need to build a barrier between here and the path to Urania, to slow them down if they arrive early. The officer agrees "We will work on it first thing tomorrow sir." "Ok, rest the men." He relaxes back on the throne as a maid comes forward and gives him a drink. He takes it happily and tells her to prepare the Princess's and Rebecca's rooms. She scurries off as he finally takes a rest.

A few days later in Norland, Princess is reviewing the troops. Laid out on a vast field in row after row of infantry. The General asks her to inspect them. She agrees and rides her horse along the front row. She asks" how many men here General"? Before you now, is five thousand, there is another forty-five thousand to review." "What "she gasps. "Ok we better move on then. She goes back to the centre as the men march of and as they leave another army take their place. This is repeated again and again until the horsemen arrive. They look magnificent and march before her, a continuous line for over an hour. By the end she is exhausted and uncomfortable being in the saddle so long. As the last passes she turns to the General "I think I better return to the castle before I fall of this horse." Very good your Highness, I will have an honour guard escort you". He points to some horsemen who surround her, and they all leave for the castle. As she is riding along with the General, she tells him "I would like to leave for Lystonia in two days, is this possible." "As you command" was the reply and she smiles knowing she will soon be home and with Geraldo.

In Lystonia, the defences have been built which will not stop, but will certainly slow down the advancing armies. Any damage to the walls by the previous battle have been repaired and the area outside cleared ready for the coming armies. Since Geraldo turned up news travelled around the country and daily more and more men are arriving to join the army, with and without armour. Geraldo camps these men down by the port, there is already nearly two thousand of them and growing daily. Also, at this time the ships arrive with the supplies. Rather than wait offshore, Geraldo arranges for them to dock and unload the supplies and store them within the city. Everything is moving along nicely.

The day arrives for Princess and her army to move out and head for Lystonia. The city come out to see them of cheering and wishing them well. There is a small group of horsemen out front followed by Princess, Rebecca, Orpheus and the Generals. They are then followed by more horsemen, and then the rows and rows of marching men, finally followed by wagons of equipment and supplies. With such a large army, it is slow progress, but Princess refuses any breaks unless it is for the men on foot. After a straight eight hours marching a plateau is reached and they pitch a simple camp. It still takes nearly an hour for everyone to reach it from the front to the back. Princess's tent is pitched, and she relaxes with her officers, who report how the men are handling the march. "I would rather push them now and give them a longer rest in Lystonia, than arrive there exhausted and unable to defend." "As you wish your Highness" is the reply from the officers. They eat and joke and then Princess excuses them so she can settle for the night. Rebecca suggests she gives her a massage to relax her muscles after the long ride. Princess lies on the bed naked as Rebecca wipes oil over her back and legs and starts to rub the oil in. It is very relaxing, and Princess is giving out little murmurs of pleasure. After half an hour it is over, and Princess sits up feeling totally relaxed. "Right Rebecca, undress and lie down, it's your turn." "But you" Princess cuts her off. "You have been on a horse as long as me, right, so let me help you." "Well, if you do not mind." Princess insists "You are my friend first remember." Rebecca undresses and lies down as Princess repeats the process. They both sleep well that night and are fresh the next morning.

The next morning everyone sets of on the march. When they have been travelling for a few hours, they are met by another army. The leader rides up to Princess and introduces himself, "General Montgomery your Highness, I bring you five thousand archers of the greatest skill." "You are most welcome general," Please join on at the end. "Very good your Highness. They move on. A few hours later the same thing happens. An army of men are waiting, these are totally different, all horsemen, but much more rough looking. The leader approaches Princess and introduces his men. two thousand wild horsemen from the mountains. "I have heard of your vicious reputation, Sir, you are most welcome." They all move on until they reach the Tarmack border and make camp. All around the camp are fires with different units of men mixing and enjoying themselves and challenging each other in strength or weapons. In Princess's tent she is entertaining the heads of the new armies. Each vying for her attention. They are telling more dramatic stories of their past battles. Princess sits listening intently then interrupts them. "Eh excuse me gentlemen, can any of you tell me of your successes against Lord Manion. This brings silence as they each look at each other. She then explains how she made him retreat on the border and destroyed half his army, before being a victim of an assassin. They look shocked and subdued at their boasting. "Well, hopefully this time we will all succeed in our battle against Manion. They all cheer and raise their glasses and cheer for Princess.

Back in Lystonia, Geraldo is well on the way to preparing everything. The city people are busy building defences and storing food for the coming armies. The ships with the stores have unloaded their goods and things, although looking up, there is a cloud hanging over the city. What everyone is missing is a Princess.

In Urania, Lord Manion is getting more and more confident as his army increases in size and his new secret weapon is improving daily. The latest test for his weapon is to hit multiple moving targets with fire. Kaaran explains to Manion that he should be held back initially so the opposition can see the strength of his army, and when in the thick of battle, they should unleash the new weapon. This will dishearten Princess's army and hopefully some will retreat. "Burn them all." Manion shouts. "Unfortunately, his power does not last for ever, after a few shots he is exhausted, like the Princess" Kaaran explains. "Then make sure you pick the right time to use him". Manion responds. "Off course my Lord, when are you looking to advance"? I think we will wait a week, give him more time to gain strength and get everyone in position to move, it takes time." "Very good my Lord." Kaaran turns and leads the weapon away. As they leave the man asks, "Why am I called weapon, I have a name you know"? "Yes, but Shirley does not exactly inspire men to fight, so Weapon it is. "I would like to be called something else"? "Well, you tell Lord Manion that, if you dare." They walk off.

Two days later in Lystonia Geraldo is out front inspecting the latest recruits. He watches their hand-to-hand skills, and the archers aim and is overall, impressed. He congratulates the officers and warns them it won't be long now. At this time a rider comes bolting towards him. "Sir, there is an army approaching." "What army is it." I could not tell, they looked vicious and on horseback." "OK ring the bells and prepare to close the gate." He turns to his officers, "set up a perimeter wall to delay them while we get everyone inside. There is frantic action as the horsemen enter the field by the wood edge and create a long line. Everyone in the City are watching from the walls and the look of concern is obvious. Geraldo rides his horse out to join his men ordering the gates to be closed behind him. The gates close as he stops by his men. "Stand firm men, it is probably just a test to check our defences. His men look to each other realising that the battle was about to start. Then there is a bright light behind the horse men as they separate to leave the shining figure of Princess on her horse. She moves forward slowly as Geraldo is shocked to see her." Stand down, get the gate open." He rides forward to Princess as fast as his horse will take him and upon reaching her holds her and kisses her passionately. "You're early" he says. "I thought you were missing me" is her reply as Rebecca and the children join her. Princess looks down to the children, "I think there are some people waiting for you kids, go on run. The children run forward as their parents run from the city gate. Princess, Geraldo, and Rebecca slowly make their way towards the city followed by row after row of men following them. The men outside the army step aside and cheer the coming Princess and army. Cheers are heard coming from the city and the bells are ringing. Princess reaches the gate, and still only a fraction of her army has arrived in view yet, they fill the field and choose their camp sites. Princess rides though the city to crowds cheering and blessing her. The children are also walking alongside her with their grateful parents. She reaches the palace and enters. As expected, a large crowd waits outside wanting a glimpse of her. There wait is rewarded when the balcony doors burst open and Princess steps out onto the balcony to a tumultuous roar. She waves and raises her hand. Everyone goes quiet, apart from the occasional "We love you princess" or other phrase. She waits for silence and speaks out. "Thank you for your warm welcome, and I am delighted to return your darling children." Another cheer is heard. She continues, "As you can see, still arriving is the largest army ever to be assembled. Once and for all, we will rid this land of the scourge Lord Manion and his followers. Her people from three separate lands have joined in a single task united in their aim to build a peaceful land. The battle will be hard, but we will avail over them and destroy any chance of any future attack from the North." Again, another cheer. "For now, help the men who have just arrived and make sure they are fed and rested. For soon we fight. May the gods be with us." She raises he hand, waves, and turns to leave. The square erupts in cheers and her name is called again and again. She makes her way inside, but the cheering does not stop, even with the door closed. Rebecca holds princess's hand, "they want more." Princess looks up and proceeds to the door. They are opened and she reappears. Again, the cheers explode, and she stands there waving. Five minutes pass before it is felt that it is time to retreat, back into the room. She turns to leave, as again the cheers build. "That's enough, I need to rest after a long ride, and I am starving." "Food will be here shortly your Highness" a maid informs her. "Good," she walks to her Throne and sits down. She then jumps up, "This is really too uncomfortable after days in a saddle, can I have some cushions. A maid quickly grabs some and places them on the throne and she re-sits. Geraldo steps forward, "Well you look amazing after that long ride, your room is prepared, and I am sure a long bath will not go amiss." "I have been dreaming of a bath" she laughs. Rebecca comes forward, "your Highness," princess throws her a look. "Princess" She smiles. Let me help you take of your armour; you can relax now." "Oh yes thanks Becky, I forgot I was even wearing it." A maid brings a tray of drinks and Geraldo makes a toast to the return of her Highness. The table is laid ready for dinner and Princess rises to eat; everyone waits for her to sit before taking their seat. Princess turns to Geraldo. "So how did you end up here"? I received reports that the garrison here was treating everyone badly, and I knew I would only need a few men to overpower them, so it seemed a good idea." "The best" Princess agrees," I am sure there are a few very happy families out there reunited tonight." The food is served, and everyone starts to eat. The conversation is positive, and everyone is amazed at the size of the army they have amassed. Geraldo speaks up, "I do not really want to talk business here, but while everyone is here it makes sense." "Go on" Princess insists. "Well as you say, we have a massive army here, quite unexpected, and it will be unexpected by Manion as well, I would suggest we move half back into the woods when the time comes in reserve, and they can attack from behind if necessary." "If that is what you think, it is your decision" "Thank you for your trust your Highness." She throws him a look.

"Well, I do not know about you, but I am exhausted, so I will make my leave." She rises and is joined by Rebecca. Everyone else stands and waits for her to leave. Once gone the room is alive with discussions on the oncoming fight, the army and mostly of Princess.

Up in her room, Princess enters her room with Rebecca and there is a hot bath waiting, along with a group of maids. "Is there a bath for Rebecca." "No, your Highness, we were not informed." "Well, she has ridden as far as I have, please prepare one for her as well." "Very good your Highness, where should we prepare it." "I think next to mine, then we can gossip while we relax. "Very good your highness." The maids all rush out to get hot water and another bath. They return shortly after and prepare the other bath. You are dismissed Rebecca tell them, they all curtsey and leave. Princess and Rebecca both undress and step into their baths. Each holding a glass of wine. They both relax back and give out groins as the hot water relaxes their bodies. They are talking about the welcome they received when there is a knock at the door. They both look at each other wondering who it could be, and whether they should answer in their baths. "It could be a maid." "Enter" Princess calls as they both lower themselves into the water to hide their bodies. Geraldo's head appears and is shocked to see Rebecca also in the room. "Oh, I am sorry, I thought." "Don't worry, come in." "I just brought you a little something" he brings a bunch of flowers from behind his back. "I am just so glad that you have arrived" he says. "Ah thank you sweetheart, they are lovely." I think I had better leave you two alone for now, enjoy your baths and I will see you in the morning." "Ok till then." Princess blows him a kiss. He turns and leaves. The two girls laugh. "His face was a picture when he saw you in the bath" Princess laughs. "Yes, he didn't know where to look, he's so proper." They laugh and Princess splashes Rebecca, "And you thought I preferred Edward"! she laughs. Simultaneously they both duck under the water to wash their hair and pour hair shampoo over them. After a few ducking's they climb out of the baths and wrap towels around themselves.

"Well, I will head for my room, get some sleep Princess." "And you Becky."

The next morning, Geraldo along with Orpheus and the officers are working on the plan to hide half the army in the woods. Geraldo explains it should be mainly horsemen so they can return as quick as possible when needed. As the meeting is concluding, Princess and Rebecca enter the room. The men all bow and Geraldo steps forward and leads Princess to the map. "We have worked out which troops will be held in reserve, mainly horsemen." Good, I was also thinking last night, we have many empty ships in dock now, could we not place some of the civilians on them so they can stand offshore and escape if everything turns bad." "Well, I certainly did not think of anything like that, I guess that's the difference between a military mind and a leader of people." Princess squeezes his arm, "So how many people could we place on them" Princess asks. "For a short time, I believe at least one thousand" Geraldo explains, who do you suggest"? Well, I believe mothers and children, as the men can help during the battle, even if only supplying weapons or building defences" she suggests "Very good, maybe Orpheus can make a list from the city population list," Geraldo suggests as Orpheus agrees. Geraldo then turns to his officers, "well you have your orders, prepare for battle gentlemen." They all salute him and leave. "So, what are your plans for today" Princess asks Geraldo. "Oh, I am completely finished, we started this meeting early, so I am totally at your disposal." "Totally at my disposal, eh., Well, let us go for a walk in the park." "As you please Princess." He agrees. Rebecca tells them "I think I will stay here and sort out downstairs." She turns and leaves as Geraldo offers his arm, and they walk out of the room to the entrance. As they are about to leave the palace they are chased by a group of soldiers, Princess's Honour guard. "We are not going to lose them are we"? she asks Geraldo. "Afraid not." They walk on with the guard walking behind them. They receive amazing welcomes from everyone they meet, and as they enter the park the children are all playing with their parents. They rush over to Princess. She welcomes them all and ask if their family were pleased to see them, the parents also approach as one steps forward and curtseys, "Your highness, we all would like to thank you personally for the love and care you gave our children." They were a pleasure and really their true carer was Rebecca. I will give her your good wishes. They all make way for Princess and Geraldo as they walk along the path and reach a small pond. "When you look at this, you would never believe there was any problems outside those walls" Princess says. They wander along the pond path and turn to return to the centre. A messenger rushes up and hands Geraldo a message. He quickly reads it. "Manion's forces are preparing to leave their base. We have a few days before they arrive." "Ok, let's get back and continue any preparations that need doing." They pick up their pace and head straight back to the Palace. They then head straight for the throne room where Orpheus and several officers are waiting along with Rebecca.

Princess takes her throne and announces," well I am sure you have all heard that Manion's men are on the move. So, everything must be finalised. Have you made the list for the ships yet Orpheus. Yes, your highness, I will have it announce in the city centre and posted to the main walls. "I think Rebecca should also be on the ship to oversee the children and be safe." Rebecca grabs Princess's arm" There is no way I am leaving you in battle again, I don't care what you say, I am staying"! Princess, taken aback by this, takes her hand and tells her, "It is your decision, I just did not want you in harm's way." "I belong next to you, always." Is the response. "So be it" Princess agrees, "but I want her to have her own guard, is that agreed. Rebecca and Geraldo instantly agree. Geraldo then turns to the officers, then you better break camp tomorrow morning for those moving so they have time to prepare, and we can arrange the defensive lines. The officers agree and leave. Orpheus asks, "I wonder what Lord Manion and Kaaran have as a surprise for us this time." "Well, it won't be an assassin, no one will get near her." Geraldo exclaims. "Yes, but she is also our greatest weapon remember." Orpheus adds. "We have enough men to win this battle regardless, so she should never be in harm's way." Geraldo repeats. "I pray you are right," Orpheus replies. "Gentlemen, Princess interrupts I will be fine regardless, please stop worrying about me, and I have Rebecca" She raises Rebecca's arm. They laugh and relax. Geraldo looks at the map. It may be a good idea to also set a line of defence 5 miles down the main road between us, to give us plenty of notice. Also, if our men's backs are going to be facing the city, Manion's will have to move along the field to the other side. Makes sense to build a defensive wall so we can pick them of with archers while they are still moving but make it plenty wide to, so they can get by the bodies. He tells an officer to put this in place, who immediately leaves.

"OK, I think one last walk around the city before the party starts" Princess says. They all rise and head to leave the Palace. As they reach the city centre, they see a large crowd all standing around the notice of who will be on the ships. A man goes up to Princess. "Thank you for thinking about our families, I will fight harder knowing my family are safe at sea." Another then another man comes over as well as many women. Then the children arrive. One of the original little girls from the school tugs at her arm. "Princess, Can I stay and fight with you." Princess kneels down to her. "If you are with me, who is going to protect all these ladies, you'll do that for me won't you." She asks Geraldo for his knife. "Here take this and be on guard." The girls' mother stands behind her and thanks Princess for her understanding. They move on to the school, which is currently an army barracks and practice field. They watch the men in different actions. On parade, hand to hand combat, all looking impressive and ready for action. I must say, the men are incredibly motivated, you have that effect it seems." "Ah another magical power you think," she jokes back. "No, it's just you" he replies as they move on. Every few steps they make they are approached by the locals giving their blesses. After a good hour of this it is decided to return to the Palace.

At this time, Manion's men have reached the mountain pass and pitch camp. They are a cold characterless group of soldiers, almost soulless. A far cry from the men of Princess. Lord Manion arrives in the camp and rides through it heading for his tent. As he passes, he is basically ignored as the men continue with the chores, not even thinking of the coming battle. There is no chatting or singing around the fires and fun fighting, just a cold silence. He enters his tent. His sits back on his enormous chair and takes a drink. So, what news of the city? Alexander steps forward, "My Lord, they are preparing defences as expected, but their numbers are not as many as we had expected, they obviously lost a lot more than we thought last time, or their soldiers have not returned." "Good, good, well hopefully this will be a short battle and we can proceed on to the other countries and see what we inherit." He laughs. "They still have her, remember." Kaaran butts in. "Yes, but she can't defeat a whole army, and you have your little secret weapon to keep her occupied, haven't you." "As you say my Lord." Kaaran agrees and backs of. "Get me a wench," Manion shouts out, "Someone around here should enjoy themselves." He laughs and goes to his back room. Shortly after a young girl is dragged in and thrown into his room. Alexander looks up. "I wonder which will enjoy themselves." He stands and leaves for his own tent. As he steps outside, he looks in the direction of the city, he has an uneasy look on his face. He shrugs and heads for his tent.

The next morning, they break camp and head out towards the city. There is an advance party followed by the main army. Lord Manion heads this group with Kaaran and Alexander. They pass the previous battle till they reach the area where princess built the previous wall." Let's take a 2 hour break her my Lord", Alexander suggests. Manion agrees and they move over to the side and dismount. The horsemen dismount and the foot soldiers just collapse where they stand. The area is quickly filled. Within a few minutes, Alexander is frustrated and get up and mounts his horse. "I am going on ahead to check everything is OK, I will meet you up ahead." He rides of as Kaaran watches and remarks" He's in a hurry to die it seems". "Not today I think" is Manion's reply. Alexander reaches the public house that Geraldo visited before, stops, and enters. He goes up to the bar and demands a drink. The barman is fully aware of who he is, as the advance party have already stopped off at his premises. "So, what have you heard about the city then," "Alexander asks. "Who me," is his response as he knows whatever he says will be wrong, "yes you, don't tell me you don't hear things while standing there"? "My Lord, I rarely visit the city and my customers are on their way to the city, not coming back." Alexander downs the drink and throws the glass across the room. He stands and leaves. The barman is motionless. Alexander expected no more, but at least had a drink and rides on. Thirty minutes later he hears a commotion ahead. He gallops forward and sees a small battle ahead. The advance party had come across the defensive line and were just charging it chaotically. Alexander rides up and calls the men back. He sees an officer. "How many men are there," not many my Lord, but they are well dug in and defended. "OK hold back and just face them; I have something that will clear the pass. He takes a notepad out and writes a note. He then gives it to the man. "Take this back to the main army and give it to Kaaran. The man immediately turns and climbs his horse before riding off. Alexander dismounts and walks along the line of men now facing the defences. He encourages his men, "Do not be impatient, we will pass soon, but no point risking your lives over nothing. Hold firm here and keep them tied down, no messages are to be allowed back to the city." An officer acknowledges his order, and he retreats to a fallen tree and takes a seat, waiting for Kaaran. During this wait a man from princess's army tries to make a run to get a message back, but ends up with an arrow in his back, they are well and truly trapped awaiting their fate.

An hour passes and Kaaran and his weapon casually ride up. They ride over to Alexander who explains what the problem is. Kaaran instructs his weapon who casually wanders over to the front and steps in front of Manion's men. He raises his arms and throws fire along the full length of the defences. The men are all engulfed and die instantly. He then turns and returns to Kaaran. Alexander gets up and walks over to his men. "Right well that wasn't too difficult, clear the pass and dump the bodies so the main army can get through." The men look astonished but encouraged that they also have a weapon like Princess. The chatter amongst them is of confidence and being on the winning side. They start clearing the road and dumping the numerous bodies along the roadside. The bodies are black and scorched and unrecognisable. Meanwhile Lord Manion is proceeding along the road and will reach then within thirty minutes.

Back at the city all is quiet, but not gloomy, there is an air of confidence. In the throne room, everyone is waiting, anxious of what will soon happen. Down in the dock the ships have been boarded and are preparing to move of out of danger. Geraldo approaches Princess, "I think it is time we arrange the men." "Very good" is her reply as a lookout comes running in out of breath. "They are here, they are here" he shouts as he reaches Princess. Geraldo takes him by the shoulder. "Report soldier". "They have been spotted no more than two miles down the road, nearer now." Geraldo asks more, "How many" "Lots, thousands." Is the frantic reply. Geraldo bows to Princess and turns to leave. "I will see you at the rear, your Highness," he marches off. The bells ring and in the parade fields there is frantic action as men gather their equipment and line up. Outside the city, the men already garrisoned there take their positions with archers along the flank wall to take out the arriving army. Geraldo places the main force as two blocks either side of the city gate. To their sides are horsemen ready to move at a moment's notice. Behind them are catapults. In the city parapets are more catapults and hundreds of archers. The two areas for the men are quickly filling up as more and more men pour through the gates. Within minutes everyone is in position and the whole army looks magnificent. Once the last man is in place Princess followed by Rebecca rides out of the city and rides along the lines of men. They are all looking up to her as some godly gift who is going to save them from the evil Lord Manion. After riding along all lines, she stops centre to appeal to the men. "We are gathered here, to defend all our lands, to defend our families and to defend our way of life. This Lord Manion has never faced a combined force as great as ours, and we will not only defeat him and force his retreat, but we will also remove him from the face of the earth. This I promise and this we will do, Together"! There is a massive cheer as all the men raise their weapons in support. Princess is approached by Geraldo "You were magnificent, now move to the back". He calls for a soldier to take her horse and lead her to behind the army. She does not fight this as she knows her time will come. As she reaches the back, dismounts, and steps onto a raised stage so she can see the battle, the first of Manion's men appear from the road. Row after row of his men march silently and menacingly along the allocated path, as archers take pot shot at them, their targets falling to the ground and being pushed aside. On and on they appear and make their way to the far side of the field. They start to take their positions as Lord Manion, Alexander and Kaaran appear and proceed. The archers stop when they appear as ordered by Princess. They stop at the rear and centre of his men. He takes a seat which is prepared for him as his officers all approach. "My Lord, it is an even match in numbers, but we have the experience and strength. Manion looks to his horsemen officers. You start and see what their reaction is". "Very good my Lord" is the reply as they turn and head for the awaiting men and horses. They make the order and from both sides they charge forward. The city catapults fire and balls land in the mix of charging horses, but make little effect. As they get nearer, Geraldo orders his own horsemen to attack, and they burst out of their places and hit the oncoming force head on. The action is frantic with men and horses falling with the cries from injured men trapped below dying bodies. This initial battle lasts for no more than thirty minutes before both sides order the retreat. The battered remnants from both sides retake their positions. Manion sits up, "well stale mate their it seems." Kaaran leaves and heads for his cannons, giving them targets and angles to shoot. He then shouts "Fire", and the noise is deafening as the cannon balls burst into the rows of men, literally cannon fodder, and the walls are hit creating holes. Princess calls to Geraldo, "they can't just stand there, move the men forward." Geraldo moves the front section of his men forward towards the enemy slowly, coming within the main arc of the cannons they are safer and then they stop, they then kneel as the archers pop up and fire thousands of arrows at Manion's men, they fall in their hundreds as Geraldo order the progression of his men. Nearer they get before Manion orders his men to attack. Without hesitation the two sides clash, and the battle is frantic. The area is covered in bodies and parts there off. The noise is horrific and the sight gruesome. This goes on and on until neither side can move on and the horns sound to retreat. The men on both sides are exhausted and stagger back to their bases. This is the end of day one. Geraldo sends out teams of men to recover injured or trapped survivors. Just picking through the dead bodies is a gruesome job. But they are, one by one, retrieved and carried back to receive hospital help. Princess, Rebecca, Orpheus, and Geraldo head back to the palace and the city gates are closed. Upon reaching the throne room, Princess rushes into Geraldo's arms. "It was awful, those poor men, how can I send them out again." "That is your job your highness, and they have theirs, they do it for a reason, unlike Manion's men, who do it purely for reward." "But so many dead." Rebecca comes over and leads Princess away to recompose herself. Geraldo and Orpheus look out the window at the sites below. "It was very even today, when Manion's men see Princess in action, they will lose heart." Orpheus explains. "She's not going out again, it is not fair for her to have all this on her shoulders." Geraldo tells him. "But she has too, how else will we win"? Is Orpheus's despondent reply. "We have twice as many men, we will attack from behind and take them out." Is Geraldo's response. "That will mean more deaths." At this moment princess re-enters and overhears them. "What are you two disagreeing about"? Orpheus quickly butts in, "Well Geraldo does not think you should join the fight tomorrow, too risky"! "I just think, "Geraldo tries to explain. "You are joking, those men are dying for me, and I am to hide behind these walls while they do! I do not think so." "But your highness, I just think.". Geraldo is cut off. "Tomorrow will be the last day, whether we win or lose, but it will be the last. She turns and returns to her seat. She sits for a moment but is too agitated. Rebecca, get me a cloak, we are going to the hospital. Rebecca runs of and returns with two cloaks, and they leave. Geraldo turns to an officer." follow her and make sure nothing happens." "Yes sir "is the reply as the man runs after Princess.

Once outside, Princess breaths in the cold night air and heads to the hospital. As she enters, she is shocked by the row after row of beds filled with dying men and the dead bodies just lying on the ground. The doctors and nurses rushing frantically trying to help everyone. She approaches some not badly injured men as she suddenly hears a crying from a corner. She goes over to see two young girls cuddling each other in tears uncontrollably. "What are you doing here, why are you not on the boat" She gathers one up in her arm as Rebecca pics up the other. "We wanted to help, but it's too horrible, I want to go home. Princess stands up and takes the girls out of the hospital and heads straight back to the palace. "You poor dears, you are so brave, but you must realise you are just children and must stay away from all the bad things. They enter the palace and Princess tells Rebecca to take them down to the kitchen where they can eat and get warm. She heads back to the throne room. Geraldo slowly approaches her knowing what she must have seen. "Are you all right." He asks. "My god, those poor men, and doctors and nurses, they have no chance. How can you expect me not to fight tomorrow"! "Well, I guess asking won't help. But please listen to me." "OK" she agrees. "I am going to bed, but I am sure I won't sleep, send Rebecca up when she returns." "I will do." Geraldo confirms and kisses her a good night.

Back in Lord Manion's tent he is discussing the situation with Alexander and Kaaran. "Well, my Lord, today we held our own, but we are losing as many as them, we need an alternative. "Why not do what they used to do in the old days, put our best against their best." "What that is crazy, one mistake and we lose. It would just lead to more fighting as I will never surrender"! "But they do not know about our secret weapon. If we make the offer to save lives, they cannot refuse, and they will honour it if they lose, so we go forward with a few very large men and some small squires like the weapon size. They will assume that the large ones are the opponents, and not having any men as big as ours, they will confidently field the Princess. Then our man steps forward and without warning strikes her down. This will shock them and force the fight out of them, they will surrender." "Interesting, it could work, she is honourable, so if we push this side, she is bound to agree, and if not, how will her army think of her not taking a risk but expecting them too. Manion laughs, "You know it just might work, just make sure your man gets in first and without warning." "We will prepare tonight my Lord. "This could end up being our easiest victory after today's disappointment." "I hope so my Lord" Kaaran explains as he leaves to discuss the plan with his weapon. Alexander agrees, "I will go and pick out half a dozen of our biggest meanest looking men." He leaves laughing.

Back in her room, Princess is lying on her bed talking to Rebecca lying next to her. "How are the children"? She asks. "They are calming down, but they really should not have been there, I just wish they had gone with the ship," Rebecca explains. "Well, it just makes me more determined to end this tomorrow. Princess states. "Well just be careful and nothing reckless, now try and get some sleep." She gives her a kiss on the cheek and leaves for her room.

The next morning the two sides stand facing each other, both looking the worse for wear. Princess takes her place on the stage and Lord Manion is behind his men. Lord Manion raises his arm and sends a sole rider forward towards where the Princess is, he slows before reaching her and stops, dismounts, and approaches the stage. "Your Highness, Lord Manion believes that

it is not in either sides interest for more men to die unnecessarily."
"That is a wise decision, please tell him, so you are leaving,"
Princess responds. "Eh not exactly, what he suggests is we do it
the old way, our champion against yours, only one death
compared to thousands, and the loser surrenders." "Interesting."
She looks to Geraldo. "Let us think about it, can we see your
champion"? He asks. "I do not believe he has been picked yet, but
I am sure I can show a short list." "Short list"! Princess exclaims.
"We will present them within the hour." He then bows and re-
mounts his horse and returns to Lord Manion. Princess, Rebecca,
Geraldo, and Orpheus return to the Palace. When they reach the
Throne room, they shut the door. "What is he up to"? Rebecca
asks. "I am not sure" Orpheus responds. "We will know more
when we see their short list, I will obviously represent us" Geraldo
states. "I don't think so, it makes more sense for me to take on any
single man" Princess orders. "But that is not necessary, you are a
Princess not a simple wrestler"! Rebecca tells her. "We have taken
enough risks with you; you stay on your throne." "Exactly"
Geraldo adds. "Looks like I am out voted then. She sits back on
her throne.

An hour passes and they head back to the stage. They take
their seats. After a few minutes twelve men from Manion's side
move forward to the centre of the field. Six are the biggest giants
ever, and behind them are six small men carrying their weapons,
with great difficulty. Princess sees the giants and is shocked into
standing and turns to Geraldo," No way are you facing any of
them, five of you could not beat them"! he takes her by the
shoulders and slowly lowers her back to her seat. "This is my
future, I am the head of the army, I cannot hide behind the skirt of
a Princess." "And I cannot allow you to lose your life and my
kingdom out of pride, I am the obvious choice." "It does look that
way" Rebecca steps in. "But this is too easy" Orpheus warns,
"there must be another angle for this, no way would Manion risk
losing everything this easy." "Well, he obviously won't stand by
the decision and surrender, that's obvious" Princess says, but his

147

men would be demoralised and that is when we attack from behind. Tell them I will send a sign for them to attack when it is over." "OK but be careful" Geraldo demands.

Princess and Geraldo ride forward to face the six men. Geraldo moves forward, so who is your champion. Manion raises his hand and five Giants and their support step back. There before Princess is this hard, mean, vicious man, who starts to threaten her. She dismounts from her horse and stands before the man mountain. Then in unison all her men start chanting "Princess, Princess, Princess." The man mountain beats his chest which startles Princess and turns to his man to choose a weapon. He takes a massive sword and a club. He then steps aside and there facing Princess is the small man now weapon less and with a big grin on his face.

Princess looks to Geraldo and shrugs; he looks confused as the small man steps forwards points at her and then unleashes a burst of flames which totally engulfs the unexpecting Princess to the shock of everyone behind her. Rebecca screams as she sees Princess engulfed, her clothes aflame, the leather holding her armour melting away and falling to the floor as she slowly before every one's eye's sinks to the ground. Rebecca runs forwards, tears in her eyes as Geraldo grabs her and wraps his arms around her. Manion's men give out a massive roar and smash their swords against their shields as Lord Manion stands and walks towards the centre. Princess's army start to drop their shields and swords totally dejected and lost. The little man starts to run around in a circle accepting the applause of his men. Rebecca falls to the floor in tears while Geraldo tries to comfort her. Then suddenly there is a small movement amongst the ashes and slowly and unsteadily a naked body, black as charcoal rises. The small man, with his back to the mound stops celebrating, when hearing murmurs coming from men from both sides, wondering what everyone is looking at. He slowly turns and sees the black body standing before him. He goes to fire again, but she raises her arms and fires a cold wind which freezes the man to a solid block. Princess then picks up her sword from the ashes and walks forward before swinging her sword at the man, who breaks into a thousand pieces. Manion turns to rush back as Princess fires another blast making a lane of ice below Manion's' feet making him slip and fall. Princess walks up to him and fires a burst of flames at him incinerating him instantly before his men. They in turn drop their swords as Princess's men pick up theirs and cheer. Alexander tries to rally his men as Princess then sends a lightning bolt up into the sky, which is her signal to her reserves, who charge out of the woods and smash into Manion's men if still holding their weapons. Princess's body is now glowing light as Rebecca looks up to see the magnificent sight before her. She grabs a cloak of a horseman and runs to Princess and wraps her in the cloak as the glow dims and she relaxes. Rebecca leads her back to the Palace, with the support of Geraldo. Manion's men quickly surrender and get on their knees. As Princess walks through the street the city people cheer her and bless her. They stagger into the palace and up the stairs to the Throne room. Princess collapses on the throne. Rebecca hugs Princess," You did it, we won"! she screams, wait here." She runs of and minutes later returns carrying a night gown which she puts on Princess. "How are you feeling"? Rebecca asks. "I am fine, just very tired, and emotional, I thought I was going to die when those flames hit me, the heat was intense, but it seems my body just compensated for it and the ice came. "You never cease to amaze me sweetheart, Rebecca hugs her and cries. "We could not have done it without you Becky, you are a real hero. Geraldo is standing before them as officers rush into the room. They have Alexander and throw him to the floor in front of Princess.

Princess looks at him and then to Geraldo, "do I really have to deal with this now"? she shrugs. "Take him away and I will deal with him later, where is that other man, Kaaran"? she asks. An officer steps forward, he has escaped but we are hunting him now, your highness. "Just make sure you find him; he dare not escape". Geraldo approaches her, "I give you my word, none of those responsible will escape, I will go myself." "No, I want you here now, we have too much to discuss. "Very good, your highness" Geraldo replies as he steps back. "Take him away" Geraldo orders the soldiers to take Alexander to the cells. Orpheus enters the room and hurries over to princess. "Your highness, I am so glad you are OK and safe." "I am fine Orpheus, please do not worry about me, the worst is behind us, now it is your time to sort out all these countries and men." "It is my honour, your highness." I think I will now retire to my room, I must stink of ash" Princess laughs as she stands and makes her way, followed by Rebecca. All the men bow as she leaves.

Down in the cells the prison guard opens the cell and throws Alexander in. He is then joined by two other guards who join him in beating Alexander close to death before chaining him to the wall a bloody mess. "That's for all the families you have abused for your master Manion." The guard tells him as they all laugh and leave him semi-conscious.

Up in her room Rebecca has called for a bath for Princess as she tries to comb Princesses hair. "This is hopeless, we will have to wash and treat it." "I am just glad I still have some after those flames," Princess says. "Oh, I never thought of that, indestructible hair as well, when will it end", she laughs. The maids arrive with the bath and jugs of water and a tray of oils. They pour the bath and stand to help. "Ok leave us" Rebecca tells them. They leave and Rebecca takes the gown of Princess and helps her climb into the bath. Princess sinks down to her neck and the bath instantly goes black. "This won't work" Rebecca says as she calls the maids back. She helps Princess out of the bath and tells the maids to empty the bath and bring two more. They rush of. Princess is standing there legs apart and arms out wide. Black water dropping from her body. "Will I stay black forever" she laughs. "No, we need scrubbing brushes, she turns to a maid and tells her to fetch some. "You are joking aren't you." "We will see" is Rebecca's stark reply.

Rebecca walks around the room looking at princess's jewellery and dresses as princess is stuck there not moving. "You know this is worse than the cells." Princess remarks as Rebecca holds back a laugh. "Patience, we'll sort it all out". Rebecca starts to brush her hair and tries some of Princess's jewellery. She holds a necklace upto her throat. "What do you think." "You're enjoying this aren't you." Is Princess's sharp rebuke. Rebecca laughs and goes and gives her a hug and when she steps back, she is also covered in ash. Princess bursts into laughter as they both collapse to the floor. The maids enter with two baths. "Better make that three" she tells the maids. They again rush off as Rebecca helps Princess into the first bath. She then grabs a scrubbing brush and starts to rub princesses arms and hers as well. Princess is screaming as the bristles run across her skin, but Rebecca does not stop and after finishing the arms, demands a leg. Princess looks at her hesitantly but raises a leg as Rebecca pours some cream over her leg and starts scrubbing. Princess continues screaming as Rebecca grabs the other leg and starts scrubbing that one. Once the legs are done, she goes behind Princess and pushes her body forward and pours oils over her back. Again, she starts scrubbing to the chorus of screams. Eventually Princess has white arms, legs and back. The bath water is black and Rebecca orders, next. Princess obediently stands and steps out and steps into the next bath. The first thing Rebecca does is duck Princesses head under the water. She then takes a bottle of liquid soap and pours over her head and rubs it into her hair. The bath is covered in bubbles as Rebecca takes a jug of water and pours it over princess's head. Princess has given up complaining or screaming and just sits there. Again, the hair is covered in soap, and rubbed in before pouring water over to rinse. The soap also cleans princess's face and Rebecca cleans with a cloth. Finally, she stops and looks at Princess, "There you are, I thought you were gone for ever," she laughs as princess goes to stand. "We are not finished yet, there is your front. Princess looks down and sees she still has black breasts and stomach. Rebecca hands her a brush. "Do you want to sort them out or…" "yes, I can handle this" is Princess's quick response. She takes the brush and starts brushing down her torso. Finally, she is clean and stands. Rebecca wraps a towel around her, and she steps out. Rebecca laughs as she wipes her hand. "Hang on," Princess interrupts. She grabs her and pushes her into the third bath and throws a brush to her. "You better come out sparkling" she laughs. "My clothes," Rebecca cries out, "they were dirty as well, I'll get you new ones" is Princesses answer. She then pushes Rebecca's head under the water and walks of laughing. Rebecca rises from the water "You're lucky I love you." She stands and undresses and finishes washing.

An hour later, the fire is warming the Room and Princess and Rebecca are sitting in front of it. There is a knock at the door and a clean Geraldo enters. He has two bouquets of flowers, "two bunches of flowers for two amazing young ladies." Princess calls out" come in." He walks in and goes straight over to Princess gives her a kiss and the flowers. He then goes to Rebecca and does the same. He sits down next to both girls as a maid appears with drinks as instructed by Geraldo. "Tonight, we celebrate"! The girls take their glasses and relax and click glasses. Princess leans back into Geraldo and leans up for a kiss. He responds as Rebecca suggests, "I guess this is my que to leave"? "No, please don't, this is a celebration for all of us, he will just have to control himself" Princess tells her with a laugh. Rebecca stands and goes over to the window and looks out, "They are still celebrating out there." "No wonder, everyone's gone through hell, especially the people." Geraldo replies. "We must go and check the injured tomorrow," Princess adds. Rebecca re-joins them. So, has anyone got any plans from now? Geraldo mentions" we still have to secure Urania, it should not be a problem, but no one knows where Kaaran disappeared to. "Yes, he is a priority, but most of their army is dead or captured, so clearing the country should not be a major problem, surely? Princess asks. I also think you should visit each country, so they know who the ruler is, no people plotting behind doors" Rebecca suggests. Yes, I also think we should spend some time in each country each year, so they do not feel isolated. Princess advises. Well, I can leave the trips to you two, and I will start work on finding Kaaran tomorrow, I don't trust him" Geraldo mutters. Well, that was easy, who needs a government"! Princess laughs.

The next morning, Princess awakens and is incredibly sore. Rebecca comes in and sees Princess struggling. "You OK, she asks. "I am so stiff, and my skin is sore as hell after all the scrubbing", she explains. "Oh, sorry about that, but it was necessary, wait here". Rebecca runs of and several minutes later re-enters with an oriental lady by her side. The lady with hands together bows. "She is a masseuse, she'll fix you. Just lie down." Rebecca clears the blankets and Princess lies face down on the bed. The lady comes over with a small box of oils. She pours some on Princesses back and legs. She kneels at her feet and starts to massage the feet, slowly moving up the body. Princess starts off making pain sounds but relaxes into it and slowly relaxes. The lady crawls up her legs to reach her back and rubs from the spine out, over and over again, creeping slowly up the back to the neck and shoulders. At this point Princess is totally relaxed and just sighing. The lady then asks her to turn over and places cloths over Princesses breasts and groin. She then stands at her head and gently starts to massage the forehead and face then turning the neck one way then the other. By now Princess is totally relaxed and on the brink of sleep. The lady stops and clears her equipment as Princess slowly opens her eyes and looks around. The lady is waiting to be dismissed and Rebecca has a big grin on her face. "I guess you liked that," she asks. "Oh my god, I have never ...." Princess responds. She thanks the lady who leaves. "Well, are you ready for work" Rebecca asks. "When I can get up, yes." She slowly rises, "my body is as light as a feather, it's amazing, you should try it." Princess suggests. "I will, later, but for now, I have an outfit for you. She brings over a light casual gown with slits down the legs. "Just in case you want to go riding" she explains. She helps Princess dress and brushes her hair. Finally, they are ready and leave the bedroom to head for the throne room. Upon entering everyone there bows and curtseys as she takes her throne. There is a flurry of gentlemen who step forward to gain her attention. Orpheus steps in "Gentlemen, please, allow her Highness to prepare before your requests." They all back of and when ready Princess waves her hand at Orpheus who summons an individual Gentleman. He kneels before Princess and starts telling her how his land was in Urainia when Manion took it, he would like to regain what was taken from him. "Oh, how much land, may I ask, and when was this." The man stands and says, "it was the whole south of the country, some 750,000 acres. It was taken some forty years ago." I see and how did you defend this land" is her next question. "We fought, but he had a much larger army, and we were easily beaten. "Oh, how unfortunate, and may I ask, how old are you Sir"? I am 48 years your highness. "So, you never actually fought for this land, you are just waiting for someone to retrieve it." "Well, your highness, my family were all forced away and had to live in Norland for 40 years". He replied. So, you have not lived there and have not fought for it, but you want me to just hand it over to you, what about the men who died fighting to retrieve it." Oh, I am very grateful your highness, I will put up a plaque to mention them". Princess rebukes "I am sure that the dead men's families will live well off that." He stutters "You miss understand, your Highness, I am the Lord of the land and," "And I am the ruler, and I did not see you out on the field fighting for this land. You will be given by your highness, 1000 acres to work as your land and appreciate it. The rest will go to the crown to pay for the costs of the war and grieving families. Orpheus leads the man away and notes Princess's order. Another man walks forward and kneels. Princess acknowledges him and he rises. Your Highness, I also claim the previous land that my family was in dispute with the previous family with." "Oh," she thinks, "please come back," she points to the previous man, who returns before her. "You never mentioned any dispute to me." She speaks. "This man has no claim to the land, his family lived on the land a long time ago, their claim is ended." "Who decides this," Lord Manion made the order before taking the land of us. "Well Lord Manion is not here anymore and therefore, why should I be so generous, I retract my previous offer, you may have 50 acres to which you will pay this man land rent. She looks to the other man" And you, you will receive 25 % of all the land, to which I will trust you will grow and employ many people and pay taxes to us". "It would be my pleasure, thank you your Highness." "So be it" Princess informs Orpheus. "Next," Orpheus barks out. Another man steps forward. He kneels and explains his problem, "Your highness, while I was away at war, my wife had relations with many men, and I am seeking an annulment of our vows and claim to all our assets." The women is kneeling at his side, in a dirty torn dress. "Please come forward," the woman rises, she comes forward and kneels again. When the war started, my husband left for an overseas trip leaving me here to the hands of Manion's men, I was locked up and abused for many weeks until you freed us, I am a good woman." "Princess stands and walks over to the woman and helps her up, she beckons Rebecca, get her help and treatment. She then looks down on the man and goes back to her throne. "So, you did not fight for me, but ran, it seems, and then you have the nerve to complain about your woman who is the victim here." "Your Highness, it was not like that exactly," "So tell me, where did you fight, with Geraldo in the mountains, by the port or in the woods with me"? I was unfortunately away and could not return to help, but"! "But nothing, You will be relieved of your vows, but you will not receive one penny of any assets held before, in fact, I sentence you to prison for desertion, you will be sentenced later, take him away". Soldiers step forward and drag him away. There is a muttering around the room as certain men who may have had questionable requests start edging back. Orpheus again steps forward, "Next." A young man steps forward and kneels. "Your highness, I have a small new farm just outside of the city. When the war started, I prepared all my crops to help in the aid, I did not ask for much, as I am aware of the situation, but instead I received a demand from a land owner, who claims the land is his and I am to pay him for the crops. What I received is a fraction of what he demands. Princess asks, "Who is this man demanding this". An arrogant man steps forward, does not bow but raises his hand. "I am the landowner, your highness." There is a shocked look around the room. "Step forward please, explain how this land is yours." Princess asks. "It was a simple land claim when he left his land during the dispute, the law clearly claims that any land left idle can be claimed by another in place to work it". "So, you can work this field, you say" she asks again. "Exactly your highness, and he sold the goods from it prior, so I am reclaiming my goods. She looks down at the other man, "Did you receive a piece of paper stating you sold the goods to the army." "Yes, your highness". So, the goods belong to my army and therefore are mine". She looks at the arrogant man, are you saying I owe you money, or cheated this man," Oh no your Highness, I would not suggest anything like that, it is clearly his debt." "Well, it is, if it is your land, so we must test this law of yours", she calls Orpheus over and whispers in his ear. "My Lord Orpheus, it seems this man is claiming the land as he is able to work it." "It would seem, your highness, "So how long do you feel we should test this theory, if it is to remain law". "Well, it should be tested thoroughly, your Highness, maybe years". "Ok, I have decided, I accept your claim that this man owes you for the goods he grew, on the understanding that you can prove you can work the field for ten years, I sentence you to 10 years working on this man's fields, then you will receive what you are owed, if you fail, you will pay him 10 times what you are asking and lose all your lands to the court, that is my final order". The man cries out, "that is not fair, this is not right"! "Take him away" Princess orders as she allows the other man up. "Return to your land and let us know how he gets on." "With pleasure your highness," he turns and walks away as Rebecca comes over, "Wow, what did that massage do to you." "I just can't stand all these greedy useless men who think they deserve everything, when real ones are working in the field." "Let's break for lunch." They both stand and dismiss the court and leave.

Orpheus runs after them. "Your highness, you know that wasn't exactly as the law works, don't you"? "If you do not want me to make decisions, just say, otherwise this is what you get" Princess responds. "Very good your Highness" he retracts his view and leaves them. Princess and Rebecca walk down to the kitchen where they see the two little girls. That reminds me, aren't the ships due back around now. "I believe so." "Come on then, let's take the kids down to the port to see their families." They both grab a girl each and head out of the palace, frantically followed by guards. They run through the streets swinging the girls and enjoying the freedom of the court. Out the gate and down to the port, they are just in time to see the ships entering. All along the ship side our families waving. The two girls are frantically looking for their parents, then suddenly they see them at the rear, waving. Un-noticed by the Princess a band erupts into music to welcome the families along with other members of their families, mainly fathers who fought in the battle. The ship ties up and the planks to disembark are put in place. The first families start climbing of the ship as the children impatiently wait for their family. Eventually after many families disembark the two girl's mother and father and young brothers and sisters climb down. The girls rush up to them. The parents walk straight over to the Princess and bow and curtsey, "Your Highness, we were so worried when they disappeared, I should have known they would get in trouble." "They have been a great help but unfortunately ended up in a place they should not have been, it was a shock for them, so be gentle with them." "Of course, your Highness and thank you for caring for them," the mother says. "Well, we better make our way back to the Palace, so no disappearing you two" she hugs both girls. "You are welcome to visit, when you are off school in the future, ok." Princess and Rebecca turn and leave as the crowd of people cheer them off. Through the gate they pass as a messenger arrives. "Your Highness, I have a message for you." He hands her the letter, it is a note from Geraldo, he has heard about Kaaran, and he has escaped back to Urania. He is going to chase him and will report back later. "Well, that's the last we will see of him for a while, he is like a dog with a bone," Princess remarks. "He's just doing his job, like you." Rebecca calms her down. "I guess so." Let's get inside. They head for the Palace.

Out on the road, Geraldo is in chase of Kaaran and the few men remaining from Manion's army. Unfortunately, Kaaran has a good lead, but Geraldo knows Kaaran has nowhere to hide. He is riding as fast as possible considering he has hundreds of men behind him. After many hours he stops to make camp.

Kaaran however has reached Manion's castle and is secure behind the massive gates. The castle is built on a mountain peak, with only a slim, rocky bridge from the mainland to the castle gate, so very hard to invade, if not impossible. He rushes into the throne room and collapses onto the throne. He calls a messenger and orders that he send messages to all their allies to send men immediately and defend the castle before reinvading Lystonia. He then makes plans to set a trap just in case he receives no help. He comes up with the idea to plant explosives within the bridge so if they are attacked, he can blow it and the attackers up. He looks at the plans and works out the number of explosives he would need. He then breaks to sleep.

The next morning Geraldo has reached the castle and places guards at the end of the bridge, stalemate. He discusses the situation with his officers, Geraldo, "what if we build catapults and smash the gates down." "The problem is that they are not accurate, and we just as easily could destroy the bridge, then there is no entry" an officer replies. "But no exit either, it would certainly cancel any risk they are to us." another officer replies. I'll contact the Princess and see what she suggests.

Kaaran meanwhile is busy manufacturing extra explosives and having them secretly hidden within the bridge. The news back from his allies was not very positive, but one offered men for an enormous cost. Kaaran had little love of money and agreed to ordered 10,000 men. They would arrive within the week.

Princess receives the message and responds, "If we destroy the bridge, they will be trapped and starve to death, which is an unholy way to die at others hands, offer them the opportunity to surrender". She sends the response and awaits his reply.

Meanwhile Geraldo received a message from a spy within the castle, he is informed of the 10,000 men on their way. Geraldo immediately sends another message to Princess. She quickly receives the message and orders 15,000 men to prepare to leave for Urania. They are ready to leave within the day and Princess leads them out of the city. There is now a race to Manion's castle.

Geraldo looks over the map, there is no clear area for a battle, and he marks out places that the oncoming army could attack, all with limited space there would not be a major battle but numerous skirmishes. He sends a few men to each place to give as much warning as possible as he did not have enough men to defend alone.

Kaaran stands on the battlements and looks down on Geraldo and his men. They alone are no threat. Princess is pushing her men to win the race and has decided not to make camp, but to just walk rather than stop. With a few water breaks. The support for Kaaran, are not however rushing as they will be paid regardless and are not even aware that Princess is on her way.

Geraldo has made his camp a short distance from the bridge but within clear site. He sits and watches the castle as he takes a drink, a man rushes into his tent. He reports that Princess is very nearby. He is invigorated and calls for his horse. It quickly arrives and he jumps on it and rides off in Princess's direction. Within an hour, he reaches Princess, and they embrace. Rebecca welcomes him as well. They do not stop but proceed to his camp.

Upon reaching it, Geraldo immediately shows Princess the castle. It is a dark dank building with flames shooting out of holes in the wall, purely for effect. Princess looks at it, and shrugs. "I would love something to eat and drink" she adds. "Come into

159

my tent, I'll have another set up for you shortly. They enter and before taking their seats, he takes Princess over to the map. He shows her the paths that they need to send the men she has brought. "Ok, you can organise this tomorrow, they need to rest, but leave enough here to take the castle. It seems that the only problem is to destroy the gates, then you can charge through and take it" Princess orders. "Catapults won't do the job" Geraldo claims. "But you have me, I can burn it down in seconds." "That is a crazy risk" Geraldo claims. "I agree" Rebecca butts in. "It's not crazy and as long as you send shielded men in with me, I should be safe from arrows or rocks." Geraldo sits down, "I don't like it, but I guess you are right, I will arrange a caterpillar to be built." "What's that"? She asks. "It's a wheeled platform with a protected roof, you can stand underneath it safely" he tells her. "OK," then it's agreed Princess claims, as she falls down onto a couch and drinks from a glass. After some food and drinks, a man enters and announces that her tent is ready. Princess and Rebecca stand. She gives Geraldo a kiss and tells him they are going to sleep after the long journey. He kisses them both good night and they leave. He stays up a while going over the map.

Meanwhile Kaaran has seen Princess arrive with her army and is rubbing his hands. He is talking to some of his officers. He points down to her tent. "They will send her onto the bridge under cover of shields or something, just keep them busy with arrows and have the men with the flames be in place underneath well before they break camp. Then just wait for her to make her move, and that is goodbye Princess" he laughs and goes back inside the castle. Have your builders ready to rebuild the bridge so we can leave when we want, and the reinforcements have arrived. "Very good sir" the officers say as they all leave, and Kaaran retires for the night.

The next morning, Princess is welcomed by Geraldo and is shown the caterpillar. "Have you offered him the chance to surrender yet" she asks. "No, I thought he should see you, just to make sure he knows he has no chance." He laughs. Well let's get on with it, send a man forward. Geraldo sends one of his messengers to make an announcement at the gate. This is met with an arrow in the head. Princess angered at this, orders the caterpillar to be made ready. It is moved to the end of the bridge and surrounded by men all carrying extra-long shields. She stands in the centre and the men start to push her forward to the gate. Kaaran watches her movement and beckons her forward. She stops about thirty feet from the gate and prepares to create a flame as she is watched at the bridge end by Rebecca, Geraldo, and the main army. Kaaran calls out to her, you won't succeed, goodbye Princess"! He then signals to his men underneath who set fire to the explosives. Geraldo senses a trap and calls out as the whole bridge explodes in flames and thousands of pieces of rock are thrown across the mountain and covering Geraldo and Rebecca and the army behind, they all duck for cover as the whole area is covered in dense smoke and the cries of dying men. Parts of bodies have been thrown across the path along with pieces of the caterpillar. Rebecca calls out Princesses' name in vain as Geraldo holds her back. "It's too late, she is gone," get back. At this moment, the smoke starts to clear and the massive gaping hole where the bridge once stood is evidence of the explosion, then as the dust above dies a bright light is shining mid-air 50 feet above where the bridge was. Unbelievably it is Princess glowing and floating in mid-air. Kaaran looks in disbelief as he orders his men to fire at her. They look at her and just drop their bows and kneel. Princess floats over the wall and is before Kaaran. She gestures and he is picked up in a gust of wind and she moves him over the gaping hole where the bridge was and releases him. His scream is heard as he falls till there is a thud as he hits the ground. Princess then lowers to the ground behind the gate and orders the men to open the gate. They hurriedly do as she says and the gates are thrown open, she steps forward, still glowing. She kneels and touches the ground and creates a flow of ices providing a thick bridge for her men to enter, led by Rebecca and Geraldo. Rebecca runs up to her, "Why am I not surprised" she screams as she hugs her, and Geraldo places his hands on her shoulders. "You are amazing, just making sure you don't fly off again." "And minimum casualties" Rebecca states. They head into the castle led by a senior Manion officer. Manion's men have all quickly shifted allegiance. They walk into the throne room and are amazed at the dismal character of the room. Princess tells the men standing by, "Strip this place, I do not want any sign of Manion and his cronies. Then whitewash it"! The men immediately start tearing down the flags and shields of Manion's history. Rebecca finds a silver silk cloak and throws it over the throne and offers it to Princess. Princess takes her place and asks Geraldo, "What is the news of the mercenaries." "They have reached the passes, but stopped, they are obviously waiting for a word from Kaaran." "Then I think you should go there and offer them a meeting to discuss, a peace agreement as they obviously are not going to be paid, and we do not want any more problems from them in the future. Ask their head man to come here to discuss." "Very good, and when do you want me to leave"? he asks. "Well, I think tomorrow morning is early enough, don't you"? she grins at him. "As you command your Highness, I will make arrangements." At this moment Rebecca interrupts. She has been talking to the Castle authorities and planning for the Princess and her court. I have arranged rooms for us all and a banquet for tomorrow so that is a good time to bring their leader here"." Excellent" Princess tells her, and what of tonight, I am starving." "That's being arranged as we speak." "Off course." Princess takes her hand and offers her a seat.

That evening there is the first relaxed meal served in the room for decades as the servants have a calm relaxed look on their faces. It is clear the hell of the past is finally over. Princess sits at the head of the table with Geraldo and Rebecca either side. They are joined by officers from her army. The atmosphere is relaxed, and music is being played, which is another difference to the past. The painters have already whitewashed the walls, which although not perfect are a vast improvement. They are all laughing and chatting as the door opens and Orpheus enters. He rushes over to Princess and kneels. "Your highness, congratulations on another grand victory, I have travelled as quick as possible so we can negotiate with the opposition tomorrow." She takes his hand, "You are welcome as always Orpheus, please take a seat and enjoy some food and drink and recover from your journey." He thanks her and a chair is provided next to Geraldo. "Has anyone got any ideas what we can do with this castle, it is the most dismal place I have ever seen," Princess asks. "Well, it can become a local government, building or even a prison, certainly it would be hard to escape from" Geraldo recommends. "You know that's not a bad idea" Princess replies. "Orpheus, how big is this actual country." It is not large about half of Lystonia, so does it need a base to run from, why not just absorb it in Lystonia and write the memory away" she suggests. Well, this is a unique opportunity to do that, I am not sure why Manion did not do that before," Orpheus replies. "To busy making trouble to worry about running a country I guess" Geraldo adds. "Well, I think this is the future here, it will also give us a securer border, wouldn't it"? she asks. "Somehow, I do not see anyone else trying to invade us your Highness, Orpheus responds. "So be it, that's what we will do." They all agree and from a side door a band arrives to play music and cheer everyone up. Geraldo turns to Princess, "Would you like to dance your Highness"? "Well, I think it would be a pleasure, thank you. They stand up and start dancing. A young Officer stands and approaches Rebecca. "Could I have the pleasure." She looks up at him, "Oh no thank you, I will remain here if you do not mind." Princess sees this and is confused. A few other people stand to dance and eventually Princess returns to her seat. She takes Rebecca's hand and leans into her. "Why didn't you dance, he was really cute"? "I did not want to, he was very nice but, no thank you." She takes her glass and drinks breaking the conversation. Princess is confused but does not push it in public. The evening continues until Princess calls the event over and makes her departure, followed by Rebecca and Geraldo. As they leave the room Princess stops Geraldo and wipers in his ear. "Stay here till I call you, I have something important I have to do." He immediately agrees and the two girls proceed to Princess's room.

There is a row of maids who Princess instantly dismisses. She goes over to a small table and pours out two glasses of red wine and hands one to Rebecca. She then leads her over to the bed. "Sweetheart, you know you are the most important person to me in the world, so please tell me, what is wrong"? Rebecca pulls back "Nothing, I am fine." "That young man was really cute, so why not relax and dance"? Princess pushes. "It just was too much, too soon." "Too soon, Becky, please tell me, what is going on." Rebecca breaks down and cries in Princess's arms. Princess is shocked at this explosion of emotion and hugs her close. "Becky tell me, it will be alright, I will be here for you." Rebecca now sobbing looks up at Princess, "It was in Tarmack, when they took you away, the king, He, he raped me, over and over again. I could not stop him." "My god, Princess holds her close "It is over now, and no one will ever harm you again, please, let it go, and continue your amazing life, he paid the price." "I know, it just flashes back when men approach me," Rebecca says. "Except Geraldo" she adds. "Well, you're not having him" she laughs, and they both relax in each other's arms. "Are you going to be ok sweetheart" Princess asks. "Yes of course, I know I am being stupid." "No, no never think that what happened was terrible, but you must rebuild and move forward, like everything else here". Princess advises. "I will, thanks" Rebecca replies. OK, go and get a good night's sleep and we will take tomorrow on as another day, you know that young officer is still cute". She smiles at Rebecca and helps her up as she leaves. Princess then calls a maid. Seconds later one appears, "Please go and summon Geraldo, thank you." The maid rushes off. Minutes later there is a knock at the door and Geraldo enters." Everything sorted" he asks. "I hope so" is her response. "Good does that mean we can have some time alone together for once." "I am sure that can be arranged." He walks over to her and leans down and kisses her deeply on the lips. Without hesitation she starts to undo his shirt and he undoes the numerous buttons on her dress. Within second, he is shirtless and he is still struggling with the buttons running down her back. "This is crazy," he mutters and takes his knife out and runs it down her back cutting all the buttons off. "Someone is going to have to fix that" Princess tells him. "I'll buy them a gift" he responds. He lowers the dress of her shoulders, and it falls onto the floor which is quickly followed by her remaining garments as he pushes her back on the bed. He then undoes his trousers and removes then and climbs onto the bed with her. He takes her in his arms and kisses her passionately and then along her neck moving down her body. She shakes in response as he picks her up and turns her over and massages her down her back followed by small kisses. He then kneels astride her and makes passionate love to her. All thought of the events of the day are gone.

The next morning, Rebecca enters Princess's room. Geraldo has gone and Princess is lying on her bed relaxing. Rebecca picks up Princess's dress and the numerous buttons lying on the floor. "Someone was in a hurry, it seems." She comments. Yes, I thought it was another assignation event" they both laugh. "I guess you want a bath" Rebecca asks and calls the maids. "Love one thanks". "Well, what do you want to wear, if things continue, I will only leave out armour" Rebecca jokes. "I'll leave it to you as always." Is Princess response. The maids rush in with a bath and jugs of hot water. They rush around Princess and prepare towels. She undresses and steps in the bath. She relaxes back in the bath and thinks about the coming day. She has already decided to arrange another meeting between the young officer and Rebecca. The morning is spent with both girls relaxing and preening themselves ready for the coming meeting. After a few hours, they both appear in the hall, both dresses in magnificent gowns. It is hard to see which is the Princess. Geraldo steps forward and takes Princess's hand and leads her to her throne. As he does this the young officer steps forward and takes Rebecca's hand and leads her to a large chair next to Princess. Rebecca blushes and takes her seat. The officer stands next to her at attention. Meanwhile, Princess has a big smile on her face.

They relax and Orpheus approaches and brings forward the leaders of the army sent to support Kaaran. They kneel before

Princess and the main man looks up at her. "Your Highness, my name is Lord Darwin, and I bring you best wishes from our leader. He is most upset about the misunderstanding between our two countries, and he wishes to secure your forgiveness and understanding." Princess leans forward, "I understand the misunderstanding and how Manion, Kaaran and their money can be very persuasive, but now they have all gone and you will be dealing with me direct, the one person who has bettered all of them." "I am humbled in your presence and ask that we can build up a new relationship between our two countries" he replies. "If you are sincere in your words, I see no reason why our diplomats cannot come to arrangements, so we can trade and have no need for concern from either side." He responds" I assure you, that this is exactly what we wish, we want the war years behind us, it is very expensive and not very profitable. I am sure that once an agreement is made it will last into the future." She rebukes "I assure you, if you break it, you will only break it once"! "I totally understand and agree your Highness." He answers. "Then let us celebrate a union between our two countries." She raises her hand and the band start playing and everyone starts mixing and talking. Princess leans over to Geraldo" Ask me to dance." He winks at her and takes her hand and at the same time nods to the young officer to ask Rebecca. He panics but goes over to Rebecca, "Can I again ask for your hand to dance." He reaches for her hand. Rebecca panics and looks to Princess who encourages her. She takes his hand, and he leads her onto the floor. Princess is watching her as Rebecca takes her position and flows a fluid dance, which totally surprises Princess and Geraldo. "Looks like she has more secrets than even you know" he laughs. Rebecca moves over the floor till the music ends. The officer is stunned and walks her back to her chair. "He thanks her for the dance and asks permission to ask her again. She responds, "I do not dance with persons I do not know." He kneels before her and introduces himself. I am Captain David Savage, and I would take it as an honour to see you again." "Well, if I know her Highness, I will have no choice, so yes I accept your request". Princess has finished her dance and walks over to Rebecca who is alone by now. "Well, who is hiding secrets miss Becky," I was taught from a young age." She replies. "And what about him"! Princess asks. "He is very nice and understanding I think." "He is gorgeous, you better hurry up and catch him." "I am not looking for a relationship." Well, we can't go on trips with partners if one of us is missing one. He obviously likes you." "We will see." As they are talking Geraldo is talking to the young officer. "She is quite a lady that one." "Oh yes, she is amazing we are all honoured to have her." "No, Rebecca stupid"! he tells him. "Oh, I thought you meant, well yes Rebecca is also quite amazing." "Well stay by her side, I can see her Highness making a few rules around her as far as positions." "Oh, what do you mean." "Let's just say, Rebecca is the most important person in the world to her highness, so anyone near her is special to her." The officer panics "Oh my god, I never thought, I should not, I never even thought, me and.. OH no". "Don't tell me you are not interested in Rebecca"? Geraldo asks, "Oh no, she is amazing, wonderful, but I am just a simple man, I have no family or name, I ...." "Nor does she, and yet everyone in this court seeks her approval, so why not you, I will guide you." "I think it is safer in battle than to take them on." He looks to both Princess and Rebecca sitting on their seats as courtiers' bustle around them. "Just be calm and supportive, and there for them." Shyly the officer agrees.

The evening finalises with the new friends leaving and all things settled in Urania. Princess and Rebecca head back to their rooms as the men stay behind to chat and drink. Around the fire is Orpheus, Geraldo, and David. Orpheus takes his drink and raises his glass," gentlemen please raise your glass to our most amazing ladies. They all raise their glasses. Orpheus continues," I hear you are joining the palace guard Savage"? "Oh, I have heard nothing of this", he responds. Geraldo smiles, "see, you cannot stop these women, congratulations, looks like you are going places." "But no one has told me anything" David replies. Geraldo laughs, you never do hear till it's too late", I was a mountain man, then head

of the army. All it took was a good beating from Manion's men."
"I have to be beaten"? he asks. "No, that is how Princess and
myself first met, I was captured, and she saved my life over and
over again." "Wow, she really is amazing," and so is Rebecca who
is always by her side." "Well, I can't wait to see their return to the
Capital tomorrow," Orpheus says. "Has a decision been made as
to who will stay here to oversee the changeover." Geraldo asks. "I
have not heard; I just hope it is not me" Orpheus laughs. "Or me"
David joins in. Geraldo looks at a map on the floor. It shows
Urania, Lystonia, Tarmack and Norlands. "Just look at this, that
little lady has taken over four countries within months and was
only a junior in a Priory before. "She always was different though,
she was the best organiser I ever met, and she is amazing at
catching chickens." David looks at him with a quizzical look."
"It's a long story" Orpheus says. "Well, we better crash for the
night, we have a long journey tomorrow" Geraldo suggests. They
all agree and make their ways to their rooms. Meanwhile up in her
room, Princess is grilling Rebecca about her young man. "So, tell
me what you know." Princess asks. "I know nothing" is Rebecca's
response. "Well, you have to admit, he is very good looking, tall,
dark and handsome" Princess throws back. "Yes, I guess so, but I
am just a maid basically, we are miles apart." "You are what"!
Princess shouts, you are the most important person in the country
to me, is this how you see yourself"? "Well, we came straight from
the priory, and it has all been a mad rush, and well you know, I'm
just a junior at the Priory." Princess takes her in her hands "You
are the most precious jewel in this land, my first thought of the
day is of you, you are always there for me." "I know we have an
amazing relationship, but he doesn't know that, and I have nothing
to offer anyone." If things had been different, I would be in a habit
at the priory in a few years." "Heaven forbid!" Princess laughs,
that's like saying Orpheus is only the head of the Priory, he hasn't
even visited since we left". "I guess so." Rebecca responds. "So,
putting that behind you, tell me what you think of this young
man"? He is kind of cute and very handsome, but you know me, I
am very new to all this, and he may not even like me"? Princess

falls back on her bed laughing. "Are you joking, just look at yourself, you are gorgeous, you have an amazing body and the kindest heart I have ever met." "Oh, you are embarrassing me." "If you like him, we can make things happen when we get back to the Capital." "Like what." "I am not sure yet, but just wait and see, but if he can make you as happy as Geraldo makes me, you have to go for it." "I just don't think I am ready." "Trust me, you are ready. We will see. Now let's get some sleep". They hug and kiss each other as Rebecca leaves as Princess climbs into bed.

The next morning Princess and Rebecca rise and enter the throne room. Princess calls to Geraldo who is talking to some men at the window. He comes over. "Your Highness, you called." "Are we ready to leave" she asks. "Not quite, I think we need a little help, he waves his hands around." She laughs "of course, I'll go straight down, can you make sure Rebecca is ready and OK." "Of course, I have arranged an escort for her." He explains. "I thought you would." She replies. They smile at each other. Princess hurries down to the gate and walks in front of the men standing there wondering what to do. She kneels and creates another bridge in seconds. As usual the men are amazed and stand back as she stands and returns to the building. She re-enters the room. "All done" she wipes her hand and goes over to Rebecca. "Are we ready" Princess asks. "Yes, your horse is waiting, I assume you do not want to go by coach." They both head down to the horses and there waiting behind their two horses are a dozen men in dress uniform, Geraldo behind Princess's horse and David behind Rebecca's. Princess looks at Geraldo and smiles as Rebecca lowers her head as she mounts her horse, embarrassed to look at David in the face. Once they are both mounted, Princess looks behind at the two men. "Are we ready." "Ready your highness." Geraldo answers. They move off and cross the bridge that men have poured sand over for grip. They head of down the road as more and more rows of men join them. Geraldo has left a small garrison at the castle along with builders for the bridge.

Chapter Ten

The Capital city is a bustle of action as everyone is preparing for the return of Princess. Everyone was aware that the wars are finally over and there was a bright future finally. The bunting and flags are out, and the bands were playing in the square. The school children had prepared a small show for the Princess and there was a stage built on the playing field.

The army has been marching for over two days back from Urania and also looked forward to returning home. The news arrives that Princess is only a short distance from the city. The field which was previously a battle ground was now a ground of fun and stalls of games and food. The bells ring as Princess and Rebecca appear from the path from Urania. The whole city erupts in cheers as they slowly ride forward followed by the rows of men behind them. They are met at the gate and two young boys take their horses leads and lead everyone through the streets, through the city centre and towards the school playing fields. The place is full of the families that had been saved and the school staff are standing on the stage. In front of the stage is a closed off area with chairs for Princess, Rebecca, and a few officials, including Geraldo, David, Orpheus, and others. They take their seats and the head of the school walks onto the stage and makes a speech. Here he announces the great thanks the whole city and country have towards her Highness and her officials. He then announces the presentation of the children of the city who love their Princess. The band starts to play, and the children run on stage and start to sing and dance a national dance. Everyone is clapping and at the end there is a big cheer. Princess stands up and applauds. Then the children run off and the two small girls saved by Princess and Rebecca walk on the stage. They make a small but poignant speech on behalf of the children. They are then joined by all the children and their parents. The show carries on for an hour with music and dance and then Princess and her entourage thank everyone and leave for the Palace. They are still cheered along the short journey to the palace gate and as soon as they pass through, the gates are closed, a crowd gather outside. Princess enters the throne room with the senior personnel. The balcony doors open, and Princess makes an appearance on her own to the cheers of the crowd. She then enters the room and grabs Geraldo. She then goes out again hand in hand with him. The people see the holding hands and cheer even louder. They again return to the room as Geraldo announces, "that was embarrassing." Princess ignores his claim and holds Rebecca and David and goes outside again followed by an embarrassed Geraldo. Princess holds up Rebecca's hand and again grabs Geraldo as Geraldo places Davids's hand into Rebecca's. Here before everyone was the base for the country's future. The cheering continues and eventually Princess makes her way back into the room and the doors are closed. It is now some 5.00pm in the day, and a long day so far. Princess grabs Rebecca, "we need to refresh, let's go to our room." Orpheus approaches them and informs them that there is a banquet that night at seven. "We'll be there," Princess states and they both run off. Geraldo goes over to David; "well it seems like your life has just changed drastically." He laughs. "So, I see" David admits. "Can we get a drink," he asks. Geraldo laughs, "Off course, wine or lager." "Oh, Lager please." Geraldo calls a servant over and they rush off to get them. They return in moments and the men sit and relax.

Meanwhile, the girls are in their room. There are two baths being poured and numerous maids rushing around sorting out dresses and jewellery. The baths are ready and both girls undress and step into the baths. The maids leave for the time. "So, what was his reaction on the balcony," Princess asks Rebecca. "Shock I think" she laughs, "he'll get used to it, Princess continued. "So, you have made your mind up then." "If Manion can't beat you, what chance do I have," she laughs. They both relax back in the bathtubs. "You know I am getting used to this. Rebecca tells her as they both lie back and relax.

Several hours later, the Throne room is full of dignitaries as the horns blow and the doors open and Princess enters followed by Rachel, both dressed in amazing gowns. They walk through the centre of the hall as the crowd separate to let them pass. They head for the throne and Princess takes her seat as Rebecca stands next to her. They both look out for Geraldo and David. Princess motions to the band and they start to play. Everyone is dancing except for the two girls. Then after a minute Geraldo and David approach and the girls prepare to dance. Both men bow before their prospective lady and hold their hand out. Princess rises and takes Geraldo's and Rebecca takes David's. Both couples walk onto the dance floor and start to dance, they are dancing around in circles. Princess looks up at Geraldo, "you know this is the first time we can actually relax and enjoy ourselves without the fear of battle to follow." "Well enjoy it, but I think you have many happy days ahead of you," he tells her. Princess looks at Rebecca and David, "Don't they make a lovely couple"? she asks. "Yes, they look amazing, and what about us"? he asks. "Well, if you play your cards right." "Yes, were will we end up"? he asks again. "How do you see the future with us," she coyly says. "I only see a future with you." "Can I really tear you away from the mountains and wild animals." She questions. "You already have." She buries her head in his chest, and they continue dancing. After the music ends, they walk back to their places. Princess leans over to Rebecca, you look amazing tonight, and a beautiful couple." "Thank you, he is rather nice." "Well fingers crossed; we could end up having a double wedding" Princess laughs. "We've only just met"! Rebecca states. "So, are you looking elsewhere"? Princess pushes. "No, but it is so early." "We have been through life and death situations, that's a lifetime." Another man comes over to Princess and asks if he could have the pleasure of a dance. She graciously agrees and returns to the dance floor. He is an older but elegant man. Geraldo is watching from the side with a fixed smile on his face. Rebecca leans over to him, "It's only duty, Geraldo, if you don't move that smile your face will crack." Geraldo relaxes and smiles at her, "guess so, I am going to get a drink, can I bring you one." "David is ahead of you there, but thanks, I am sure Princess would like one," she tells him. The music ends and Princess is escorted back to her throne. She takes her seat and immediately looks for Geraldo. "He's gone to get you a drink" Rebecca tells her. "Oh, thanks, just checking." Rebecca smiles of the comment. "You've got it bad, haven't you." "Is it obvious" Princess cringes. "The room reeks of sexual tension" she laughs." I don't envy the position he is in though". "I'm hardly going to have his head cut off or something if we argue," Princess points out. "Maybe but you could burn or freeze him in a temper," Rebecca retorts. "Oh, I never thought of that, he doesn't think that does he"? Princess looks concerned. "No, and he is the bravest man I know, so if anyone is going to be with you, it's him." Rebecca reassures her. "You are right, he is perfect for me." At this moment, Geraldo returns with Princesses drink. She takes it and thanks him. She leans into him and whispers, "Can we talk." He nods agreement and offers his hand as they walk out of the room, onto the balcony. There is a beautiful night with a full moon. Princess looks up at it as Geraldo wraps his arms around her. He whispers, "So what do you need to talk about in private"? "Oh, I just wanted to get your thoughts on us as a couple." He turns her towards him, "It is all I think about, I know there will be obvious problems, and god help me if we disagree, but I very much love you," Her face lights up as he takes a ring out of his pocket. I have been carrying it around for days, even before the bridge"! "Oh my god, you make me so happy," is her response as he formally asks her, "Will you marry me"? She throws herself at him and hugs and kisses him and shouts out "YES"! He laughs, "Well we won't have to announce it." They both laughs, kiss again and re-enter the room. Princess rushes up to Rebecca and shows her ring off. Rebecca jumps up and hugs her as they dance around in circles as everyone watches them. Geraldo stands silently by as David asks him what is happening. Geraldo points to the ring. "Oh, Congratulations I guess." Rebecca then rushes to Geraldo and hugs him and gives him a kiss on the cheek. Orpheus sees all the commotion and goes over to them. "What is happening"?

Princess points to her ring. "We are getting married" she blurts out. "What it hasn't been discussed, there are no arrangements made, I mean." Rebecca interrupts him. "All you have to do is announce it here formally and put it on a sign in the city centre tomorrow. "Oh, very good, I'll do just that. He stands before the throne and bangs his staff, "Ladies and Gentlemen, I have a rather important announcement to make, I am delighted to announce the formal engagement of her Royal Highness the Princess and The Honourable Geraldo Templeton of the Queens Guard. The room burst into applause and cheers. The band break out again in music and Geraldo takes Princess's hand to lead her onto the dance floor. They start to dance as they are joined next to them by Rebecca and David and then everyone else. David leans over "Congratulations," they both thank him. Rebecca whispers in David's ear, "It's so romantic," "Yes, you must tell me how they met." "Later she responds."

The evening continues and everyone is in a great mood. After a while, Princess turns to Rebecca, "I think I am going to turn in, I'll see you tomorrow." "I'll tell the maids to keep out till called, she replies." Princess gives her a kiss and heads for the exit with Geraldo following. They enter Princesses room and immediately kiss as soon as the door is closed. They paw at each other undoing the numerous buttons and clasps holding their clothes together. Once completely naked Geraldo lifts her up and carries her over to the bed and lies her down. He then leans over her, and they embrace and kiss. They then spend the night making passionate love. Down in the throne room, people are leaving, and Rebecca and David are seated alone near the bar. He hands her a new drink. "You know they really make a great couple," he says. "Yes, from day one they have placed each other before all else, I have lost count of how many times they have saved each other's lives, from the time they first met, when Geraldo was apparently a mountain man." David looks shocked at this, "A mountain man, never"! Yes, he was captured by Manion's' men and tortured and Princess found him and saved him and treated him, that's when it all started. "I never knew, I assumed they met in court." "Hardly, it was all by chance, if she hadn't secretly left the priory to help the victims, he would probably be dead." "No wonder they have such a bond." "Yeah, it's pretty unique, and I came along to help her, we have known each other since childhood, we are like sisters." "Well, she is very lucky, I think." "We all are having her here." They clink glasses and then Rebecca puts her glass down. "I had better retreat to my room; we have a busy day tomorrow." "Oh," I thought we could...," he tries to continue. "I am sorry, but this is all a bit new for me, I will see you tomorrow." She gives him a kiss on the cheek and leaves. He just watches her leave before pouring another drink and sitting down contemplating his future. Rebecca walks to her room, trying not to make any noise and trying desperately not to listen. She looks out her window at the moon lit sky and thinks of her future and possible relationship with David.

The next morning, Rebecca knocks on Princesses door and finds her still asleep in bed. Geraldo has left. She wakes Princess who is very happy and just relaxes as Rebecca calls for the maids. They quickly arrive with Baths and hot water. They are in the routine quickly and Princess rises from the bed and walks naked over to the bath and steps in. The maids place out her dress for the day and prepares her hairbrushes and combs. Princess quickly washes and stands as Rebecca wraps a towel around her and she steps out. She then sits by her desk in front of the mirror. She is looking at her ring. "What do you think of its Becky"? "It is beautiful, you are very lucky, a brave, elegant man with great taste." Princess sighs "Yes I know, now we have to think about you and your man." "Oh, I'm not rushing, I hardly know him, he hasn't even saved my life yet" she jokes. They both laughs "Well I'm not starting another war, just so he can" Princess jokes. Rebecca helps Princess dress, and they head for the throne room. Upon entering everyone bows and curtseys and Princess takes her throne. She calls Orpheus over and discusses something privately in his ear. He goes to his desk and brings out a map of the land they now control. He points to several areas and Princess picks one. She then stands erect and calls for Rebecca to stand before her. Rebecca looks confused and David steps forward and is stopped by Geraldo. Rebecca stands before Princess with a curious look on her face. Princess announces, please step forward and kneel. Rebecca stumbles forward and lowers to her knee, Princess takes a sword handed to her by Orpheus and places it on Rebecca's shoulders. I pronounce you the Duchess of Romarnia and Lady over the lands and people thereof. Arise Lady Rebecca. She stands and looks around as everyone cheers. Princess rises and gives a hug and kisses her on the forehead. "You will always have a future sweetheart. Orpheus, Geraldo, and David congratulate her along with others and Orpheus shows her where Romarnia is, a beautiful area along the coast of Tarmack with its own castle. "So, when are you going to invite us to your new home"? Princess asks. "My god, I don't believe it, when shall we go"? "Well, I think that we can put a small party together to travel there, a small Royal guard would be handy." Princess suggests. She turns to Orpheus; can you send a message to the castle to let them know we will arrive in two days and they should prepare to meet their new Lady". "It would be a pleasure your Highness." "Let's go out and celebrate," Rebecca suggests. "OH, does this come with any money, how will I pay for everything"? Orpheus steps in, Lady Rebecca, the land is quite substantial, with many landowners, and industries and a major port, so your title comes with substantial taxes." "Great, then lunch is on me, let's go." Princess sends a maid to get their cloaks. Geraldo says" I will get a small guard to escort, I assume myself and David are invited." "I dare you not to come" Princess laughs. Are you coming Orpheus, you are like a father to us both." "I would be honoured, thank you." They all prepare to leave the Palace and head into the city centre. They approach a fine restaurant and as they enter, the owner nearly faints in shock. He clears a long table and offers the chair at the head of the table to Princess. Princess against protocol offers the chair to Rebecca, "This is your day, Becky." They all sit with Princess to one side and David to the other. The Owner brings over some fine wine and the food starts to be delivered. Rebecca talks to Orpheus, "What do you know about this Romarnia place, Orpheus." "I understand it is quite beautiful with amazing beaches. You should spend many happy days there." He explains "Oh no! I will be at the palace with Princess, won't I Princess"? "If you wish, but I am sure you will want to visit it occasionally, especially when you marry and have a family." "What, family, does this all come with the Lady thing"? Princess laughs, "no, but in time you will want to settle down and every woman wants children, don't they"? "I, I don't know, I never thought, I guess so." Rebecca stutters as Princess laughs, "it's no harder than becoming a real Princess, so you know roughly what it's like." "These are changing times" Geraldo cuts in, "I'm having to give up my mountains," he laughs." See" Princess jokes, "let's eat." They tuck into the food which keeps coming with several servings and deserts. After a couple of hours, they are all relaxed and happy and full. The restaurant owner comes over and asks if everything was to their liking. "It was excellent" Rebecca replies. He then hands her a long bill for all the food and drinks. She looks at it with shock on her face. "Oh, I never thought, Orpheus, how do I pay for these things. "Well usually the Lord or Lady have a purse full of Silver." "Oh, I don't have one of those. David leans over and takes the bill, brings out a pouch and throws some silver coins to the restaurant owner. "Please let me settle this as a congratulations gift." Rebecca thanks him. Geraldo pats him on the back in agreement. Princess rises and everyone else follows and they head out of the restaurant where they are met by the guard still waiting outside. "Oh, I forgot about them, Geraldo can we let them go" Princess suggests. "No, your Highness, this is their duty, they can relax when you are back safe in the Palace, then I will relieve them. "As you say" she agrees. They walk back to the palace in a good mood and through the gates. Geraldo then turns to the guard. "You are dismissed and have a round on me in the bar. He throws them some coins. The party heads indoors. They go into a smaller lounge room with a large fire blazing. It is warm and cosy. Orpheus makes his retirement known and leaves as the other four sit around the fire. The men remove several parts of their uniforms for comfort. "So, what time will we leave tomorrow. "I suggest before noon. Then we can make camp at a decent time." "So, you are coming with us aren't you David"? Princess asks. "If you wish your Highness," he replies. "Oh, I do, I have lots for you to do when we arrive there." Rebecca looks at her curiously. "I will be honoured." I think twenty-four men to accompany us should be enough" Geraldo suggests. "I would be happy just us four" Rebecca suggests. "That can't happen I am afraid, my Lady. Rebecca ignores him before she realises, he is talking to her. "Oh, of course, you know better, those days are all behind us now, Get used to it Becky" Princess advises.

Princess nods to Geraldo to go. "We are breaking for the night, see you tomorrow," They stand and leave Princess giving Rebecca a kiss on the head. Rebecca is embarrassed being alone with David for the first time. "Thank you for the meal, it was very generous of you". "It was my honour, and I hope the first of many." "You are too kind, I am just a simple girl," she replies, "Well I hope it will be the first of many, maybe some just the two of us"? he questions. "I think I would like that" she responds encouragingly. "Can I get you a drink or something" he asks. "Oh no, I think I should make my way to bed now, we have a long journey tomorrow, but it has been a lovely night" She thanks him and rises to leave. He quickly also stands and approaches her, "I was wondering, Could I possibly, if you would not object, to a good night kiss." She instantly blushes but has been thinking this thought also. She nods in agreement, no words mentioned, and he takes her in his arms and kisses her passionately. It is a long strong kiss." She then turns and leaves him standing. As she staggers back few steps, "Wow, that was unexpected" she stutters, He interrupt," I am sorry I am rushing you, I just thought." She stops him, "No, it was very nice, please do not worry." He breaks out in a massive smile. She laughs back, let's leave it there for now and I will see you tomorrow morning". "Excellent" he replies and opens the door for her, do you want me to escort you to your room." "I don't think so, I'll be ok, good night" She leans forward and gives him a small peck on the cheek, "I'll see you tomorrow morning." "Good night." She turns to leave as he stands there in the doorway spell bound.

The next morning there is a Royal guard and two wagons of equipment plus Geraldo and David waiting by Princess and Rebecca's horses. Eventually they appear stepping down the steps to their horses. "Sorry for the delay, had some last-minute packing." They are both helped onto their horses and the parade moves of, out of the city.

Princess rides alongside Geraldo and Rebecca, David. This is a perfect time for bonding. Princess is discussing their upcoming wedding, which Geraldo has no ideas about and David is trying to encourage Rebecca, talking about how exciting it will be to explore her new castle and lands. They have been travelling for several hours when Geraldo suggests that they have ridden enough and make camp. They all agree and stop by a river side. The wagons are unloaded of tents and the men erect them and they also build a large fire. Princess and Rebecca lounge on two large couches and watch the men working and maids preparing food. An hour later the tents are ready, and everyone can relax. The men are sitting around the fire, joking, and telling stories. Geraldo sits behind Princess with his arms around her. And David sits next to Rebecca. They are talking about their coming wedding. "I hope you will be my maid of honour, Becky." "Don't dare ask anyone else," Rebecca says, and maybe some little boys and girls to throw flowers. "Geraldo, what family will you invite." "Eh I will invite my parents and brothers and sisters." "What, you have a large family" she asks, surprisingly. "Yes, we never had the chance to discuss them before." "Well, it will be nice to meet them, as they will probably be the only ones, we both know" she laughs. "Are you going to invite everyone from the Priory. "Of course, they are my family." Rebecca asks, "what about the honeymoon"? Well, I understand that we will have to tour the new countries we now lead, so I guess that will be our honeymoon." "So, I guess we will be joining you then" she laughs. "Looks like it." Princess confirms. "Well maybe we can arrange a few secret days at my new castle away from the crowds at the end" Rebecca invites." Well, if it has beautiful beaches as they say, that would be lovely," Princess responds. They retreat to their tents and prepare for bed to rest for the coming day.

The next morning, they are awake early and packed to move on. After the recent weeks, the ride is a welcome break from the pressures of war. Everyone is feeling relaxed and excited at seeing the castle. After several hours they finally come across the city the castle is based. They slowly enter through the city gates to the amazement of the city dwellers. It is as if they were not known to be coming. They make the way towards the castle and enter through the castle gate. A team of people rush out and help Princess and Rebecca of their horses. A man comes forward, who introduces himself as Jaytor, the head of household within the castle. While he introduces himself, the number of soldiers in armour rush forward and stand in a row to present themselves to the Princess. The guard are introduced to the two ladies who are then followed by Geraldo. Once they complete this task they are led into the castle to the main hall. Here there is a large chair where the throne would be. Rebecca looks around the walls at the flags and pictures hanging on the walls. It also has an amazing painted ceiling of angels flying across a waterfall. "it's beautiful" Rebecca states. Jaytor points out certain areas as the maids and servants line up to be introduced. Jaytor leads Princess followed by Rebecca along the line. The maids all curtsey as they pass as the men bow. When the last is past, Jaytor claps his hands and they all rush of, he claps again, and a servant appears with a tray of drinks. He hands a glass each to Princess and Rebecca, it is a red wine. He explains the wine. "Your Highness and My Lady, this is a wine produced on our land. The girls take a sip each and nod reassuringly, "it is very good, I think" Princess says, not really knowing. Jaytor then hands Geraldo and David a mug of beer each. "This is also produced within the castle, gentlemen." They swig back a taste each and agree it is a fine brew. He then turns to Princess and Rebecca. Would you like to see your rooms ladies. "Love too," Rebecca replies. He leads them to the stairs and up one floor. The first room is Rebecca's. This was the master of the castles room, prior to his demise in battle. Rebecca looks around, it is a large room with a four-poster bed, large furniture, and fireplace with a raging fire. In the far corner is a bath. "It's lovely thank you. There is a young maid standing by the door." This is Sarah, she is your personal maid," he informs her. "Nice to meet you" Rebecca says. They then head to the guest suite. This is another large room with the expected four poster bed and grand seats and fireplace. "This will do fine, thank you" Princess tells him. "If you require anything just ring the bell, I have arranged dinner for seven." Jaytor informs them. "Fine, see you later" Rebecca tells him. They both go back into Rebecca's room. She is totally excited and rushing around it, looking into drawers and cupboards. "This is amazing, I can't believe this is all mine"! Princess   grabs her and puts her arms around her, "You deserve it," and they both jump back on the bed. "This is a big bed for one little lady alone, don't you think." Princess taunts her. "Don't rush me, I'm not in a hurry." Rebecca replies. "Well, you have a hell of a room, when you are" Princess laughs. Rebecca leans over to a table and picks up a bell and rings it. Immediately two maids rush in. "Can you get us some wine and also bring up our luggage." The maids curtsey and leave. "I could get used to this" she laughs. Moments later the maids and a couple of servants return with a tray of drinks and two boxes of luggage. Rebecca points to one box. "Take that to Her Highnesses room, thank you. The maid asks her, "do you want us to unpack for you". "No thank you, but you can arrange two baths." "Together or apart," the maid asks. Rebecca looks at Princess, "together" they both say in unison. The maids again disappear and return shortly after with an extra bath and hot water. The baths are prepared as the girls sit in front of the fire drinking their drinks. The maids finish preparing the baths and line up to assist the girls undress and bath. Rebecca tells them to leave as they can look after themselves. They curtsey and leave. Rebecca and Princess start to undress and look at the ointments by the side of the baths. They are smelling the ointments and when they agree on one, they pour it into the baths. They then climb into the baths and relax. "I wonder what our men are doing"? Princess questions. They are probably relaxing and unpacking their bags.

Down in the stables the men have been barracked. It is cold wet and filthy. "I thought we might get a room, didn't you" David asks Geraldo. "I guess they think we are just soldiers, leave it with me, he leaves the stables and heads for the main hall. "Where is Jaytor," Geraldo asks. Within seconds Jaytor appears and asks what Geraldo is looking for? "I am expecting to receive a decent room for myself and my assistant for the head of the army and future husband of her Highness." Oh, my goodness, I was not told, I just assumed you were a normal officer. Please wait a moment and let me organise rooms for you." He rushes off and then returns shortly after with a team of servants. They will show you to your room sir and bring your bags up." "Don't forget my assistant." He has been sent for sir. Geraldo is shown to a room which, although not as impressive as the girls is a great improvement. He then checks the other room which is similar. "These are fine" he informs the servants and goes back to his room. He is quickly joined by David and their bags. "This is better" he comments. "Yeah, I bet it's nothing like the ladies' rooms though." Geraldo responds. "Maybe we should pay them a visit" David suggests." No give them some time to climatise, we'll meet them at dinner. Geraldo recommends.

An hour later the ladies come down and are met in the main hall by the men. "What's your room like" Rebecca asks. "Well initially it was quite cold and windy and wet and had unwanted guests, but we left the stable and moved to two rooms on the second floor." "Ours are lovely" she replies. At this moment Jaytor arrives and asks them if they would like to see the rest of the castle and its little pleasures. "OH, I'd love to." Rebecca responds. He raises his finger. "Then follow me. They do as asked. Rebecca leading with David and Princess with Geraldo. He leads them down to the cellars and shows of the caskets of wine and beer. "Now this is my type of place" David comments. "There is more, follow me." Jaytor adds. He leads them down a corridor and it opens into a large, tiled room with a pool heated by the steam from the nearby mountain. It has painted tiles showing the history of the country. "This is amazing" Princess comments. "Well, I recommend we finish the evening here after our dinner" Geraldo suggests. "Got my vote" princess adds," "Oh definitely" David adds. "I guess that is unanimous then" Rebecca laughs, "But for now, I am starving." They all agree and head back to the main hall for dinner. There waiting is a long table and standing by it several courtiers. Jaytor leads Princess to the main chair and offers Rebecca the next. "May I introduce your guests, your highness. The next thirty minutes was spent with Jaytor introducing them to everyone. During this, Princess was presented with many gifts to impress and gain favour. When the introductions are over everyone moves to the table to eat. A grand feast if offered and Jaytor stands at the side of Rebecca during the whole event. Every time she is asked something, he advises her or tells her about the history behind the request. As it comes to the end of the feast, Rebecca turns to Princess, "Being important is exhausting" she exclaims. Princess laughs, you'll get used to it. Jaytor certainly seems to have your back." "I hope so" Rebecca replies. The dinner is over and Princess and Rebecca both send of the guests. Jaytor comes over to them, "Is there anything else I can do for you." "Well, I think we would love to try the pool." "Oh certainly, will you require masseurs and assistants"? I don't think so, just make sure there are plenty of towels and robes and wine." Very good my Lady". He departs and the four of them head down to the pool. They head for the two different changing rooms and undress. Geraldo appears with a towel wrapped around his waist. He is shortly joined by David. In the ladies changing room Princess is standing with a towel wrapped around her waist and another draped around her neck falling in front of her breasts. Rebecca appears wrapped from head to toe in a massive towel. Princess holds back the laughter and walks over to her. "Sweetheart, you are here with two of the sexiest men in the land, you do not want to look like this. She pulls the towel of her to reveal her still wearing underwear. Princess bursts into laughter. "Oh my god, you are going to be a virgin forever," "I'm not" Rebecca responds. "But it was not David, and you have a new life now." Princess tells her as she grabs two small towels and gets Rebecca to remove her clothes. She then wraps her up in the two towels and they head for the pool. The men by now have slipped into the pool and relaxing. Princess stands by the pool turns her back to the men and removes her towels and jumps in. Rebecca stands on the steps. Princess reappears from under the water and calls to her. "Jump in" she calls out. Rebecca pulls of the towels and jumps into an enormous splash. As she rises to the surface she throws her arms around, "I can't swim." David is pushed towards her by Geraldo. David grabs her and cradles her in his arms. Princess swims over to Geraldo and asks. "Oh, lucky David was here". "Who would have guessed she could not swim," he asks. "Don't look at me" she smiles. Rebecca cradled in David's arms reaches up and kisses him. Princess looks at her, "And my work is done," she turns to Geraldo, so where is my kiss"? He dutifully complies. Princess and Geraldo are happily playing in the water as David is helping Rebecca with her fear of water and teaching her how to swim. Each lesson seems to be interrupted by a kiss and embrace. After a period, Princess, and Geraldo swim over to them. "How are you two progressing"? Princess asks. "I am floating and can swim under water." "Oh, swimming, yes of course, good, keep up the good work," Princess turns away and smiles as Geraldo looks at her and grins. "I think we should break for the night, don't you" she asks Geraldo. "You mean leave these to rabbits alone" he laughs, and they head for the side and grab their towels. "We are off, see you tomorrow" Princess calls out." "Oh but, you can't go, I mean. "Rebecca tries to make an excuse for them to stay. "Sorry really tired, have a nice swim." Princess and Geraldo leave. David turns to Rebecca," well that was subtle, but not being one to waste an opportunity," Rebecca frantically looks for an excuse, "It looks like it's time to go." "Just one moment, this is the first chance we have really been alone, and, well you are naked, and I am naked, and we obviously feel a lot for each other, and I thought." She interrupts him" OK, I can't fight all three of you, she grabs him and kisses him passionately and pulls him out of the pool. Let's at least be in comfort. She grabs the towels and heads for her room, he rushes after her. They reach her room and enter. She goes over to the bed and lies back on it. He comes up to her and leans over and kisses her and runs his fingers over her body, removing the towels. They wrap themselves around each other and make passionate love. At the same time Princess is lying with Geraldo and she sniggers as she hears the banging of Rebecca's bed. "My work was better than I thought" she whispers to Geraldo. She then wraps her legs around him and they embrace and make passionate love.

The following morning, they all appear at breakfast. David has a big smile on his face and Rebecca is blushing but content. Princess comes up behind her and kisses the top of her head. "Good night" she whispers. Rebecca looks up, "It was very comfortable." Quite a first night in your new home it seems." So, what are the plans for today, Rebecca asks. "Well, this is your home, but I would suggest we look around and meet the locals" Princess suggests. "I'll arrange the horses and men to escort." Geraldo tells them. "Do we really need to take the guard"? Princess asks. "Rules are rules, and you never know where an assassin might be," Geraldo explains, she gives in. Geraldo leaves and David sits and watches Rebecca. Fifteen minutes later Geraldo returns. "Everything's ready, shall we make a move." Rebecca responds excitedly" Can't wait" They all head outside and mount the four horses waiting for them. They then head out of the castle to the city followed by the guard. They head down the main high street and are staired at by the locals, there is no excitement or any real reaction from them. "This is strange,"

Princess mentions to Geraldo," certainly is, I suggest we stop of somewhere and gage the atmosphere inside" is his suggestion. They reach an inn. Let's stop here. Geraldo raises his arm to his men. They dismount and he posts men at the front and back and six enter the property with them. They go to the bar and ask for a booth to drink. The barman looks up at them and waves to a booth the far side of the inn. They all move over there and take seats. A waitress walks over and asks what they would like. "I would like to see some respect for her Highness the Princess. The waitress looks at them and looks confused, who are you, Geraldo stands up, this is her Royal Highness the Princess. The girl instantly changes her attitude, "What, no one said we would be expecting any Royalty, what can I get you." He demands a bottle of best wine and beers for all the men. She scurries of and sees the barman, who happens to be the owner. He comes creeping over and introduces himself and tells them that they have heard no news of any Royalty arriving in the city. Princess stands up and points to Rebecca, "Well you better be introduced to the new Lady of Romania and your Mistress who you are answerable to! The man buckles at the knees and begs forgiveness. "We were not told of any changes; everything has been the same since before the war. The castle runs everything. "What do you mean, the castle, the previous lord and the king have died, who has been running this county. Well, the administrator your Highness, Sir Jaytor. "Sir Jaytor Geraldo repeats," yes, my lord, we send all our taxes to him, even after the big increase recently, it is really hard at the moment, that's why this place is empty, no one has any money." "I see." Can you show me any documents of the taxes you have paid recently." "Well yes of course Sir, I will go and get them, in the meantime, are you intending to eat"? "I guess we had better, I am not sure what our food will be like when we return to the castle. The man rushes off to get the documents as the waitress comes over again. What would you like my Queen." "I prefer to be called Your Highness or Princess, but we will all have the today special, whatever that is." "That's all there is, I am afraid, stocks are low is seems." "So be it," Geraldo interrupts. "Well, it seems we have found a little area of corruption here" Rebecca says. "This is why it is so important to travel the land to see what is happening," Geraldo tells her. "This is quite an introduction for you." "We'll sort it out" Princess adds. The waitress comes over with the drinks followed by the owner and a bag of documents. He hands a note from the bag, it is the latest tax amount and then he hands another from the previous tax period, the difference is thirty percent. "Wow," Geraldo says. He shows Princess and Rebecca. "You will be reimbursed the difference when we sort this problem out" Princess tells him. "Thank you, Your Highness, it would be greatly appreciated, everyone around here has been hit hard." "Not for long Rebecca adds. Enjoy your food. The waitress returns with a tray of food, which is anything but appealing. They start to eat it, but no one finishes their meal. "I think this news has destroyed my appetite, Rebecca claims. "Yeah, let's get back to the castle and sort this mess out." They all stand and go to leave. Geraldo hands the barman a few coins and tells him he will return his documents and sort the problem out. The landlord thanks them and invites them back. "Yes, thanks David says as he leaves. They mount their horses and ride back to the castle at a pace and head straight to the main hall. Geraldo has also called for more men to join them. They barge through the doors and Princess marches over to the main chair and takes her place. Jaytor rushes over, your highness, what can I do for you, how was your trip"? Geraldo throws the documents at him. "What is the meaning of this" Princess demands. "They are local taxes, it has been hard times here it seems, these are dated after the Lord was killed along with his King, who authorised them. Why I believe I was asked to keep an eye on the county while his Lordship was away. There was a war to support. "Yes, and how much of this has been received by the crown. She demands. Well, it is awaiting collection, it is all stored in the vaults. Show us, Geraldo grabs him by the collar, and they head for the vaults followed by Princess, Rebecca, and David. Jaytor opens the vault, and everyone is stunned by the enormous amount of gold and currency is stored inside. "This can't be all from one tax payment surely" Princess asks. "Eh no, this is over the last five years, the tax was not exactly forwarded to the crown. He answers sheepishly. "So, this is all the crowns, mine"! she shouts back at him. "I believe so your Highness." "Well, I am glad that we came here by chance, Rebecca you have a job here, you will have to remain for a while and sort this out. Everyone who can supply their last tax form will be fully refunded, that should change the attitude around here. Then send 50% back to my Capital and invest the rest in your land, schools, hospitals, and the people's wellbeing". "I understand Princess." "David, you will remain here and protect her and run the army." "As you order your Highness." Now let's get upstairs and get some food, I am starving, OH Geraldo, sort him out" She points to Jaytor. Geraldo grabs him by the shoulder and throws him towards some guards, "Take him to the cells till further notice, they drag him away, pleading his innocence. They make their way upstairs again and Rebecca calls over the most senior looking servant. "Can you organise some food for us to eat and drinks." "Off course my lady" he rushes of as maids arrive with drinks. They all sit around the table. "Well, that was quite a trip" Princess claims. "Fortunately, you have a fortune to rebuild this land and turn it into a really nice resort, so we can visit regularly." "I hope so Princess." Rebecca replies. "I'll keep a close eye on her, your highness" David adds. "I am sure you will" Princess jokes. The maids arrive with food, and everyone starts eating as they are really hungry after the terrible meal earlier. "I think you can be really happy here, when you have sorted everything out, sweetheart" Princess tells Rebecca." Once we have removed the obvious corruption, I am sure it will be fun, she responds. I think tomorrow we should proceed onto the Capital of Tarmack and see what other things we will find." OK, we will leave a garrison here. Call Orpheus and tell him to send another five hundred men, keep one hundred her under David's authority and send the rest onto the capital. "I will do, your Highness, this all seems so real, all of a sudden," Rebecca claims. "Sure does" Princess agrees." "But you have a pool and a beach" she jokes. They enjoy their meal and Rebecca is sitting trying to rap her mind around all the information she has just received. After the meal they all decide to retreat to their rooms, Geraldo goes with Princess and Rebecca invites David. Tomorrow is going to be a busy day.

The next morning Rebecca and David see off Princess and Geraldo. Princess and Rebecca give each other a big hug and kiss, as Geraldo Shakes David's hand and tells him to look after Rebecca. They then mount their horses and move of through the gates towards the capital city. Rebecca and David head indoors and David asks her what they will do now? Rebecca tells him "I think we should sort out Jaytor now, then sort out the tax refunds. David agrees, "and a big refund will certainly help your popularity. They head for the main hall and Rebecca takes her seat. David calls for his men to bring Jaytor to Rebecca. She in turn is having a small panic attack as she has never been in a position like this. David reassures her as Jaytor is dragged into the room and forced down onto his knees. Rebecca looks down on him. "So, tell me Jaytor, what is your defence against this claim of fraud and theft. He pleads "my Lady, this is all an understanding, I only did as I was instructed to do by my Lord." She responds" Well I can't accuse you of this before the Lord died, and I have no doubt that he was corrupt, but you certainly learnt from him and abused, the people even more. I therefore find you guilty and sentence you to five years of hard labour. All your assets will be impounded to go towards refunding the people, which is my order". She gestures to David, take him away"! David orders his soldiers to take him back to the cells. Once he is removed, David turns to Rebecca, "Congratulations, you handled that very well, no one would have thought it was your first time". "Thanks, I learnt from a natural, so what shall we do now"? She asks him." Well, we can go out again to see your city, or look for someone to go through the papers we have." She suggests "I guess we can do both, there must be an administrator somewhere around so let's go out. They head for the door and are followed by her guard. "I'm beginning to know how Princess feels" she laughs. Outside they mount their horses and head into town. Word is getting around that there is a new Lady in town, and everyone is treating them with respect. Bowing and curtseying. They head through the street and Rebecca is looking in the shop windows. She sees a dress shop, "Oh let's look in here" she tells David. He raises his arm, and the men stop. He dismounts and helps Rebecca of her horse. They enter the shop. Rebecca looks around as a lady rush to greet her. "My Lady can I welcome to my shop" she welcomes Rebecca. "Thank you, I need some night gowns" Rebecca asks. "Certainly, come this way and take a seat." She takes Rebecca to a seat and then rushes behind a curtain to find possible outfits. She quickly returns. "Here My Lady, feel this." She hands Rebecca an outfit which is made of a fine cotton. "It looks nice, do you also have swimsuits." "One moment." The lady rushes of again and returns with boxes of swimming outfits. "Here, these are very popular my Lady." Rebecca stands and holds all the products against her body. "They are very nice, I'll take the night gown and two swimsuits, please deliver them to the castle tomorrow and you will be paid." "Thank you, my Lady," David intervenes and asks the lady, "Do you have your tax forms available also." She looks at him as if in trouble, "I paid them fully weeks ago, my lord." Rebecca reassures her, "Do not worry, it is that we have found out that the taxes have been increased illegally, so if you send them along with the outfits, you will receive a refund." "What, that's amazing, things have been really hard, no one has any money to buy things lately," the lady tells her. "Things should be a lot more comfortable in the future for the whole city" Rebecca tells her. She rises and prepares to leave the shop. The lady shows her out and thanks her again for her help. As they step outside David notices there is an accountant shop a few shops down. "My Lady, look, just what we are looking for." They head straight there and enter. David rings the bell, and an old man comes from the back room. "Welcome, how can I help you," he asks. David introduces Rebecca, "This is the new Lady of Romarnia." The man bows, "I am honoured to have you visit me, but how can I help you"? Rebecca steps forward, "Well I am sure you are aware that the taxes have increased substantially in this county." "Oh no, you are not going to increase them even more, there is nothing less," the man panics and interrupts. Rebecca takes his hand. "Please calm down I am aware that the new taxes were illegal, and I have already imprisoned the person responsible, but now I need someone to go through the tax forms so the people can be refunded." "I would be honoured to help in this matter my Lady" he replies. "Good can you visit the castle tomorrow so we can discuss further" she asks. "I will be honoured my Lady. "Excellent, please arrive at noon" David tells him. The man bows and Rebecca and David leave. They mount their horses and move on. There next stop is the local school. They dismount at the school entrance and enter. An old lady approaches them, "Can I help you" she asks. David introduces Rebecca as the new Lady of Romania. The lady curtseys and introduces herself as the headmistress of the school Mrs. Standish. "I was wondering if you could show us around your school, "Rebecca asks. "It would be a pleasure, the lady answers and leads them into the main hall. Here they see some children playing a ball game in two teams. "They do at least an hour of sport and activity a day, to keep their fitness. They also use this room for eating their lunches." "Oh, does the school supply them," Rebecca asks. "Oh no, we can't afford to do that, it would be far too expensive, it does mean however that some survive on tiny rations." "That's a shame, they can't keep fit if they are starving." "Unfortunately, our grant was reduced by over 50% last year, so we can hardly survive". Standish informs her. They move on. They enter a classroom, and the class is studying local history. They are discussing the recent war in Lystonia. Mrs Standish introduces Rebecca to the class. Rebecca asks the children what they know about the battles. A boy sticks his hand up, "My father told me that our King was killed by an evil witch and that let the baddies invade our country. Rebecca is taken back by this. "This is not true at all, I was there, the Princess was fighting the baddies on her own while the King was not even there. She destroyed over 250 ships and thousands of men on her own and saved the country. The King arrived later and betrayed her and locked her in a cell." "How can a girl destroy 250 ships the boy arrogantly argues". "She has magical powers and controls, fire, water, wind, and the land. She created a giant wave which destroyed the ships." A girl raises her hand "Do you know her miss." "Yes, she is my best friend, and we have had many adventures together." Maybe I will come back one day and tell you what really happened". "You would be most welcome Mrs Standish assured her. They leave the class and Rebecca turns to Mrs Standish, "I have asked a local accountant to look into the city accounts, can you make sure he receives the schools accounts, and maybe we can help with the school lunches." "That would be very helpful my Lady," she replies. They exchange farewells and Rebecca and David leave and head back to the castle. "Well, quite an eventful day" David says as they enter the castle gates. Yes, we have a lot to do, but I do not want to be away from Lystonia for too long, so the more we do now the better.

Approaching the capital of Tarmack, Princess and Geraldo enter the city gates and are met by the City Elders who had heard she was visiting. She stops at where they are waiting and the elder statesman steps forward. "Welcome your Highness, my name is Lord Senna, you are eagerly awaited and welcome." Princess turns to Geraldo, "Well this is a better welcome than the other town. "Please follow us" the elder asks her. The all proceed down the lane to the Castle entrance and Princess and Geraldo pull up at the main doors. The unmount and the gates open and they are led to the throne room. As they are walking the Elder tells Princess that he was present at her coronation and that everyone is very pleased she is visiting them so soon". They enter the Throne room, and she is led to the Throne and takes her place. May I introduce your welcome party to you Your Highness. "Briefly, it has been a long journey, and I am tired and hungry, make it swift and maybe to can talk more at dinner". "Very good your highness." He then runs of the names of the Elders present and they individually bow to her. "Thank you, can you have someone show me to my quarters now." He calls over a servant and some maids and tells them to show Princess to her room. "Dinner will be in one hour your highness. He steps back as she follows the servants accompanied by Geraldo. They open the bedroom door, and it is a massive suite. It has separate lounge, bathroom, bedroom, and maid rooms of it. Standing by her bed is a maid. The servant tells her this is her main maid who will organise all the others. "Can you organise for my things to be brought up immediately, along with General Templeton's things. The maids look at each other in surprise. They all nod agreement and rush of. Princess falls back on the bed. "Well, this is rather nice, isn't it." "Yes very, but don't you think I should have my own room." Why, would you spend any time there"? "I guess that's a point, it just seems strange." "A lot of things are going to feel strange initially, you should have seen my shared room at the priory, nothing like this she laughs." The maids return with all their bags and start to unpack their belongings. Princess and Geraldo sit on a couch by the fire drinking wine. "I wonder how Rebecca is doing, it is strange not having her here." She asks. "I am sure she is coping as well as you are princess." "Yes, she is so capable, miss her already." "It won't be long to her. The maid comes over to Princess, do you wish to bath and change before dinner your Highness"? Do we really have time, I would love to but"! "You are her Royal Highness; I can tell them to wait for an extra hour if you wish. "OK, do that, thank you." The maid claps her hands, and the other maids start to fill the bath with hot water and oils and lay out a new dress for her. "You see this is where I could do with my own room" Geraldo tells her "You don't want to rub my back for me, you know Rebecca is not here." "Well, if you put it that way, I guess I can hang around." "Thought you would" she smiles. The maid comes back and informs her that everything has been arranged. "Thank you" she tells her. The maid then starts to undo princesses dress and removes it. She then wraps her in a large towel. "Please follow me" the maid requests. Princess follows her into the bathroom and the maid takes her towel and helps her into the large bath. "Thank you, you can go now, I have all the help I need from here." The maid curtseys and leaves. Geraldo pokes his head around the door and enters. "So, what is this extra service I have to offer" he asks. She raises her leg. You can start here if you want. He takes her ankle and a cloth and soap and lathers it up and rubs it on her feet, she wriggles as it tickles. He then slowly starts to raise the leg higher and soaping up the leg. She leans back and relaxes. One he has gone as high as possible he lowers the leg and moves to the other side of the bath and is presented with the other leg. "Well, I have to ask, where did you learn to do this, not in the mountains." "Oh, I've been around, the odd massage, sauna, you know." "I can imagine, well don't stop now she giggles. He moves again to behind her and leans her body forward and soaps her back, slowly bringing the soap around to the front. She rests her head b ack in his arms" Well Rebecca never did it like this" she laughs. He then takes the cloth and places it over her face. She is motionless and waiting for his next move. She then feels a motion in the water and a foot touching her leg and then another. He is climbing in naked. "Well, this is very nice. She leans forward and gives him a passionate kiss. At this moment, the maid enters the bathroom and sees Geraldo in the bath. "Oh sorry, I did not think." "Don't worry, he didn't have a bathroom, so it was only fair" she laughs. The maid giggles and curtseys. Are you ready to get out or should I return." "I am ready, and I think he needs more time to cook after all that riding. The maid holds up a large towel and Princess stands and climbs out of the bath. She is lead to the dressing table and the maid brushes her hair. The maid is drying her hair and back as Geraldo walks out covered in soapsuds and holding the flannel in front of his private area. "I couldn't find a towel" Princess bursts into laughter and the maid giggles and rushes to a   cupboard and hands him a large towel. He thanks her. He goes back in the bathroom to dry of. He comes out again and looks for his bags. He takes out a new uniform. The maid helps Princess into her fresh clothes as Geraldo struggles into his clothes. Eventually they are both ready and the maid leads them down to the throne room. As they enter the trumpet players blow their horns. The congregation all bow and curtsey and princess walks to her throne and Geraldo stands next to her. Lord Senna` approaches her, "Your Highness, would you like me to bring up each Lord and Lady to introduce them to you. "I think everyone must be hungry by now, why not let them stand by the seats and I can walk along them, much quicker." "Very sensible, thank you your Highness. He turns and mutters to the servants to inform the courtiers as he leads Princess and Geraldo to the 1st person standing to princesses right after a spare seat. This is my wife, Lady Senna. She curtseys to Princess who acknowledges her. They then move onto the next and next until all parties have been introduced. Then Princess takes her seat and Geraldo sits to her left. Lord Senna stands and makes an announcement "Your Highness, we are all honoured that you should visit our capital so early in your new reign and offer you are sincere allegiances. The city is yours. ". He sits as princess stands, "Thank you for the kind welcome and I am delighted to meet you all and find out more about this lovely country. We have some important tasks we need to investigate with your help and hopefully we will agree to plans to make this city and country thrive." She takes her seat as everyone claps her. The servants all step forward and pour wine and serve the food. While waiting, Lord Senna asks the Princess," Is there anything in particular you are concerned about, I should be aware of." "Well on route here, we visited Romania and found a lot of corruption there, and the people being taxed ridiculously high, but the revenue receiving none of it." I was wondering if this was commonplace in Tarmack." "I can assure you that I am aware of nothing like this here, as you will see by how well the people of the city live and the country is run" he responds. "Well, that is very reassuring to hear Lord Senna, tomorrow we will travel around the city and meet the people to see how they feel as well". "Certainly, would you like me to join you." "That would save time, if you would not mind, maybe your wife would like to help as well, us ladies like to window shop you know." "I am sure she would love the opportunity" he replies. "Good, then we will leave at 11, this food is very nice, I must say". Lord Senna then turns to Geraldo. General Templeton, would you like to visit the barracks and inspect the men." "No, not necessary, I have met plenty of the Tarmack soldiers in the field, they are very well trained and equipped" Geraldo replies. "But you can show me a few of your bars later in the day if we have time," he adds. "Very good" Lord Senna smiles. The dinner runs well and there are no obvious problems and after a short period of dance, princess excuses herself and heads to her quarters followed by Geraldo.

The next morning, they enter the Throne room at 11 exactly and are met by Lord and Lady Senna. They make their way to the castle entrance where a large carriage is waiting. The four of them take their seats followed by the Queens Guards and Castle Cavalry. They proceed down the wide roads into the city centre welcomed by all the locals. Senna points out the theatre, sports area, and the shopping mall. "Well, I guess it is the shopping mall as the first point of call" Princess suggests. They stop at the entrance and Geraldo and Senna exit the carriage and help Princess and Lady Senna out of the carriage. The soldiers dismount and Geraldo tell them all bar four to wait. They enter the shopping area and princess is impressed by how modern and clean it is. Senna points out these points, "As you can clearly see your Highness, there is no starving or hardship here, I do not understand what happened in that other city." "Well, it certainly was not like this one" is her reply, "tell me, who paid for all this"? He points up to the name over the Malls entrance, Senna Shopping, "it was paid for by investors who receive a little from each shop as rent, it keeps all the shops in one area and the area under one management." "It seems very impressive, she looks along the shops, bakers, butchers, numerous clothes shops, household goods, ironmongers and pharmacies" He points out one shop in particular, it is a jeweller. "Please let me show you into this shop," they all enter, and he introduces Princess to the man behind the counter. He shows her all the fine jewellery. She is impressed and points out certain pieces to Geraldo. In particular, a beautiful ruby and gold necklace. The manager takes it out from the counter and shows it to her up close. "Try it on, your Highness" Senna suggests. "Oh, I couldn't, could I." She looks to Geraldo. The manager opens the clasp and asks her to turn around and lowers the necklace over her head and fastens it around her neck. He brings a mirror and shows it to her. Lady Senna tells her it looks beautiful. Princess looks into the mirror and is surprised how nice it looks. She turns to Geraldo, "What do you think." "It looks very impressive and very expensive your Highness" he assures her. She turns to the manager, "It is beautiful, but I can't." She goes to undo the necklace as the manager, stops her, "Please your Highness. Accept this as a gift from the people of the city." "Oh, I can't, can I." "I insist" he confirms to her. "Well thank you I accept your gift." She looks at it again in the mirror. "Shall we move on your Highness," Senna asks. Oh yes, lets. She thanks the manager again and they exit. They walk further into the mall and Geraldo sees an ironmonger. He goes over and looks at the swords all hanging in the window. "I have never seen weapons and armour sold like a clothes store" he remarks. "There are very many different things in Tarmack you will find. "There certainly are, Geraldo admits. They walk on and as they walk all the people shopping are greeting them and smiling. Princess smells the distinct smell of the bakery. She looks into the window and sees hundreds of different dainty cakes and sweets. "These smells wonderful" she tells them. "Our baker sold bread and bread" she laughs, "Can we go in" she asks. "Of course, your Highness," they enter. "I must take some cakes back to the castle she says." "Just pick what you would like to try, the castle has an account here, it will be delivered within the hour. She goes up to the counter and starts picking out cake after cake, till Geraldo reminds her of why they are here. "Sorry, that will be enough," she tells the girl behind the counter. Senna tells her to deliver them when we leave. She curtseys as they leave. Princess turns to Senna," this is so different to Lystonia, you must tell me more while I am here." "Of course, your highness, just ask anything you want clarified." "I want to know who organised all this, how does it work." "Well modesty stops me saying too much, but most of this I organised. It is very profitable for the people and the city." "Could this be done anywhere" she asks. "Anywhere where people are willing to try new things and work together." "It is very impressive" Geraldo adds. Lady Senna takes princesses arm "I have to show you a wonderful dress shop down here," she leads her to a large shop with amazing dresses in the windows. "How do you stop people smashing the windows and stealing them," "very simple your Highness, every entrance and exit has guards and the whole area is closed after eight o'clock. "Let's go inside" lady Senna suggests. They enter and the assistants rush to help them. Princess is shown numerous gowns from overseas and local. She is looking in amazement. "I have something you may be interested in; lady Senna suggests. General Geraldo, you will have to wait outside, he looks puzzled, but Senna reassures him and exits with him. "Women" he says. Lady Senna tells the assistants to bring out the special order. They come out with a large box and open it. Under fine crepe paper, they take out a stunning wedding dress covered in Jewels. Another assistant brings out a very long veil. "Oh, it is beautiful" Princess tells her. "Why don't you try it on, your Highness Lady Senna offers. "Oh, can I" Princess questions," Off course, she is told. Lady Senna tells the assistants to take her to the back room to change. They lead Princess away and help her undress and put on the gown. They tie the corset up tight. It has a low cut which complements her bust. She looks in the mirror. She is shocked at how amazing she looks, like a princess! She goes out front and shows lady Senna," you look stunning my dear, you have to have it, please accept this as a gift from myself and Lord Senna." "I shouldn't, but I cannot say no, thank you so much," Princess tells her. "You better take it off before General Templeton comes back in and sees it. She rushes to the back room with the assistants as Lady Senna tells the manager to charge her accounts and bring it to the castle later. Several minutes later, Princess returns and they leave the shop after Princess thanks the assistants and Lady Senna. Princess joins Geraldo with a big smile on her face. "Well, you look pleased with yourself." He tells her. "Yes, I love this place"." Well, it is lunch time your Highness can I suggest a fine restaurant just along here. "If it is anywhere as nice as everything else, I have seen, I can't wait". He shows her to the restaurant, and they are given a private booth. The maître de greets them and shows them to their seats. It is a round table. Can I tell you the specials of the day. "Please do" Senna instructs. The maître de has a soft low voice with a foreign accent. As he describes the dishes it all sounds totally unreal. Princess asks him, "What do you recommend." He suggests a delicate starter and a fish main course." "I haven't had fish for a long time, and then it was cooked by the river side on a stick she jokes. Lord Senna suggests to everyone that they all enjoy the same and they agree. The maître de then brings over a fine bottle of red wine. "May I recommend this, our finest vintage, would you like to taste. Senna agrees and he pours a sample in Sennas glass. He tries it" Very nice if you agree your Highness"? "Oh, I am sure you know more of wines than I do" she concedes. He nods to the man to proceed to pour. Senna then makes a toast "To your Highness and may you reign over us gloriously." They all raise their glass to her. "Thank you, you have both been so kind" she responds. The waiter brings over the starters and places it on their plates. They all try it, and it is super delicate and delicious but very small. Geraldo finishes his in seconds. "Well, it was very nice, but I could not run an army on it" he jokes. "But you will taste it for hours" Senna suggests. The atmosphere is totally relaxed, and they talk about the country and do not mention the war. The main course arrives, and each person is offered a whole trout stuffed with herbs and a selection of vegetables. They start to eat this and again everyone is totally impressed with the quality of the food. "I have never had food like this before in my life, maybe we can get the chef for our wedding Geraldo." "It seems nothing is impossible your Highness, and I cannot imagine us finding anyone better." "Could you see if it is possible Lord Senna." She asks. "I will move heaven and earth to make sure he is there, with his full staff" he replies. "You are so kind" she replies. She turns to lady Senna. "We must talk about our wedding; I am sure you have lots of advice I can use." "It would be a pleasure your Highness." Princess claps her hands together. "This just gets better and better." After the main course is cleared and maître de brings over a large tray of deserts. Princess looks at them all finding it impossible to choose. She decides on strawberries and cream. Geraldo has a chocolate cake and Lord and Lady Senna both have trifle. By the end, Princess feels totally full, "I can't move, that was amazing". Geraldo jokes, well if an army marches on it stomach, you must be undefeatable" they all laugh and thank the maître de. They rise from the table and Senna tells the maître due to charge it to the castle account. He shows them to the door, and they thank him again and leave. "Well, I cannot go on, I think we should return to the castle." "Very good your Highness." Princess links her arm with Lady Senna and they walk of together, Princess pointing into numerous shops. "I think she enjoyed herself, thank you," Geraldo tells Senna. "It was an honour; I feel she will bring so much life and pleasure to the country." "I think my problem will be to get her to leave," they both laugh. They reach the entrance, and the guards mount up and they climb into their coach and head back to the castle.

Upon arrival, Princess thanks Lord and Lady Senna for the day and bid them farewell. They then head up to their quarters to relax. Upon entering, Princess goes over to the mirror and inspects the necklace. "It's beautiful, don't you think." "Very, a King's ransom." He remarks. "What do you mean" she asks. "Well, there are an awful lot of shops with castle accounts don't you think" he suggests. "You must remember how pompous King Alphonso of Tarmac was, so I'm not surprised, but I am impressed with how everything is organised. "I guess that's true" he admits. "So, what was the dress you bought." "It was a gift from Lady Senna, it was my wedding dress, it is amazing." "So, I guess I will have to wait till the wedding to see it. "Exactly" she tells him, it's a surprise". She then tells him she is exhausted, and she is going to rest. He tells her he is going to check on his troops. She lies down and he leaves.

The next morning Princess calls a meeting with Lord Senna, and the city administrators. She is joined and all sit at is organised. the table. She starts" I would like to thank Lord Senna for the information I gained yesterday, and I must say how impressed I am in the way this city is organised. I do have some questions though; I am confused at how this city can run like this and Rumania was such chaos. I therefore have thoughts that maybe there are other cities in terrible conditions. Lord Senna speaks up," Your Highness, thank you for your kind words, and I agree that a lot of work has gone into running this city. It was certainly an experiment, and I believe a successful one. This city brings more funds to the exchequer, than the rest of the country. "I can believe that, from the little I have seen, I therefore ask, can we not bring the same organisation to the other cities, I must admit that I was expecting to find nothing but trouble here, so this has been a pleasant surprise," she asks. Senna adds "I should show you where all this organisation comes from, we have a large office of accountants, who check all bills and taxes, it is not a simple thing, but I certainly would look at it as a challenge to try to recreate it elsewhere. Princess asks, "well, can we take a look at this office"? "Certainly, your Highness," He stands and offers his hand. Princess stands and takes his hand and is lead to the back of the castle. They reach the office and Senna opens the door. There before her eyes, Princess sees row after row of desks with men and women checking pages of documents. "I see what you mean, where did you find all these administrators." We were fortunate to come to an agreement with the church and they trained their juniors who then had the choice to join us." "So, If I was from Tarmack originally, I could have ended up here." "Possibly your highness" he smiles. "Ok, I have seen enough, it is very impressive, let's get back to the others." They return to the meeting. "I would appreciate it if you could work on the other cities." "I will see what I can do"." I think I will leave to return to Lystonia tomorrow, via Rumania, maybe you could send someone to join me there to explain this to the new lady". She asks. "Certainly, Your Highness, I am delighted you are happy with our hard work." She finishes with "This meeting is over, you are dismissed, thank you gentlemen." She stands and they all stand and bow then she leaves the room. She heads to her room.

Upon entering, Geraldo is there waiting for her. "How did your meeting go sweetheart"? He asks. "Oh fine, I think we should head home tomorrow via Romania, and pick up Rebecca." "As you wish, and what about tonight"? "Well let's have a last look at the city." She responds. "Ok." He stands. "You get ready, and I will tell the men to prepare to leave tomorrow." He leaves and Princess calls her maid. She rushes into the room. "I need to change, something comfortable would be nice." "Certainly, your Highness, I will see what there is available. The maid goes over to the wardrobe and pulls out a lilac dress. "How about this one your Highness"? "Yes, that is fine. She stands and the maid helps her take her dress off and place the new one on. As she finishes brushing her hair, Geraldo enters. "All done, when do you want to go out"? he asks. "I'm ready, let's make a day of it." She tells him. He offers her his arm, and they leave the room and make their way to the stables. Waiting there are the horses and guard. They mount up and head out of the castle. "So where are we going" Princess asks. "I thought we would just ride out into the country and maybe finish of down by the port" Geraldo answers. They ride out through the gates. After a while they have reached the outskirts of the city and come across a beautiful lake. They stop here and dismount and walk along the side of the lake. They come across a small house, where they see a little old lady sitting in front of a pot cooking. Princess walks up to her and says "Hello, you have a lovely location for your home here"! "Thank you, who are you, you are not local." She asks. "I am the new ruler of this country as well as Lystonia and Norlands" she tells her. "I never heard that, so the King has gone"? "Yes, he was killed by Manion. "Good"! the old lady laughs. "I take it you never liked him" Princess asks. "He only cared about the rich, us poor never received anything"! "But the city is so clean and tidy, and run so well." "In the city yes, but the people do not get much." She answers. Geraldo interrupts "Why do you say that"? "Well, all the youngsters are taken to work in the factories, so the countryside is empty. I had five sons and have no one to care for our land, and I am alone." "Oh, I am sorry, princess tells her." "It is not your fault, you are new here, but maybe you can do something to sort it out." "We leave tomorrow, but we will look into it" Geraldo tells her. "Thank you, Sir," She responds. They remount their horses and move off. When out of reach, Princess asks Geraldo, "So what do you think"? "I really do not know, she may be just a bitter old lady, but we should investigate." "We leave tomorrow, so how can we." Let's get back and you stay in the castle, and I'll venture out into the city and see what I can find". "Ok." She replies and they head back to the city. Upon reaching the city, Princess heads for her room while Geraldo asks a couple of his men to join him casually dressed. They change out of their uniforms and head into the centre of the city. Princess keeps busy arranging for her things to be packed ready for tomorrow. The maid informs her that there will be a banquet at 8 o'clock to celebrate her visit and to say goodbye.

In the city Geraldo has moved beyond the city centre and into a less affluent area. Here he finds many warehouses and factories. The buildings are all lit and obviously working, while the streets are empty. They come across a small bar and enter. They go up to the bar and Geraldo orders drinks for himself and his men. They relax and Geraldo asks the bar man, "We are new here, what is this area, it's totally different from the centre." "The centre would not be like it is without us." "Where do you think all the goods come from for the shops, this country is a major exporter, not importer, so everything comes from here". "Well, that should be good, isn't it"? Geraldo asks. "If everyone benefitted, but the people here hardly get paid, and work hours are crazy. The only reason I can work here is due to my injury. He kicks out his wooden leg, lost it in a battle years ago." "Oh, I am sorry, so who owns the factories"? "The castle of course, that Lord Senna and his cronies, they live the good life on our backs." "Is it really that bad" Geraldo asks. "You have been here a while now, have you seen anyone else come in." The barman asks. "No, but I assume they are at work." "Yes 16 hours a day, and no one has the time or money to spend in a bar". "I see, I am surprised." "Yes, it is well hidden to strangers, they have their little act, visit the Mall, give gifts, no one asks" he explains. "We will have another round, let me buy you one as well. The bar man pours out more drinks and Geraldo and his men go and sit around a table. I want you two men to stay here for a while and of checking. The men nod agreement. Geraldo calls out to the barman, "Do you rent rooms here". "Of course, plenty of empty rooms." He answers. "Good we will take two for a week." Geraldo informs him." Shall I show you to them now." "No, we will finish our drinks first, thanks" Is the reply. Geraldo again talks to the men. "Come back to the castle and gather your belongings, and move out tonight, I'll give you funds for your stay, no one must know of this though." They both agree. They finish their drinks and head back to the castle. They call out to the barman. "Be back soon"!

Back at the castle, Princess is in her room relaxing as Geraldo enters. He goes over to her and kisses her forehead. "How did it go"? she asks. "Interesting, there is a whole area of factories and warehouses, totally different to the centre, I have arranged for two men to stay behind to check things out and report back in a week." "Ok, well get ready there is a goodbye banquet tonight" she tells him. That night they entertain everyone and give their fare wells, not mentioning what they suspect. The next morning, they leave and head back to Romania to see Rebecca. While they travel, Rebecca goes back to the school to see the children and tell them of the battle against Manion and the hero Princess. The children sit on the floors and Rebecca starts to tell the story. How princess destroyed the Manion fleet and saved her army with the wall, and how she was betrayed by their King Alphonso. Also, how she was locked up and escaped and Manion killed the King. Then the return of Princess from Norland and the final battles, and how she won all the battles almost alone. The little girls were in ore at the story, but a few boys did not believe it. One boy puts his hand up. "No one can do that, it is impossible, this is not true." The other boys agree with him. "Are you calling me a liar," Rebecca asks. He holds his place, "Yes, it's impossible and you should not lie to us." The teacher tells him to be quiet. Rebecca laughs and tells him we will see. She then leaves and the boys are full of arrogance and shoving the girls. She heads back to her castle and awaits Princess. Late that night, Princess and Geraldo arrive, and Rebecca runs up to them." Princess, I missed you, how was the Capital"? "Interesting, is the short answer" she replies. "Come in." They enter the castle as the servants gather their belongings and take them inside.

In the main hall, there is a large table prepared for a private dinner. "Just us for dinner tonight, thought it might make a change," Rebecca tells them. "You are a mind reader," Princess tells her. Geraldo puts his arm around David, "So how have things been here." "Good, looking into the accounts etc, and Rebecca seems happy here." He replies. "I was talking about you and her," Geraldo tells him. "Oh good, fine, yes, very good. He stammers. Rebecca calls," let's have a drink, and celebrate. The maid brings the drinks, and they all sit around the fire. "So how was the Capital"? Rebecca asks. "It was difficult to say, initially we were very impressed, run very efficiently and had an amazing shopping mall, but then we went further afield and heard some disturbing things, so Geraldo has left two men there to investigate", Princess explains. "At least it is efficient, this place needs a good shake up, but we are getting there." Rebecca responds. The meal is prepared, and they move to the table to eat. Princess tells them of her visit to the school today and that the boys did not believe her. "Maybe I should turn up tomorrow and prove it, could be fun." Princess suggests. Rebecca laughs, "yeah why not, give them the shock of their life."

The following day Rebecca and princess supported by 50 guards arrive at the school. The men march in and order the boys onto the playing fields. Rebecca introduces Princess to the teacher and the girls who sit in ore. Princess suggests they all head out to the playing field and there the boys are huddled together surrounded by guards. Princess goes upto the boys and introduces herself. "Kneel for her Highness Princess" Geraldo shouts. The boys all quickly kneel on both knees as the guard's step back several yards. "I understand that you doubt the information told to you by Lady Rebecca, please explain"? The boys say nothing and are shaking. A small girl shouts out. "They said you did not have powers and saved everyone." Princess turns to the boys "Are you calling Lady Rebecca a liar"? the boys all nod their heads. She turns and heads back to the girls and Rebecca she winks. She then turns towards the boys and fires a wall of fire around them. The boys scream and beg forgiveness. She stops the fire and then forms a wall of ice around them. They are all shouting apologies. She then raises her arms to the sky, and it rains just over the boys. The girls laugh as the teacher goes over to her. "I think they are convinced." Princess laughs, stops the rain, and makes the area above the boys heat up and dry them. She then melts the ice and lets the boys out. They are led to Princess and Rebecca. "So, what do you have to say to your Lady Rebecca"? They all shout out, "We are sorry, we believe her, Princess." Princess turns to Rebecca, "I think we are finished here, let's get back and prepare to travel." They head back to the castle.

Upon reaching the main hall, Princess asks how the accountant is getting on. "I'll call for him, he is in the castle," she goes to a servant and asks him to fetch the accountant. The four of them are sitting around the fire as the accountant arrives. He bows to both princess and Rebecca. Rebecca asks him "Can you tell her Highness what you have found out to date. "Your highness, I have received some thirty accounts and tax bills from different traders here. All of them have been taxed an extra 30% of which is still in the vault. I am expecting another fifty, before making my full report. I have not bothered with individual families, as I am aware that they all have been taxed extra, he tells them. When do you think you will be finished"? Princess asks. "I hope no more than two weeks." He answers. "Very good, I would like you to report to us in Lystonia in two weeks then and we will hopefully authorise the refund to the traders and families". "As you wish your highness, he responds." "Thank you, you are dismissed," Rebecca tells him. He bows and leaves. "Lucky there is a lot of funds in the vault really, I think we should take are portion back to Lystonia as well, as you have the men with us." "good idea "Geraldo agrees. "So, I suggest we have an early night so we can leave at a good time". Rebecca suggests. "In that case, I will go and inform the men to be ready by 9a.m." Geraldo tells them. He rises and leaves as Princess also prepares to go to her room. "I'll see you in the morning, sweetheart" she tells Rebecca. "Sweet dreams" she replies.

Next morning, they proceed out of the castle and head for Lystonia. "Well, how do you enjoy the life of a Lady" Princess asks Rebecca. "I'll get used to it; I will be happier when the taxes have been sorted". Maybe we can spend next summer there as a holiday" David suggests. Rebecca agrees "that will be nice, especially if everyone is happier with their refunds". "Maybe next time we can travel by ship and bring some of your belongings down here." "What belongings," Rebecca laughs. "Well look at the fun we can have shopping now" Princess tells her.

Back in Tarmack's capital, the two men left behind have been busy mixing with the locals in bars and restaurants. The information they have received is of a city built on slave labour, with the rewards going to the rich elite. They have learnt that men are forced at late teens to move into the factories, where they live, eat and sleep. The women work in the service industry as maids, shop assistants and waitresses. It is evident by the lack of men in the bars that they have little or no money. The two men have found nothing positive in the outskirts of the city, but when they visit the centre and malls, it is totally different. They have found out that virtually every shop, hotel or factory is owned by a dozen of the lords, who run the city as their own. They feel they have enough information, so decide to head back to Lystonia as well.

In Lystonia Orpheus has been busy arranging the wedding of Princess and Geraldo. Invites have been sent out to all Lords and Ladies and other important people. He has arranged a banquet for Princess's return and is looking forward to her return. Around 5pm princess arrives at the gates of the city and rides through with the others and her guard. The city folk are all waiting for her and cheering, happy to see her return. She enters the Palace and goes straight to the throne room where Orpheus is waiting for her. He welcomes her and escorts her to her throne. "You have been missed your Highness, but I have been busy organising things for you." I had no doubt you had she replies smiling. She sits and he asks her what new information she has. "There is a lot, a lot of corruption, but we have started rectifying things, we will discuss in detail tomorrow." "Very good your highness, if you wish to rest, the banquet is at 8PM". He informs her. "Yes, I think I need a long bath and chance to relax, we have ridden many miles." She tells him. She rises and leaves the room, followed by Rebecca, Geraldo and David stay behind to inform Orpheus of what they have seen.

Princess enters her room and throws her arms out, "Home"! The maids enter and Rebecca tells them to arrange two baths. They rush of as usual to fetch the baths and water. Both girls help each other out of their dresses, and they relax by the fire and drink wine. The maids return shortly after and prepare the baths. They are then excused. Princess is lounging in the large armchair. "I can't move, my body, I'm as stiff as board." She moans. "Same here, come on let's soak and I'll call for a masseur." Princess gets up finishes undressing and climbs in the bath. Rebecca goes to the door and tells a maid to get a masseur in 30 minutes. She then has her bath. After their baths and massage, they both have a good night's sleep.

The next day there is a meeting with Princess, Rebecca, Orpheus, Geraldo, and David and the two soldiers. They are discussing their trips and the concerns they have concerning the running, and taxes of Tarmack. Orpheus is told of how the Capital is run and the slave labour and shopping malls. Rebecca explains the taxes of Romania and the fortune in the vault. Well, when you get married, all these people will be here, so we can complete our investigation now and arrest them when they deliver themselves to us then. Princess says, "That will change their attitudes for sure." I would like to invite the accountant in Romania as well if possible." "He will be needed for statements anyway, so that makes sense" Orpheus advises. "So, what will happen on the day"? Princess asks. "There will be a march past of the military in front of you outside the city. Then there will be a parade with you through the city, before ending in the Palace. Then all the guests would arrive and welcome you for the wedding. This is when Geraldo appears in public and meets you before the Archbishop and get married. Then there will be an appearance on the balcony, followed by a gala evening of music and dance. Then you and Geraldo will tour the three countries to be seen by your subjects." "Is that all" Princess jokes. "Eh how long is the tour they will go on" Rebecca asks. It will be several months, but as there is no threat, it is a good time to build relationships and grow relationships". Orpheus explains. Geraldo then asks, "what and when will we sort out the Lords from Tarmack." "I think just before the wedding," Orpheus suggests. "Well, that'll be fun" Geraldo laughs. "I am assuming there will be a rehearsal of all this" Princess asks. "Off course" Orpheus replies.

Chapter Eleven

The time has arrived for the wedding, the city is in a carnival mode and dignitaries from all three countries are attending. The main hall is crammed waiting for the arrival of the wedding party. David is supporting Geraldo and both wearing dress uniforms.

They walk down the aisle and stand in position awaiting Princess. The trumpets blast out as the doors open and Princess being escorted by Orpheus make their appearance. Rebecca is behind Princess, followed by 12 young boys and girls. In front are two flower girls who start walking down the aisle throwing petals. The congregation are all standing, and there is a buzz as everyone first sees Princess who looks stunning although under a veil. They proceed down the aisle towards the awaiting Geraldo. She reaches his side and Rebecca pulls the veil back over Princess's head. She looks stunning and Geraldo confirms this in a whisper. They both kneel before the archbishop who reads out the wedding statement. They then stand and take turns making their oaths and statements. They exchange rings and kiss. And the whole hall bursts into a cheer. The two married couple then head down the aisle and onto the balcony to the awaiting crowd outside. The cheering is deafening and both Princess and Geraldo wave to the crowd then upon demand from the crowd "Kiss, Kiss, Kiss," they kiss, to an enormous cheer. They are then joined on the balcony by Rebecca, David, and Orpheus along with the children who are busy throwing flowers and waving. After a solid ten minutes of waving and noise, they all go indoors. The doors close but the crowd do not stop cheering. The doors open again, and the crowd are rewarded when they are calling for. The reappearance of Princess and Geraldo. They step out and the crowd erupt again. There is no point in making a speech as they could never be heard. They wave and then go back inside.

"We have to go on a carriage ride around the city next" Geraldo tells her. "No problem, give me a few minutes," are you coming Rebecca!? Princess asks. "No, this is your day, I'll make sure things are prepared for tonight's banquet" Rebecca replies. Geraldo takes Princess by the arm, and they head for the Palace entrance to meet the carriage. They exit the palace and there is the carriage and two hundred guards waiting. Fifty guards go out in front then the carriage followed by the rest of the guards. They exit the palace gate, and the streets are cleared so the crowd are standing along the street cheering. Both Princess and Geraldo are waving as they turn into the city centre where there are thousands waiting to see them. The guards in the street are having trouble holding everyone back, but there is no incident. They carry on the route, while back at the palace the hall is being prepared for a massive banquet with two long rows of tables. The guests include the Lords and Ladies, plus senior military officers and several the juniors and staff from the Priory. Before the meal, Princess and Geraldo will sit in their thrones and will receive the gifts from numerous guests and foreign leaders.

They arrive and go to their room to change into formal wear. An hour later they are escorted down to the hall and take their thrones. Princess is sitting on the right with Geraldo to the left and Orpheus is standing to their left. He announces the arrival of a messenger from the far of land of Stanmore. The messenger steps forward followed by six servants carrying three chests. He kneels and introduces the best wishes of his King and hope they accept these gifts. The chests are thrown open and are full of gold coins. The audience are stunned by the value of the gift. Princess thanks the messenger and sends her thanks back to their King. The messenger rises and steps aside. Orpheus then introduces another messenger from the land of Gorland. The messenger again walks forward followed by four servants carrying chests. He sends his best wishes from his King and offers this wedding gift to the happy couple. The servants open the chests to reveal fine oils and scents. The room fills with the smell of this gift. Again, they are thanked for their gift and like before rise and leave. Orpheus then introduces another messenger from Claris. He walks forwards, kneels, and gives his message. The doors then open and two magnificent white horses are brought in. His King is thanked, and they leave. Then Orpheus introduces a Lord within the room. Lord Markle of Norland steps forward. He calls for his servants, they enter the room and bring forward bundles and bundles of fine silk cloth. Lord Markle offers his gift and his allegiance to her Highness. He is thanked by Princess and then he steps back.

Orpheus then introduces numerous other Lords from the three countries. He Then calls Lord and Lady Senna forward. They step forward and kneel. Lord Senna offers a set of two fine swords for Princess and Geraldo and Lady Senna offers them a fine set of dinner settings for banquets. Princess leans forwards and speaks direct to them. "Lord and Lady Senna, you have again been very generous with the assets of the people of your city." There is a silence in the hall and a curious look on The Senna's faces. Princess continues, "I was very impressed with the way your city runs, so efficient, and it was only after a secret investigation that we discovered the slave labour camps, and that all the profits of the city are split between the lords of the city." Lord Senna tries to stop her and defend himself, but she stops him. "Please do not interrupt me, I am removing all titles awarded in this land till further investigation. Until the matter is finalised all the Lords and Ladies will be held in house arrest at Lady Rebeca's Castle. All assets of the factories and shopping malls will be transferred to the crown until further notice. Lord Orpheus will move to the city to oversee the transfers and the investigation awaiting my arrival in six months, officers take them and the other Lords and Ladies of Tarmack away." Lord Senna tries to object but is seized by two soldiers and escorted out of the hall, along with his wife and the other Lords and Ladies. The remaining guests are stunned into silence. Princess continues, "I apologise, for bringing this matter to an event like this, but it made sense to handle it here while all were present, please do not let it change the atmosphere of this celebration. The crowd applaud and Orpheus continues introducing the guests and their gifts. After the last one has been introduced, the happy couple stand and head to sit at their place at the banqueting table. The guests stand and applaud them, then once Princess and Geraldo sit the rest join them. There are then several toasts and responses from the married couple and the evening is finished with a massive feast and music. After the meal, the tables are cleared and the evening ends with music and dance. The evening opens with the married couple having the first dance and are then joined by Rebecca and David. The evening ends with everyone on a high and finally Princess and Geraldo make there exit and head for their room. Geraldo lifts Princess up and carries her over the door threshold. He carries her over to the bed and lies her down there. He then goes over to the table and pours two drinks. Princess rises to accept the drink when she suddenly doubles up in pain and falls to the floor. Geraldo rushes to her and helps her to the bed. He then rushes to the door and calls for help. As usual, Rebecca is the first there. She rushes in and sees Princess clutching her stomach in obvious pain. Rebecca starts to undo Princess's corset to relieve the pressure and take the heavy dress off. As she removes it, she sees two glowing lights deep in Princess's stomach. She Touches the area, and it is incredibly hot. "My god, I think I know what this is." Rebecca says. "Is she poisoned" Geraldo asks. "No, I think she is pregnant, if her children have inherited her powers then they would possibly not control them at this stage, but Princess should be safe." "Pregnant"! Princess scream, I've only just got married"! Geraldo bursts into laughter, "Well that's what you call timing sweetheart, congratulations." He takes her into his arms and gives her a hug. The pain disperses and Princess feels immediately better. All three of them have a group hug and look forward to the future.

The End.

Printed in Great Britain
by Amazon